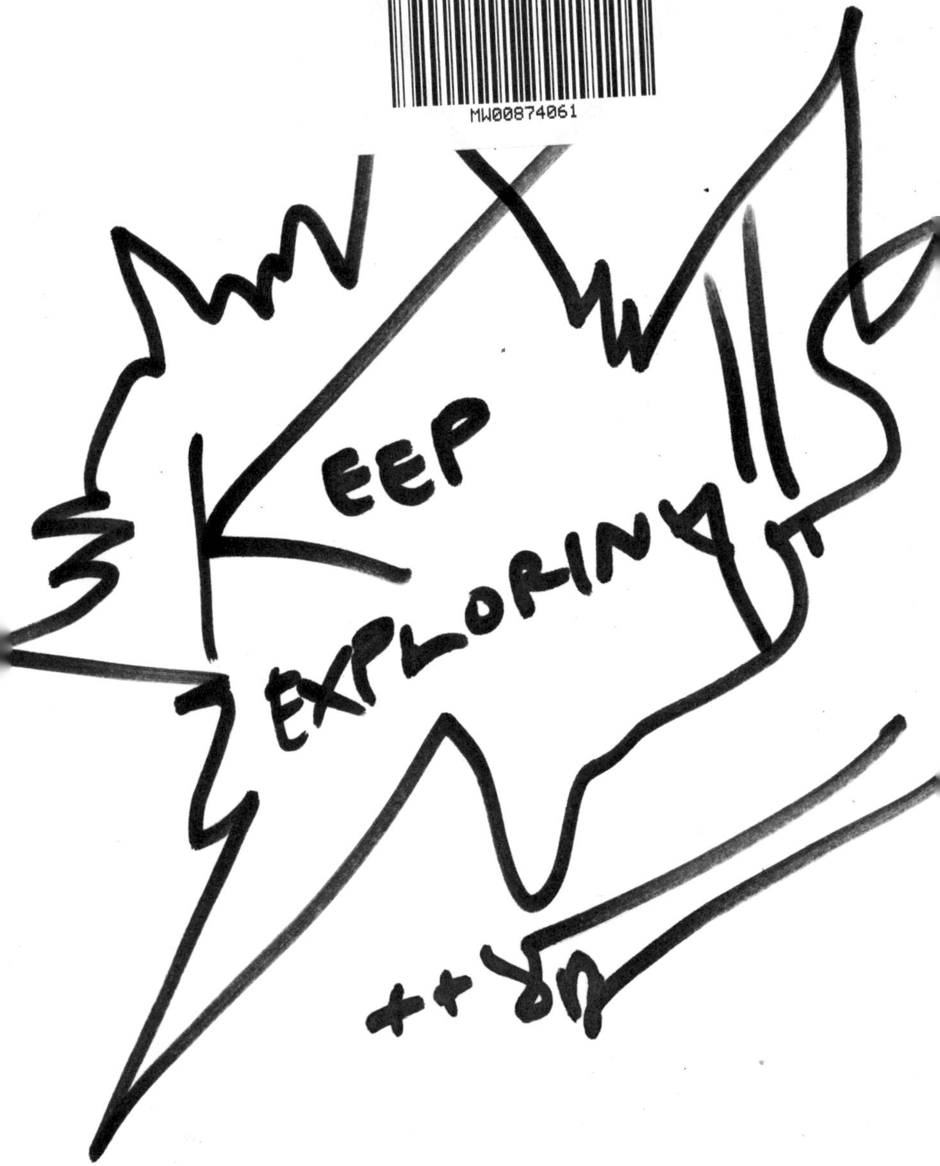
KEEP EXPLORING!!

RACE FOR THE RUBY TURTLE

Also by Stephen Bramucci

The Danger Gang and the Pirates of Borneo!
The Danger Gang and the Isle of Feral Beasts!

RACE FOR THE RUBY TURTLE

Stephen Bramucci

BLOOMSBURY
CHILDREN'S BOOKS
NEW YORK LONDON OXFORD NEW DELHI SYDNEY

BLOOMSBURY CHILDREN'S BOOKS
Bloomsbury Publishing Inc., part of Bloomsbury Publishing Plc
1385 Broadway, New York, NY 10018

First published in the United States of America in October 2023
by Bloomsbury Children's Books

Library of Congress Cataloging-in-Publication Data
Names: Bramucci, Stephen, author.
Title: Race for the ruby turtle / by Stephen Bramucci.
Description: New York : Bloomsbury, 2023. | Audience: Ages 8–11. |
Audience: Grades 4–6. | Summary: When his parents send him to spend
the summer with his great-aunt, Jake suddenly finds himself on a quest to
change the way people see him and his ADHD, and to protect the wonders of nature.
Identifiers: LCCN 2023028226 (print) | LCCN 2023028227 (ebook) |
ISBN 978-1-5476-0702-0 (hardcover) | ISBN 978-1-5476-0703-7 (e-book)
Subjects: CYAC: Nature—Fiction. | Attention-deficit hyperactivity disorder—Fiction. |
Adventure and adventurers—Fiction. | LCGFT: Action and adventure fiction.
Classification: LCC PZ7.1.B7513 Rac 2023 (print) |
LCC PZ7.1.B7513 (ebook) | DDC [Fic]—dc23
LC record available at https://lccn.loc.gov/2023028226
LC ebook record available at https://lccn.loc.gov/2023028227

Book design by Yelena Safronova
Typeset by Westchester Publishing Services
Printed and bound in the U.S.A.
2 4 6 8 10 9 7 5 3 1

To find out more about our authors and books visit www.bloomsbury.com
and sign up for our newsletters.

The author would like to acknowledge the traditional custodians of the region where *Race for the Ruby Turtle* takes place, the Nehalem Band of Tillamook, as well as all Indigenous peoples of the Oregon Coast.

A percentage of the author's proceeds for this novel were donated to the Siletz Tribal Arts and Heritage Society.

For Julien River and Zeela Sky—in hopes that Oregon's endless green spaces will course through your veins, as they do for me.

RACE FOR THE RUBY TURTLE

1

Rainiest Town in the State

If there was one thing Jake Rizzi didn't want to do on one of the last Sundays of the summer, it was pack a bag for the rainiest town in the whole state of Oregon.

If there was a second thing he didn't want to do, it was stay in that soggy town for five days, cooped up in a tiny cabin with a great-aunt he barely knew.

And if there was a *third* thing he didn't want to do, it was think about the giant catastrophe back in May that led to this whole trip in the first place.

Which at least sort of explained why Jake had given up packing altogether. Instead, he was sitting on his bed, flipping through a book about reptiles, eating cheese twists, and wondering how often it must rain in the town of Nehalem to add up to 120 inches every year.

"Probably almost every day," he muttered to his red-bone hound, Singer. "And Mom said it's been extra rainy this year."

Jake snatched a balled-up pair of socks and winged them across the room. Singer padded over to get them and dropped them at Jake's feet with a strand of drool attached. There was a knock at the door; Jake's mom leaned her head in.

"Honey, you're supposed to be packing."

"Snack break," Jake said, holding up the cheese twists and giving the bag a little shake.

"Jake. Focus. Please."

Jake's dad poked his head in next. "Gotta focus, buddy. First the shirts, then pants, a few sweatshirt—"

"Bring lots of socks!" Jake's mom interrupted. "And underwea—"

"Guys!" Jake said. "I got it."

As his parents retreated, Jake looked down at the random clothes piled on his bed. He dropped the drooly socks inside a duffel bag. Then added some sour-smelling swim trunks and a crumpled sweatshirt.

"I bet *they* aren't packing sweatshirts," he muttered to Singer.

While he was at his aunt's cabin, ten miles from the Oregon Coast, Jake's parents would be in Joshua Tree, California, for a workshop called "Reawakening Your Sacred Bond." And sure, that name *sounded* very serious, but Jake had seen the retreat center website—it was definitely a vacation.

"I don't even *know* Aunt Hettle," Jake complained to Singer. "Not really."

It was true; he'd only met his great-aunt three times—once for Thanksgiving and twice when she drove all the way to Portland to watch basketball games at the Rizzi house. Her cabin didn't have a TV.

"No internet either," Jake said to Singer. "Not even a phone. Dad says Aunt Hettle goes to the grocery store to make her calls. How weird is that?"

"Fo-*cusssssssss!*" a voice trilled from downstairs.

Jake scowled. Ever since he'd gotten diagnosed with attention deficit hyperactivity disorder—ADHD for short—his parents and teachers had thrown the word "focus" around a lot. Sometimes it seemed like all anyone talked about.

As if someone telling a kid to focus fifty times a day could actually make them pay attention better. As if Jake *liked* not being able to block out small sounds or tiny movements. Or being so impulsive that sometimes he did things that made absolutely no sense to him later.

Things like the Whole Saturday Market Fiasco.

Don't think about that. Not now. Do. Not.

"Five minutes 'til blastoff!"

Jake sprung to his feet and stuffed three pairs of pants, five pairs of underwear, and four more pairs of socks into his bag. He also grabbed five of his favorite animal books. Or he was *about to*, until one of the books fell open and a photo of a strawberry poison-dart frog caught his eye. When Jake saw the tiny, slick-looking, neon-blue-and-red amphibian, he couldn't help but crash back down on his bed and read the text box next to it. Also the next page, on the golden poison frog, which was the size of a paper clip but secreted venom so powerful it could kill ten people.

"Nine . . . eight . . . seven . . . ," his dad called from downstairs.

Jake slapped the book shut, tossed it in his duffel, popped up, and raced around the room, looking for anything else he thought he might need. Finally, he zipped the bag halfway closed, flung his bedroom door open, and made a little "coo-eee" sound to get Singer's attention.

"Rainiest town in the state," Jake said as they raced downstairs, the hound's nails clicking on the hardwood steps. "By the end of the week, the whole cabin is gonna smell like wet *you*."

2

The Whole Saturday Market Fiasco

"Although we've *COOOOME*, to the *ENNNNNND* of the *ROOOOAAAD*!"

The car was twenty minutes out of Portland, and Jake's parents were singing oldies. Badly.

"How's it sound back there?" Jake's dad called over his shoulder.

"Boyz II Men should take you on tour," Jake grumbled, forcing a lopsided grin.

I'd be singing terribly too if I was about to spend a week at a place with daily pottery classes and four different types of hot tub.

As the city's suburbs thinned, the scenery changed. There were big, rolling patches of farmland between stands of towering evergreens. Then, when the highway headed into the Oregon Coast Range, the landscape shifted again. The trees grew thicker together, blocking out the sun completely.

"Expect a lot of moss," Jake muttered to Singer, about an hour into the drive.

Every time she'd come over, Aunt Hettle brought Jake a gift, and it almost always seemed to have moss attached. She'd give him some twisted piece of driftwood with a little tuft of dried moss or a speckled rock with some mint-green moss still growing on it. The last time Aunt Hettle had visited the Rizzi house, she told Jake a story about finding a hatch of baby salamanders in her front lawn.

Inside a mossy log, of course.

"Salamanders or newts?" Jake had asked.

Aunt Hettle eyed him closely. "I am not fully certain of the difference. Are you fully certain of the difference, Jacob?"

"Newts are a type of salamander," he said. "But they have webbed feet and thick tails because they spend more time in water."

"I failed to notice the feet," Hettle said. "But they were enchanting and lustrous creatures. Perhaps that tells you something?"

Jake thought for a moment. "They're both enchanting."

He hesitated.

"What does 'lustrous' mean?"

"That they reflect or radiate light," Jake's dad called from across the room. He was busy trying to beat his record of correcting fifteen fourth-grade math tests during halftime of a Portland Trailblazers game.

"Oh, then that's not a newt," Jake replied. "The only newts in Oregon have rough skin."

"Jake must know a million animal facts," his mom said with a smile. "He's got a great memory."

Hettle eyed her grandnephew closely. "Jacob, is this correct? Do you know one million facts about various mammals, birds, fish, insects, mollusks, and so forth?"

Jake *did* know a lot about animals. Not mollusks, but definitely mammals, birds, fish, and insects. He'd always had a knack for remembering little things that he found in books or online but he was pretty sure his mom had just said that to make him feel good. He'd seen a section highlighted in one of her books about raising kids with ADHD that read: **"REMEMBER: Kids with attention difficulties need their 'focus reminders' balanced with plenty of praise!"**

Whatever the case, the conversation struck a nerve with Aunt Hettle. In the spring, she'd written a letter to Jake's mom inviting him to come visit her cabin deep in the Nehalem Valley, about ten miles out of town. She sent another letter four days later. And one more a week after that.

The next week, she called the Rizzis from the Nehalem Food Mart. Three afternoons in a row. By June, Hettle had convinced Jake's parents to send him to visit her at the end of August.

"Newts have rough skin," Jake whispered in the back of the car, playing back the conversation while massaging Singer's head. "That's all I said."

"I heard that."

Jake caught his mom eyeing him in the rearview mirror and looked away. It wasn't that he didn't want his parents to have a vacation. Or spend some time "soaking away your stresses in one of our four serene mineral baths after a morning spent crafting ceramics." He just didn't want to be left behind with a relative he barely knew.

Maybe they would have brought me . . . if it weren't for the Whole Saturday Market Fiasco.

Jake winced at the thought. The Whole Saturday Market Fiasco was literally the last thing on earth he wanted to have in his brain at that moment. Or really at any time. But the weird thing about ADHD was that you could almost never get distracted when you actually *wanted* to.

Jake tried to think about something else. Anything else.

List animals that mimic other animals. Okay, snake's head moth and . . . kingsnake . . . and—

No luck. All Jake could think about was how, three months earlier, he'd caused absolute mayhem in the middle of Portland's famous weekly craft fair, the Saturday Market.

Okay, wait—I'll list animals that mimic plants. That's easier. Number one, leaf-tailed gecko. Number two, stick bug. Number three . . .

It all started when a bunch of kids in Jake's class met up at the Skidmore Fountain to eat kettle corn and complain about a really long math test at school. They'd all agreed that they could barely finish before the bell rang—which made Jake feel restless and sort of jittery, because he had forty-five extra minutes to finish his test after school. As the other kids went on and on, it started to seem unfair that Jake got more time.

One of the other kids even joked that he wished *he* had ADHD.

That made Jake's face feel hot. He wanted to explain how homework took *forever* and how, when you get distracted a lot, you never feel like you're getting to take a break, even though your brain focuses on other stuff while you're supposed to be working. Plus, getting distracted wasn't the only part of it—he also had too much energy sometimes or did things without thinking about them or seemed rude by accident because something grabbed his attention away from whatever someone was saying or forgot assignments and plans and birthdays and—

List your favorite Italian foods. Or practice rhymes. Italian food rhymes! Fettucine, linguine, tortellini, rotini . . .

But Jake hadn't said any of that to the other kids. Instead, as they started to walk through the booths at the market, he'd decided to try to change the subject. And his method for changing the subject had been—

Macaroni, rigatoni, cannelloni . . .

Jake cringed remembering how he'd randomly decided to try a handstand. He double cringed thinking back on how he flung his legs too far over his head and tipped backward. Into someone's booth.

Then there was shattered glass. Yelling. The kids from school backed away and drifted off. But Jake had to stay with the three burly security guards who rushed over and made him call home.

Minestrone . . .

Next came the worst part. The look in his mom's eyes when she came to pick him up. The tone in her voice when she asked, "Honey, why on *earth* did you do that?" She wasn't mad. Or even disappointed. It was worse. It was something else, a look he didn't quite recognize but left a lump in his throat.

"THE FLYER!" Jake practically yelled.

He'd finally thought of something that really might take his mind off the Whole Saturday Market Fiasco. He jammed his hand into his jeans pocket and dragged out a flyer that Hettle had sent to the Rizzi house a few days earlier.

3

The Turtle

Join us for the . . .

NEHALEM BLACKBERRY MOON FESTIVAL

AUGUST 23–28

MONDAY, 2 p.m. – OPENING CEREMONY (Weather permitting!)

TUESDAY, 12 p.m. – NATURE HIKE & FORAGING
(Hope for sun!)

WEDNESDAY, 12 p.m. – LONG-NECK CLAM BAKE!
(With new rainproof tents!)

THURSDAY, 12 p.m. – BLACKBERRY JAM CONTEST &
MAYPOLE DANCE (Postponed if wet!)

FRIDAY, 12:30 p.m. – INNER TUBE FLOAT!
(Fingers crossed for clear skies!)

SATURDAY, 10 a.m. – MUSHROOM COOKING & CLOSING
CEREMONY (No, if raining. Yes, if drizzling!)

ALL WEEK LONG
(RAIN OR SHINE):

THE 72ND ANNUAL SEARCH FOR
THE RUBY-BACKED TURTLE!!!*

*Best turtle receives $45.50 in Nehalem Bowling Lanes
gift certificates.

The flyer was for a local festival that overlapped with Jake's trip.

"I've been meaning to ask you guys," Jake said from the back seat. "What's the Ruby-Backed Turtle? I looked in all my animal books and didn't see anything about it. Is it related to the diamondback terrapin, from Florida?"

"We wondered if you'd notice that," Jake's mom said with a wry smile in the rearview mirror.

His dad half turned in his seat. "Sounds cool, right?"

"Definitely. But what is it?"

They were coming down from the Oregon Coast Range now, and the rain started slapping against the windows harder than ever. The wipers whacked back and forth noisily. Jake felt a little surge of giddiness—he was glad to have his mind off the Whole Saturday Market Fiasco.

"The Ruby-Backed Turtle is actually connected to a book written by Aunt Hettle's grandpa Gustav," his mom began. "That's my great-grandpa and your great-*great*-grandpa. I still remember the cover from when we would visit as kids—it was cloth and . . . forest green—oh, there was a silver fern embossed on the front—and it was . . . probably at least three hundred pages."

She glanced at Jake in the rearview mirror again.

"It was a housekeeping book," she went on. "Or more like a 'how to keep a house from rotting and falling into the river when you live in such a rainy place' book. Gustav had come to Oregon all the way from Finland and built the cabin on his own, so he had all these tips for protecting the wood from rain damage and drying clothes by the fire . . . stuff like that."

"Guys," Jake said, "if Aunt Hettle tries to get me to read a book about drying clothes next to a fire, Singer and I are coming to meet you in California."

His dad let out a jolt of laughter.

"Seriously," Jake joked, "we'll just head to the beach and start walking south."

"*Most* of the entries were like that," his mom said. "But there were a few old folktales inside—like this one about a boy who refused to wear a coat when he went out in the rain. Pretty soon, his hair turned to thick cedar needles and they started falling off his head, so his parents brought him into the front yard and planted him." She chuckled. "Great-Grandpa Gustav's stories were all a little strange."

Jake's dad grinned. "We might be going to California without you, but at least we've never left you outside to turn into a tree."

The road curled left, then rolled back to the right. The rain continued to thrum against the windshield. The wipers slashed back and forth and still couldn't clear the glass fast enough.

"What about the turtle?" Jake pressed, scratching Singer's belly.

"Well, the Ruby-Backed Turtle was one of the stories from the book," his mom said. "It was about this tiny turtle that Gustav and his wife claimed to have seen out in the forest. To tell you the truth, I don't really remember."

"How could it compete with the tree boy?" Jake's dad joked.

"Gustav was really proud of his book," his mom said. "So he had copies printed for a few neighbors and friends. At some point, looking for the turtle became like this local tradition each August. People came from all through the Nehalem Valley to explore Gustav's homestead, looking for the turtle, hiking, and having picnics before the heavy fall rains started. Then they added a clambake and a Maypole dance . . . We used to love going as kids—I just sort of assumed that no one really did it anymore after the pandemic."

Jake was suddenly interested. "Do people ever find the turtle? I wonder what the habitat is? What does it eat? Are there photos? How come no one told me abou—"

"Oh . . . no, honey . . ." His mom flashed him a "sorry" look in the rearview mirror. "The stories in the book were fables. Folklore. When we'd go to the cabin when I was a kid, the adults would send us on 'turtle hunts' to get us outside after dinner. Hettle would even make us tell her exactly where we'd looked, and she'd write it down like it was all super scientific. But I remember my parents giggling in the kitchen whenever we came back to report our findings."

Jake watched the rain slat across his window. He leaned his face against the glass, feeling the cool condensation on his cheek. "Made up. Got it."

"But they *do* give out gift certificates to the bowling

alley every year for whoever makes the best pretend turtle out of rocks and sticks and stuff!"

The car wound toward the coast, tracing the North Fork of the Nehalem River. The water crashed and tumbled toward the Pacific Ocean, washing up over mossy boulders and plunging past fallen logs.

Jake turned to Singer and spoke over the pelting rain. "So, pal, what do you think of all this?"

Singer moaned. It was a very specific sort of redbone hound moan. The kind that seemed to say, "I think I'm going to be carsick soon. *Very* soon."

Scrub Pine, Texas—3:34 p.m., SUNDAY

It definitely wasn't raining in Scrub Pine, Texas. In fact, it hadn't rained for seventy-seven days and counting. Not a cloud in the sky for forty-three of those seventy-seven days.

The weather could be described with one simple word: hot. "Fry an egg" hot, if you liked metaphors. "Melt the tarmac" hot, if you wanted to get flowery. The red quicksilver in the thermometer had skittered past 100 at 9:53 a.m. and kept climbing 'til it hit 109.

Just the way the tall man sitting in the small, stuffy office liked it. He leaned back in his chair and kicked his snakeskin cowboy boots up on his desk. In his right hand, he held a nineteen-inch bowie knife.

"My Texas toothpick," he said, admiring its gleaming, razor-sharp edge.

The man sank the blade into a leather sheath resting on his lap and snapped the button that held it in place.

Click. He flicked it open.

Click. Buttoned it again.

Click. Open. *Click.* Closed.

His phone buzzed. The man had been expecting this call. He sat up, mopped his forehead with a kerchief, set the bowie knife on his desk blotter, and let the phone rattle a second time before answering.

"You got Stick," he drawled.

The voice on the other end of the line began to speak. Stick reached into the top drawer of his desk for a leather notebook and a chewed-up pencil.

As the voice raced on, he scrawled the name of a state: OREGON

Then a town: NEHALEM

And next a person: HETTLE OLSSON

"I am not partial to rain," Stick said when the voice finally paused to take a breath. "If I'm fixing to drive all the way to Oree-gone to search for some creature from a book that no one has seen for seventy-some dang years . . . Well, I reckon the payment—"

The caller interrupted with a dollar amount. Stick mopped his brow again. He drew a long breath of hot, stale air and spun the knife sheath on his desk.

"And suppose I *do* find what you're looking for? For that, I'd figure—"

A second dollar amount was spoken. This time, Stick stopped fiddling with his knife altogether. He let out a low whistle.

“Ma’am, are you serious about this?”

The voice on the other end of the line answered “As serious as life and death.”

“Well then,” Stick said, “I believe I’ve got some driving to do.”

4

Hettle's Cabin

After pulling over to let Singer out of the car for a few minutes, the Rizzis drove another half hour down the Necanicum Highway, to where the river widened and finally straightened out. The water's surface flattened like a sheet—looking slick and metallic. The rain gradually faded, then stopped altogether. Clouds blotted the sun but it battled to break through.

"We're almost there," Jake's mom said, beaming.

She hooked a left and Jake noticed a sign that read "Foss Road." There was the river again, but it was on their right now. On their left were steep hills, tangled in soupy fog and covered in a sea of trees, ferns, and nettles. This wall of green was only broken once—by a wide gravel lot filled with excavators and earthmovers. At some point, the machinery had chewed deep scars into the hills, leaving slate-gray rock exposed.

After a few more minutes, the car slowed.

"I'm pretty sure it's this one," his mom said, slowing the car. "I think I sorta remember it . . ."

The turnoff for Hettle's driveway was marked with a pile of glass fishing buoys, wrapped in a ragged net, heaped alongside the road. A sign leaning up against the pile might have had words on it once, years ago. Now it just looked like battered driftwood.

The car *clunk-clunked* over train tracks and crossed through a gap in a wall of hedges. Jake's parents both looked back at him with big smiles.

"Here we are!" Jake's mom announced. The car tires crunched across the gravel driveway. "Honey, remember to grab your bag."

The yard was overgrown with spreading ferns and blackberry brambles. Three humongous chickens strutted in circles, pecking at the ground. Jake hopped out of the car and Singer bounded out to stretch.

A two-story cabin stood in front of them, built from wide pine slats. The roof seemed to sag in the middle. Emerald-green moss sprouted between every shingle.

"Remember, Aunt Hettle can be a little . . . *gruff*," Jake's mom said, leading the way to the front door. "But that's just her way. She was very excited to have you visit and told me that she—"

The door swung open. Standing in the doorframe was a large woman. There was no other way to say it and no reason to ignore it. Her face was large. Her hands looked like they might weigh ten pounds each. She was both tall and wide.

Jake had met her before, of course, but she seemed even bigger here, in her home.

"Hettle!" Jake's mom said. "I know you're not much of a hugger, but . . ."

She smiled and threw open her arms, clearly offering a hug.

Aunt Hettle's eyes narrowed. Her mouth was a thin line. Her pink cheeks seemed to redden. "Is this something my relatives spend their precious moments on earth discussing? Whether or not Hettle Olsson is a hugger?"

Jake remembered that his great-aunt had a very peculiar voice. There was clearly an accent—maybe a couple of different accents—even though he knew she'd been born in Oregon.

"Oh no!" Jake's mom said, forcing an awkward laugh. "I just meant . . . it's more of . . ." Her arms had fallen a little, but she raised them again. "Do you *want* a hug?"

Hettle reached out a heavy hand and wrapped it around one of her niece's outstretched arms, shaking it up and down. It wasn't a cold gesture. But it definitely wasn't a hug.

"Perhaps you are right. I suppose I never have been much of a hugger."

Jake laughed before he even realized he was doing it. The way Hettle said the line felt like some joke you'd see on TV—where one person says something and the other person has a perfect comeback right away.

"Jake," his mom said.

He stopped. But looking up at his aunt, he felt like he saw something in her eyes. A glimmer of mischief. The hint of a smile.

Maybe it was a joke? For all I know, she could be the hermit comedian of the Oregon backwoods.

Jake's dad broke the tension with a light whistle. "I can't believe this is all your land," he said. "And it goes upstream *how* far?"

Hettle turned to him. "I do not agree that it is my land. There was someone occupying it before me and someone before them and so on. I am sure there will be someone here after me."

"I just meant," Jake's dad said, "it's amazing that you own all this."

Hettle frowned. "Who decided that land can be owned, I wonder. The Tillamook people have a better claim to it than me. Or, if you consider animals, the deer could make quite a strong case. My friend Myron would tell you that the mushrooms send their networks of mycelium under every inch of this region. Is it not their land, also? Do I have more or less ownership than the chanterelles that emerge from the soil year after year in the same spot for centuries?"

Jake watched his dad's eyes widen. This clearly wasn't the answer he'd expected.

"I am a temporary caretaker of this homestead," Hettle finished. "That is my only title."

"Well," Jake's mom said with a cheery smile, "thanks for welcoming Jake to join you."

Hettle's gaze had locked on something in the distance. She drew her hand up to her mouth, jammed her thumb and pinkie past her lips, and let out a piercing whistle. Jake winced at the sound, then followed her sight line.

Singer stood beside the towering cedar in the front lawn—frozen, gaping back at them. His leg was lifted right above a weather-beaten bell-shaped buoy tied around the tree trunk. Hettle took her fingers out of her mouth and waved him away.

"Jacob, that tree has family history," Hettle said. "I would prefer that it not be urinated upon by you or your canine during your stay."

Jake bit his lip to keep from smiling at the word "urinated."

"Yep, got it."

Singer watched this large, stone-faced woman for a moment, then set his leg down. His red coat shimmered, and his tags clinked and jangled as he looked for a new spot to do his business. As Jake kept an eye out to make sure his dog didn't pee on some other family landmark, he saw something moving across the road.

Or rather *someone*.

A person. Watching them between the gap in the hedges.

Through the drizzle and fog, Jake could barely make the figure out. It was a kid or maybe a teenager. Definitely taller and older than he was with deep brown skin, tightly braided hair, and a green windbreaker.

Whoever it was saw Jake, too, and leapt back into the sea of ferns that lined the road. Jake opened his mouth to say something, but Hettle spoke first.

"It seems the hound has completed his urination. Let us go inside."

Jake couldn't tell whether his great-aunt had seen the person spying on them or not. Maybe he was the only one who caught it. He was always noticing little movements and sounds that other people missed. Those were the exact sorts of things that distracted him when he was supposed to be focusing in class. Some tiny click or rustle of fabric or the whisper of a classmate always seemed to trip him up at exactly the wrong time.

Jake's parents took a step toward the cabin door. Hettle didn't move to let them in. And she wasn't the sort of person you could just squeeze past.

"I apologize if I was unclear," she said. "I meant that Jacob and his hound should come inside. We have four guests coming for dinner and quite a bit of cooking still to do. There will be no time for idle chatter."

"Oh . . . ," Jake's mom hesitated, taken aback. "We thought we might stay for an hour. Maybe two. Our flight doesn't actually leave until tomorrow morning."

"I'm an excellent sous chef," his dad added with a friendly smile. "You remember my famous nachos, right?"

"With a whole can of olives on top," Hettle said. "Yes, I most definitely recall their distinct flavor."

She looked down at Jake. Her wide frame had shifted just a little so that he could see past her and into the living room. Bookcases lined the cedar-slatted walls all the way to the ceiling and there was a fire crackling in the hearth. Two leather chairs and a sagging couch piled with knitted blankets faced the fireplace.

"Would you prefer that your parents stay awhile, Jacob?" Hettle asked.

Water slid from the roof in fat drops, tapping out a rhythm on the gravel. Every few seconds one of them would hit the back of Jake's neck and slide down his collar, making him shiver.

Everyone was watching him.

"It's fine," Jake said, looking at his mom first, then his dad. "Go get ready for your trip."

"You sure, buddy?" his dad asked.

Jake glanced at the flames dancing in the fireplace and thought of how Hettle's eyes had crinkled at the edges when he'd laughed at her line about not being a hugger. He dropped a hand to his side; Singer trotted forward and moved underneath it, so that Jake could rub the hound's ear.

Five days. I've got my dog. And she's got all those books.

"I'll be fine," he said, swallowing hard.

His mom knelt down and gripped him by the shoulders. It was her trick for getting him to focus—one he actually liked.

"Remember," she said, "the retreat center doesn't allow cell phones or internet. If there's an emergency, Hettle has a number for the office that can get through to us."

"We'll check our phones and email once a day in the

reading room," Jake's dad added. "And if we mail you a letter on the day we get there, you should get it before the end of the week."

It was raining again. Sweeping in diagonally from the road. Jake's parents hugged him tight and started toward the car. He shielded his face with his hand to watch them go.

"Make me some pottery," he called with a half wave.

Once the car had crunched back onto the road, Hettle turned and stepped into her cabin.

"Come along, Jacob. We have a busy week and not a second to waste."

5

"An Aficionado of Acrobatics?"

Jake lingered at the cabin door, waiting for Singer to shake off. He noticed that the main part of the house was basically one wide room. Almost everything was cedar—from the walls to the bookcases to the mantel. Woven woolen wall hangings and dangling plants crowded in the corners. There was a record player on a cedar table and two old speakers standing tall on either side of it.

It smelled . . . *warm*. If warm could have a smell.

"You are quite likely to enjoy my neighbor Myron," Hettle called over her shoulder. "Most people do—he is a very charismatic fellow."

She sauntered into the kitchen, which was separated from the living area by a half wall, and drew four onions out of a basket. She lined them up on a butcher block that stood alone in the middle of the room.

"And I will be quite curious to see if you get along with his youngest daughter, Mia," she added.

"Why curious?" Jake asked, still standing at the door.

"In my perception she is a very strenuous judge of character," Hettle said. "Now, are you coming inside or would you prefer to sleep on the porch?"

Singer had finished shaking off and trotted over to the fireplace. Jake grinned at her and stepped across the threshold. He closed the door behind him, unshouldered his duffel, and set down Singer's bag of dog food.

The kitchen floor was tiled with smooth river rocks. A table made from one giant, polished slab of tree stood beside a row of windows that looked out on the overgrown front yard.

"Myron and Mia are bringing two guests with them," Hettle said. "Zoology students from Sweden."

Jake felt his brow crease. "What brings zoology students all the way to Oregon from Sweden?"

"This is quite an interesting and perhaps crucial question," Hettle said. "I think you should ask these young gentlemen precisely that."

She opened a drawer, drew out a knife, and set it on the butcher block.

"Now then," she said, "this knife is very sharp. I would prefer if you did not cut your finger off." She paused. "If you do, the nearest hospital is only one hour away."

Jake let out a laugh. That one had to be a joke—the timing was perfect. He was sure of it. *Mostly* sure.

Hettle stepped over to the oven and opened its heavy iron door. The rich smells that escaped drew a moan from Singer.

“We are having merimiespata,” she said. “It is a Finnish stew. Tonight I have made it with venison meat, hunted on this very land.”

“Venison?” Jake asked.

“Deer.”

Before Jake could react to the news that he would be eating deer for the first time, Hettle was halfway across the living room.

“I will leave you now to get dressed for our meal,” she said. “Hold a crust of dry bread in your mouth if the onions bring tears to your eyes.”

She lumbered upstairs and Jake was left alone. He’d never chopped onions before. And definitely never chopped anything with such a giant knife. He tried to remember what his dad did when he was making Bolognese sauce—bracing the onion with one hand and cutting with the other. When it made him cry, he tried Hettle’s advice—sure enough, the tears stopped.

“That’s a cool trick,” he said to himself, wiping his cheeks while biting the bread crust.

Soon, Jake had made a pile of odd-shaped onion pieces. He had a feeling they were bigger than how his dad chopped them, but his fingers were all still intact. He set down the knife, picked up his duffel bag, and went to find his room at the back of the house. It was small and felt like a ship’s cabin. There was a single bunk, built right into the wall, loaded with quilts.

Jake dropped his duffel on the bed and dragged Singer’s

kibble bag over to the far corner. On the way back to the kitchen, he stopped to look at the framed black-and-white photos that lined the shadowy hallway.

The first picture that caught his eye was of two young men, standing on either side of a giant tree. They wore trousers with suspenders but no shirts; both looked very serious. There was a big chunk cut out of the middle of the tree trunk, and a long saw lay flat inside the gap, sharp teeth facing out.

Underneath the photo it read "Christoph and Olaf cut timber on the North Fork of the Nehalem. 1956."

Jake stepped close to peer at a few other photos. There were more colossal trees, fog-covered hills, an iron ship washed up on the beach, and the ruins of an old restaurant. He looked at them one by one before drifting into the living room to browse the books.

After reading the spines of a few books, Jake found a paperback called *Bring 'Em Back Alive*. He pulled it out of the shelf. It smelled musty. The cover was different shades of faded yellow and green with an illustration of a man trying to lasso a tiger.

Jake crashed down on the couch with the paperback. The pages felt brittle in his fingers. He flipped through, scanning chapter titles like "Tiger Revenge," "Tapir on a Rampage," and "Man-Eater."

That last chapter title reminded Jake to feed Singer. He set *Bring 'Em Back Alive* on the end table, but what he saw there kept him locked in place. It was a green, cloth-covered book, just like his mom had described on their drive. He reached for it. *Homesteading on the Nehalem* and a curling fern were embossed on the cover in flaking silver.

Jake had just flipped to the table of contents when the stairs gave a heavy groan. He looked up to see Hettle, dressed in a blue housedress and a thick fisherman's sweater. She was wearing fur-lined leather boots that curled up at the toes.

"I see that you have located my grandfather's book," Hettle said as she steadied herself against the banister. She noticed *Bring 'Em Back Alive* on the end table. "And also his least favorite book ever. Two very intriguing selections, Jacob."

For the first time, Jake saw that his great-aunt was favoring her right leg. Not terribly but definitely noticeable. He snapped *Homesteading on the Nehalem* shut and set it back on the table as if he'd been caught snooping.

"I brought that volume out specifically to discuss with you," Hettle said, arriving at the bottom of the staircase. She sniffed the air. "However, I have a suspicion that our dinner requires some attention."

Jake followed his aunt into the kitchen and watched as she opened the oven again, lifting a giant iron pot from inside. When Hettle tipped open the lid, the smells flooded the cabin.

"Jacob, do you mind bringing *Homesteading on the Nehalem* to your room?" she asked. "It is quite old and delicate."

"No problem," Jake said.

He was turning to go when his aunt whipped a dish towel off a mixing bowl on the counter. Inside was a giant puffy mound of risen bread dough.

Jake hesitated. He'd always been curious about bread making. He watched as Hettle cut the dough ball in four parts and rolled one into an egg-shaped loaf. Next, she used a knife to slice the top of it three times.

"So that it can expand while it bakes," she said, without facing him.

She shaped another loaf, then turned and motioned for Jake to do the next two. Once the bread was in the oven, Hettle wiped her hands on her apron and took out two bottles of root beer from the fridge; she handed Jake one of them and he twisted off the cap.

"Kippis," she said, clinking her bottle with his.

The root beer was frosty and crisp. Jake reminded himself that he had to bring *Homesteading on the Nehalem* to his bedroom but he wanted to drink up while it was still ice cold.

Warm root beer is the worst. Everyone knows that.

"So," Hettle said, after drawing a long sip, "your mother told me that you were recently apprehended for destroying seven hundred dollars' worth of glass figurines at an outdoor craft fair."

Jake almost spat out his root beer. He hadn't expected Hettle to know about the Whole Saturday Market Fiasco. Who else had his parents told? Did his dad's cousin Rob the Party Magician know, too?

"It was . . . really stupid," Jake said after a pause. "I was trying to do a handstand. Or like, walk on my hands, I guess."

"Fascinating," Hettle said. "And are you an aficionado of acrobatics?"

Jake looked down at his shoes. "I don't know what that word means."

"An aficionado is someone who is very passionate about something—like reading old books or making rye bread or performing feats of contortion and strength in the middle of crowded outdoor marketplaces."

"I'm not an aficionado of acrobatics," Jake said.

"I can see that the subject is not enjoyable for you," Hettle said. "I have no right to tease—I have my own impulsive mistakes to be concerned about. One, in particular, that demands our attention as soon as possible."

Jake frowned and started to form a question but was interrupted by a brisk knock at the door. Hettle's expression shifted.

"The time to discuss my grave errors will be upon us soon enough," she said. "Unfortunately, now is not that time."

6
Myron and Mia

Jake was still trying to figure out what his aunt meant as he swung the door wide. He found himself face-to-face with a man who practically had to stoop to get in the door. He was at least a full head taller than Hettle.

"Jacob, meet Myron."

The man's skin was deep brown, and he wore his hair in locs. Not the thin twists that some kids at school had, but thick, heavy strands that framed his entire face. He had a grown-out beard that was flecked with gray and wore eyeglasses with delicate gold frames.

The commotion at the door stirred Singer, who clambered to his feet, trotted across the room, and slipped outside as Myron stepped in. A girl, maybe a few years older than Jake, came in next. Her skin was a shade darker than her dad's, and she wore braids with beads on the ends.

Jake noticed that the two of them had very similar eyebrows. Not that eyebrows were really a feature he made a habit of noticing. It was just that both Myron and his daughter had turned to watch Singer and their curious expressions looked almost identical.

"Jacob, this is Myron's daughter Mia," Hettle continued. "Jacob is the grandnephew I told you both about who is an expert on animal facts. The hound belongs to him."

"People call me Myron the Mycologist," Myron said, stomping his feet a few times on the doormat and reaching forward to grip Jake's hand. "That's someone who collects and studies mushrooms."

His voice was deeper than any voice Jake had ever heard, but it wasn't loud. It felt warm, as if Myron drank a glass of maple syrup before coming over.

"Like study them in a lab?" Jake asked.

"Not much anymore," Myron said. "These days I usually just sell them to high-end restaurants in Portland."

"You sell every single specimen?" Hettle asked. "Not a solitary mushroom remains?"

Jake noticed his aunt had an interesting way of emphasizing certain words by leaving more space between them.

"Not *every* one." Myron reached into the pocket of his coat, drew out a brown paper bag that was stapled shut, and tapped it with one long finger. "I always keep a few for my friends."

Hettle's eyes glowed. She led the others into the kitchen, and Myron scattered the bag's contents on the butcher block. Jake looked down to see twelve heavy mushrooms tumble out. Their caps were turned up, instead of down, and they were the color of taco chips that had been sprayed with fake cheese—except maybe a little more pinkish than pure orange.

"Lobster mushrooms," Myron said, elbowing Jake lightly. "The first of the season."

"Do they actually taste like lobster?" Jake wondered.

"Close," Myron said. "More like if lobsters grew underground. But . . . y'know, in a good way. Your great-aunt loves them. I'm the only one who gets to hunt for them on her property—except this week, because of the festival—so I figured I'd gather a few now before they get trampled."

"Let us please not ruin this evening with talk of trampling tourists," Hettle said. "It will put me in foul spirits."

She snatched up her knife from beside Jake's onion pile and sliced a mushroom in half, lengthwise—revealing its dense, creamy-looking flesh. Jake realized that he hadn't said anything to Mia yet and turned to his left. She was scribbling something in a spiral notebook.

"What's that?" Jake asked.

Mia only half looked at him. "Words I want to look up. Notes about interesting things that happen. First impressions of people."

Jake's mom bought him the exact same brand of notebook at the start of every school year. He always seemed to lose it by October.

"Have you been keeping it for a long time?" he asked.

Mia's eyes narrowed. "It's just a journal. Don't make a big thing out of it."

With Hettle slicing the mushrooms and Myron over at

the stove, investigating the stewpot and cooling bread, Jake searched for something else to say. There was so much to process that it felt like the cabin was buzzing around him.

"Hello?" Mia said.

Jake realized he'd spaced. "Sorry . . . I zone out sometimes. Was that you watching from the woods when I arrived?"

Mia scowled and motioned Jake over to the living room with a jerk of her head. He followed, stopping at the door to let Singer back in, and they stood on the rug by the fire.

"Of *course* it was me," Mia said, sounding annoyed. "Who else would it be?"

Jake shrugged. "Um . . . I don't know anyone in Nehalem. It could be a lot of people. Literally anyone. Why were you watching me, anyway?"

Mia ignored the question. "Hettle keeps saying you're some kind of animal expert. Is that true?"

"I just like them and know some stuff; it's not like I work at a zoo or anything. How old are you?"

"I'm turning thirteen on October 8. How old are you?"

"I'm turning twelve on September 9," Jake said. "Hey! We're one year, one month, and one day apart!"

"Actually," Mia said, "we're one year and one day *less* than a month apart."

"Oops . . . yeah," Jake said. "I have a good memory. Not as great at math, though."

Over in the kitchen, Myron shuffled a deck of cards and Hettle stirred a pan piled with lobster mushrooms, the onions Jake cut, a whole stick of butter, and a glug of white wine. The adults hadn't seemed to notice anything unusual happening over by the fire.

Not that anything *was* unusual. Except for the hushed tone Mia was using. And the fact that she seemed slightly annoyed with Jake, even though they'd just met.

"Look, kid," she said, "I need an animal expert who is good with subterfuge. Is that you or not?"

Jake could feel the heat from the fire warming his legs through his pants. Mia's eyes gave off a certain heat too—it made him not want to say the wrong thing.

"Ruses," the older girl said. "Trickery. Schemes. Ploys. Stratagems."

"Stratagems?"

Mia frowned. "You know a lot about animals or not?"

Something about Mia made Jake want to help her. "What do you need me to do?"

"Here's the scenario . . . ," Mia began.

She sat down in one of Hettle's leather armchairs, and Jake sunk into the sagging couch beside it. Singer stretched out on the rug in front of the fire.

Speaking under her breath, Mia explained: "These two zoology students emailed my dad's website a few days ago. I help him with the site, so I saw it first. The email was full of questions about the area. Very specific questions. It made me think they're looking for something."

"Probably mushrooms," Jake said, "right?"

"Nope," Mia said. "They were asking more about the river and the different streams. I think that they're looking for the Ruby-Backed Turtle."

Jake could tell by Mia's own reaction that he'd failed to hide his surprise.

"So you know about it?"

"I heard about it on the drive here," Jake said. "But my mom said that turtle doesn't exist."

He tried not to look at the table, where *Homesteading on the Nehalem* rested within arm's reach.

I can't believe I forgot to put that away! Focus, Jake!

"Yeah, I've never once heard anyone say that the turtle actually exists," Mia said. "But the email was *full* of turtle-related questions."

Hettle and Myron had started a cribbage game; their conversation fluttered across the room. Jake did his best to concentrate on Mia, even though the book was right there, calling to him.

"So my dad emailed them back—told them what he knew—and guess what they did next?"

Jake shrugged.

"They showed up. Here in Nehalem," Mia said. "Brought donuts to our house, first thing this morning. Then hung around as we ate them—asking us even more questions. But of course, there's not much to tell because—"

"There's no such thing as the Ruby-Backed Turtle," Jake said.

“Exactamente,” Mia said. “But check this out, because it gets stranger. When they asked about what animals live in the area, I told them how there’s a family of beavers upstream. And my dad said, ‘Yeah, they can be a *dam* problem.’ ”

Jake grinned. It was the exact type of pun his own dad would have liked.

“See, you smiled,” Mia said. “Because it’s clever. But it’s not *ha-ha* funny, right? These Swedish dudes gave big belly laughs, as if it were hysterical.”

“So?”

Jake snuck a glance at the table. He wanted to remember to put the book away the second Mia was done with her story. Leaving it sitting out in plain sight was making him feel jittery.

I can’t believe I didn’t pack a fidget spinner.

“The point is,” Mia said, “that no one thinks that joke is laugh-out-loud funny.”

“Maybe they just like puns,” Jake said with a shrug. “There’s this kid in my class who keeps a book of jokes in his desk. He’s always laughing out loud about puns.”

“*Dam* problem?” Mia said. “That reaction is suspicious. It makes me think they’re hiding something.”

Three loud knocks made by a single, heavy knuckle rang out—*clack, clack, clack*—on a rectangular stained-glass window set high in the cabin door that Jake hadn’t noticed until now. It rattled in its frame, like it was about to pop out and shatter on the ground. Myron pushed out his chair and crossed the room.

While her dad's back was to them, Mia leaned close to Jake's ear. "During dinner I want you to say three animal facts. The first two should be real; the last one should be fake. If they agree with the fake one—"

The door swung open, and she never got the chance to finish the thought. It didn't matter—Jake knew where she was headed. If the visiting zoology students agreed with the fake fact, it would mean that maybe they weren't zoology students at all.

7
Mia's Gambit

Two young men with wide smiles, bushy blond mustaches, and almost fluorescently white teeth clomped into the cabin. Jake could see that they were twin brothers. Also, that they had similar taste in clothes. One wore a mustard-yellow tracksuit with maroon stripes down the side, and the other wore a maroon tracksuit with mustard-yellow stripes. They both wore white sneakers speckled with mud.

"Jake, Hettle," Myron said, "meet Angus and Ragnar Magnusson. They're zoology students."

Both men had rose-colored cheeks and hair so blond it was practically white, which they wore spiked with gel. It looked like it had been cut just hours earlier.

"Yes, exactly," said the one in the maroon tracksuit, flashing his perfect smile. "I am Angus Magnusson, a zoology student, quite pleased to make the acquaintance with you both!"

Jake smiled a greeting, then glanced to his right and

saw Mia, eyebrows arched, watching closely. She clutched her notebook to her chest.

"I am Ragnar Magnusson, also a zoology student," the brother with the mustard tracksuit said. "And the twin brother of Angus, though I am older by eleven minutes. Ha-ha!"

Jake looked over at his great-aunt. She set the stew pot down on the table and gave it a final stir. With the two men focused in her direction, she wiped her hands on her apron and stepped forward with a nod.

"Hallo," she said gruffly. "I have heard that you two young men are Swedish."

"Yes," Ragnar said. "And we have been told that you're Finnish! We are neighbors! What a very pleasant connection!"

Jake noticed a crescent-shaped scar on Ragnar's left cheek. He thought to himself, *Rag-nar, moon-scar.* It was the only difference he'd noticed between the two Magnussons so far, besides the tracksuits.

"My family line goes back to Finland," Hettle said. "And I lived there for seventeen years, in my younger days. But I am a woman of the Oregon woods before all else."

Myron gripped Angus and Ragnar by their shoulders and steered them toward the table. "Hettle has stories for days! She's the best cook in the region, too—so let me suggest that we eat while everything's hot."

Mia grabbed a pitcher of ice water from the counter and Jake picked up the breadbasket. They sat down next to each other, on the side of the table facing the kitchen.

The Magnusson brothers sat across from them, facing the window. Hettle and Myron sat at either end.

The six of them passed around the stew, the bread, the water, and a plate arranged with thin slices of lobster mushrooms and the onions Jake had cut.

"A very nice slicing job," Hettle remarked, with a sly glance at Jake. "And it seems no fingers were lost."

"Hey, Jake," Myron said, while chewing, "want to see something wild?"

Jake was distracted, tracking the plate of mushrooms and onions. He was excited to try them, but the plate had stopped moving once it got to the Magnussons. He wondered if he should ask them to pass it.

"Nephew," Hettle said, "did you hear Myron?"

"Oh, sorry, I— Can you tell me again?"

Myron pointed to the mushrooms with the tines of his fork. "Lobster mushrooms—a type of fungi." He pointed to the bread. "Bread made with yeast—also a type of fungi." He pointed to the beer bottles and wineglasses. "Beer and wine—sugars converted to alcohol, by, you guessed it—"

"Fungi," Mia finished.

"Exactly," Myron said. "Fungi is everywhere. Literally all around us. Especially in these forests."

Mia did a jokey voice like a presenter on TV. "And if you visit Myron's Fungal Jungle dot com, you can get a lot more fungi facts from this . . . wait for it . . . *fun guy*!"

She giggled and smiled a little at Jake, like they were in on some private joke. Jake flashed a smile back. For seven or eight long minutes after that, everyone was mostly silent—except for a few mutters about how delicious everything was.

"Ragnar," Jake finally said, "could you pass the . . . ?"

He trailed off when he saw that the lobster mushrooms were gone. There were just a few odd-shaped onion pieces left.

So much for that idea.

Singer wandered across the room and lay down under the table at Jake's feet. Every few seconds, when no scraps fell to the ground, he let out a morose sigh.

Angus opened his mouth to say something. "Hettle, I—"

"Do you know that redbone coonhounds can smell up to a hundred thousand times better than humans?" Jake blurted. He wanted to get one of his animal facts out of the way as soon as possible.

Ragnar swallowed his stew and gave Jake a broad grin. "Of course we know this."

"After all," Angus added, "we both are zoology students at a very prestigious Swedish university."

Mia's brow was furrowed. Hettle was also watching the Magnusson twins closely from the other end of the table.

"Is there a particular focus to your zoological studies?" Hettle asked, tearing a hunk of rye bread off one of the loaves.

"We are studying amphibians," Angus said, flashing a gleaming smile. "This is why we told Myron that we are very interested in the story of the Ruby Turtle. It was written about by your grandfather—is that correct?"

Hettle didn't answer. Jake noticed Mia's hand moving out of the corner of his eye—scribbling notes without ever looking down at what she wrote.

Myron dipped a crust of rye in his stew and smiled across the table. "That's what I was trying to tell you, Hettle. These boys came all the way here because they heard something about that old yarn your grandfather wrote way back when. Wild, right?"

"It is most certainly curious," Hettle said, chewing. "Though perhaps not a wise use of their resources."

Angus and Ragnar smiled at the older woman, ready for anything else she might add. But the words simply hung in the air for a few seconds before Hettle rose to her feet, picked up the water pitcher, and stepped into the kitchen to refill it.

"The mushrooms were a hit!" Myron said, pointing across the table with his fork. "They're already gone."

A shoe, belonging to Mia, tapped Jake's foot. When he didn't move she did it again—once, twice, three times.

Jake looked over at her. She motioned down to her notebook with her eyes. He leaned forward to slyly glance down at it but couldn't make out what was written. Mia tapped his foot again, and he leaned down a little farther, pretending like he was reaching below the table to pet Singer.

ASK THE NEXT TWO QUESTIONS!!! was written in big, capital letters across the page.

As he sat back up, Jake saw the Magnusson brothers staring right at him. They were both smiling with those glistening grins.

"Jacob," Angus said, "what do you think of this tale of the Ruby Turtle? Does it capture your imagination and spark your curiosity, as it does for my brother and me?"

"I . . . I guess I don't really know much about it," Jake said. "I just heard about Gustav's book for the first time on the drive here."

"That is a tremendous shame," Ragnar said, slurping a spoonful of stew. "You must have your aunt share each detail of this fantastic tale with you!"

"Or perhaps you might ask her to share the story with *all* of us?" Angus pressed, eyes widening with excitement. "My brother and I have only heard whispers of it from other very accomplished zoologists at the prestigious zoological school we attend in Sweden."

"Yes, we have not yet seen the book that the story comes from," Ragnar added.

"You guys sure know how to drop a hint," Mia muttered, almost under her breath.

Both brothers were sitting up so straight and smiling so bright that it reminded Jake of a cheesy commercial playing late at night. They were clearly waiting for him to ask his aunt to tell the story of the Ruby-Backed Turtle. Meanwhile, Mia was tapping his foot again and Hettle was lingering in the kitchen, looking increasingly upset by these tall, mustachioed strangers.

You're ramping up. Calm down.

Jake's thoughts flitted away—pinballing off in a whole new direction. He had a split second of wondering what his parents were up to, then Singer rolled over onto the foot that Mia wasn't tapping, and there was something from a few minutes earlier still bouncing around in his brain, something Angus had said.

You were distracted. You probably didn't hear him right.

Jake tried to replay the exchange back in his head but Mia was practically stomping his foot now and the other one had fallen asleep because of Singer and the book was just resting out in the open on the table and the Magnussons were waiting for him to ask Hettle about the turtle and he really needed a fidget spinner or a squeeze ball or *something* to do with all his energy and—

"I have to walk the dog!" Jake declared, a little too loud.

Everyone gaped. Even Myron looked taken aback.

"I . . . uh," Jake said, "have these . . . concentration issues . . . and I get too many thoughts running through my head. Sometimes my mom has me walk the dog . . . It helps."

"Why don't you do that," Hettle said, returning to her seat. "Perhaps you would like Mia to go with you?"

"Yeah," Jake said, "that'd be great, actually."

He pushed out his chair, rose to his feet, and made his little "coo-eee" sound. Singer slid out from under the table and trotted toward the door. Mia slyly pocketed her notebook and stood up, flashing Jake an annoyed glare as she exited the cabin.

The sky was slate gray and there was a foggy mist so fine that it was hard to tell if it was falling from above or rising from the ground. Jake, Mia, and Singer crunched across the gravel in silence for about fifteen steps.

When they were parallel with the giant cedar, Jake realized he'd been too overwhelmed to remember Singer's leash. It wouldn't be safe to walk along the road without one. Besides, he wanted to be out of the sight line of the Magnussons. He glanced over his shoulder and sure enough, Ragnar was staring right at him.

Without talking, Jake doubled back and headed toward the river, walking upstream. Mia followed but he could feel her eyes burning a hole in the back of his head. Singer passed them, loping ahead.

When they reached the sloping riverbank, Mia wrenched Jake's shoulder. "Listen, kid, I asked for your help. It was a small thing. Now I'm out here with you and your dog when I could be figuring out what's going on with those two Swedes."

She took a small tape recorder out of her pocket and dramatically pressed STOP.

She was recording all that? This girl is like some kind of secret agent!

Jake tried to calm down and gather his thoughts. He watched the water eddy near the bank for a second, then looked up at Mia.

"I'm not going to try to trick Angus and Ragnar with a fake animal fact."

Mia's face hardened like she just might push Jake into the surging Nehalem River. "I knew I shouldn't have—"

"I don't need to," Jake interrupted. "Didn't they say they're studying amphibians and that's why they're interested in the story of the Ruby-Backed Turtle?"

Mia flipped to a page of her notebook and started reading her notes. "They call it the 'ruby turtle,' but yeah. Why?"

Jake offered a crooked grin. "Turtles aren't amphibians. They're reptiles."

It took a second for Mia to register what Jake meant. Then her eyes lit up. "You're one hundred percent sure?"

"It *seems* like they would be amphibians, because they live on water and on land," Jake said. "But real zoology students wouldn't get confused about that."

Mia broke into a wide smile. It was the sort of smile that made Jake smile too. "So we now know, for sure, they aren't who they say they are."

Jake whistled to Singer, who came bounding through a wall of emerald ferns. He felt glad to be officially on Mia's side. Even if he was still a little confused about what was actually going on. Or why it should even matter if the Magnussons wanted to pretend to be zoologists to look for a turtle that didn't exist.

"Now we have to figure out who they *actually* are," Mia said.

"And," Jake added, pushing aside his questions and letting himself get caught up in the moment, "why they decided to lie in the first place."

8
Homesteading on the Nehalem

Jake and Singer followed Mia back inside the cabin. The whole house smelled of butter, sugar, and vanilla. Hettle was busy getting dessert ready in the kitchen; a fresh log crackled away on the fire.

As if everything was normal. As if they were among friends.

But Jake knew everything was different. They'd caught Angus and Ragnar in a lie. Now nothing was certain. Were those even their real names?

Are those even their real teeth?

Mia walked over to the butcher block, cool as could be. Jake admired how calm she was, the opposite of the ramped-up feeling he had when his mind raced in too many directions. Hettle had made some sort of dessert he didn't recognize, and she was busy scooping up servings of it. Without missing a beat, Mia started spooning a little ring of caramel around the outside of each plate, then dolloped fresh whipped cream on top.

In the living room, Myron was settled in one of Hettle's plush reading chairs. He wore half-frame reading glasses over his regular glasses, and his face was shielded by his locs. He was reading *Homesteading on the Nehalem.*

Jake kicked himself for not taking the book to his room before he went outside with Mia. It was the exact sort of situation where his mom would say "Honey, *slooooow down* and think it out."

Singer settled in front of the fire with a soft groan. Someone had set a bone on the rug and the dog immediately started gnawing on it. The Magnusson brothers were still at the table, spoons clinking against their bowls, wiping the bottom of the stewpot with torn hunks of bread.

"Angus, Ragnar," Mia said while fixing the desserts, "what are your favorite amphibians to study?"

The Magnusson brothers froze, mid-chew. Their eyes met for a fraction of a second, almost too quickly to notice. But Jake caught it.

"Actually," Ragnar said, face breaking into a wide smile, "my brother misspoke earlier. We are studying reptiles, not amphibians. That's why we're so interested in the story of the Ruby Turtle. Because it is a *reptile.*"

Angus's eyes widened. "Exactly, yes! It is a reptile. I meant to say this, and my tongue was tied."

It was quiet for a moment. The only sounds in the room were the pops and crackles of the fire.

"I have found myself tongue-tied on occasion," Hettle said, still completely focused on plating her dessert. "It never seems to leave me saying the exact wrong word."

Jake saw a flicker of panic in Ragnar's eyes. His mustache gave an odd shiver. The eleven-minute-older Magnusson brother cleared his throat.

"I didn't want to embarrass Angus, my brother, by pointing out his mistake," he said. "We are still perfecting our English."

"Yes, precisely that," Angus said, nodding eagerly. "In Swedish, amphibians is 'amfibier.'"

He looked desperately over to his brother, who refused to meet his gaze.

"What are 'reptiles' in Swedish?" The question was out before Jake even knew he was speaking.

"It's . . . ," Angus said. "It's . . . um—"

"Reptiler," Ragnar muttered into his lap.

"Amfibier and reptiler," Mia said. "Those don't seem too easy to mix up."

Her voice had an edge that she couldn't hide; her dad looked up from his reading.

"Everything okay over there?" Myron called, turning a little in his chair.

"Quite fine," Hettle replied, her gaze steadied on Jake and Mia. "Our guests were just sharing the nuances of the Swedish tongue with us. An extraordinarily complex language, it seems."

Jake felt his face start to curl into a smile but caught himself. Myron waved the green cloth cover of *Homesteading on the Nehalem* in Hettle's direction.

"I had no idea your grandfather knew so much about mushrooms," he called. "Who cares about the turtle story—I want to see these chanterelle spots that he writes about!"

Every eye in the room snapped to the mycologist. Every eye except Jake's. Instead, he watched Hettle for a reaction. She was already back to plating desserts.

"You cannot trust every story in that old book," she said. "My grandfather was known to be a lover of fables."

"Well, I'm going to check out these places he mentions anyway," Myron said. He glanced at the faded silver fern on the book's cover with admiration. "Really fascinating stuff."

"He is holding *Homesteading on the Nehalem*?" Ragnar asked. He pushed his chair out and stood up so fast that his thighs banged the underside of the table, making the dishes rattle. "I would love to have a look at—"

"Dessert is ready," Hettle said, voice calm and flat.

Myron rose to his feet, setting the book down on a wooden table beside the plush leather chair. He rubbed his hands together eagerly. "Now for the real treat of the evening, Hettle Olsson's sticky toffee pudding!"

Hettle looked directly at Ragnar. "Let us all sit."

The gangly twin ignored her and started walking toward the fire, eyes focused on the book that Myron had just put down.

"I am not much for sweets," he said cheerily, covering the distance in long strides. "Perhaps I might just sit in that comfortable chair and—"

“I also do not have a sweet tooth,” Angus said, standing up.

Ragnar was all the way to the table now, looking down at *Homesteading on the Nehalem*. Angus was only two steps behind him.

“I would quite prefer that you join us,” Hettle said firmly.

The brothers turned toward her and smiled in unison, wider than ever.

Angus gave an odd little bow. “As we say, we’d rather—”

“You will sit and watch us eat then,” Hettle said. She spoke with a force Jake had never heard in her voice until now. “Similar to how my nephew and I watched you eat double your portion of the mushrooms and never got any for ourselves.”

Ragnar stared at her for a moment, smile frozen on his face. He tugged on his mustache, as if deciding what to do.

“Of course,” he said, trudging back to the table. “And apologies if I ate more than my share of . . .”

Angus followed his brother and crashed back down next to him. Hettle motioned to Jake and Mia, and they carried dessert plates to the table two at a time.

“I’m sorry,” Myron said, “is everything okay with you all? Did I miss something?”

Jake tried to answer it for his great-aunt. “Aunt Hettle is . . . She’s just worried about the book getting damaged.”

He looked to Mia for help.

"Because Ragnar was sopping up his stew with bread," she added. "His fingers could be greasy."

This was only a little better. Mia and Jake both turned to Hettle now.

She nodded solemnly. "Greasy fingers concern me greatly. Jacob, if you would not mind putting the book away . . ."

Jake sprung to his feet, walked straight to the living room, slid the book off the table, and started down the hall, feeling the eyes of everyone in the house on him. When he got to his tiny bedroom, he scanned around for a spot to hide *Homesteading on the Nehalem*. Finally, he lifted up the mattress and began to slide the book underneath.

Behind him someone gave a disapproving *tsk*. Jake wheeled around. Mia stood in the open door.

"That's the first place anyone would look," she said, arms folded across her chest.

"Also, always close the door when carrying out covert operations," she added. "It's starting to seem like you've never had to be sneaky before."

Mia stepped inside and shut the door. It latched with a crisp *click*.

Jake frowned. "How did you—"

"I said I needed to go to the bathroom. They're going to suspect something, but we'll have to risk it." She stepped farther into the room. "They came all the way from Sweden because of a made-up turtle, which is weird. And your aunt doesn't want them to know anything about it, which is double weird."

"And your dad somehow hasn't caught on to any of it so far," Jake said. "Triple weird."

Mia grinned. "That's just the way he is. My sister always teases him about it . . . When she's home."

When she mentioned her sister, Mia's gaze flicked down to the floor for just a second. Jake looked around the room for another place to hide the book. There was a desk, but it was built into the wall like the bed and didn't have drawers. The dresser had drawers, but he hadn't unpacked yet, so they were empty.

"I've got it," Mia said.

She went to the bed, took the pillowcase off Jake's pillow, and reached for *Homesteading on the Nehalem.* He handed her the book and she dropped it inside, folding it up like a package. Then she opened the bag of Singer's dog food, buried the pillowcase under the kibble, and rolled the bag shut.

"There," she said, spinning on her heels and smiling at Jake. "Who's gonna check inside a dog food bag?"

"Great idea," Jake said, looking at the bare pillow on his bed, covered in yellow sweat rings. "Plus, now I get to sleep on a thousand-year-old pillow without a pillowcase."

"You're funny, when you want to be," Mia said, giving him a half smile as she dusted off her hands and breezed out of the room. "I like it."

9

"The Ruby-Backed Turtle, Nature's Oddest Creation"

The Ruby-Backed Turtle wasn't mentioned again until all the guests had gone, the dishes were done, and the fire was just embers. Jake glanced at the clock. It was almost 10 p.m.

"Sorry I forgot to put the book away before people got here," he said to his aunt. "I get distracted sometimes . . . it's called ADHD . . . and anyway, I didn't mean to—it's just the bread seemed so cool and then the root beer and then Myron and Mia came and then—"

"Am I correct to presume that you have it well hidden now?" Hettle interrupted.

Jake thought of the book—rolled up in his pillowcase, buried deep in a bag of kibble. "You could say that."

Hettle let out a yawn loud enough to make Singer stir and started up the first few steps toward her room.

"Then no harm has been done," she said. Halfway up the stairs, she turned toward Jake. "In the meantime, I think you should read my grandfather Gustav's writing. Specifically, the chapter about the Ruby-Backed Turtle. That way, you will know what all of this commotion is about."

She wavered for a moment, as if there was something more to say, then turned back and continued up to the second floor, gripping the banister. The stairs creaked under her weight.

After hearing Hettle's door click shut, Jake let Singer outside one more time. Then he grabbed *Homesteading on the Nehalem* from the kibble bag and put a log on the fire. It had dried droplets of red sap spread across its bark; soon, they began to crackle and throw sparks.

Singer yawned and splayed out on the rug. Jake curled up on the couch—jamming his feet into the gap where the seat cushion met the back pillows. According to the table of contents, "The Ruby-Backed Turtle, Nature's Oddest Creation" was chapter 27 of *Homesteading on the Nehalem*, the second-to-last chapter in the book.

Jake flipped to the page, dug his feet deeper into the crack between the couch cushions, and started to read.

XXVII—The Ruby-Backed Turtle, Nature's Oddest Creation

After the long, wet winter of 1936, spent mostly indoors, the family and I took to exploring the deep woods around the homestead. We would keep a

weather eye open for the yellow trumpets of chanterelles hidden by leaf litter, but mostly these hikes were simply to draw fresh air into our lungs.

Life is a dance and the natural world is the human being's eternal partner. The choreography must not be allowed to grow stagnant. New steps must be added or a certain electricity of the spirit will be extinguished.

The paragraph struck Jake. He liked the way the words flowed, but he'd been reading too fast to catch their meaning. He read it again. Mouthing each word. "The human being's eternal partner . . . electricity of the spirit."

As we explored the deep woods, the children would oftentimes join Hildy and me. If ever they dared whinge about being cold or tired, we were quick to send them padding right back down the track. On those occasions, the two of us would walk along the thin paths, ferns sweeping against our legs with each step.

We were always happy to have a few moments alone, marveling at the greenery that surrounded us.

Rain pattered on the cabin roof. Jake liked the sound of it. He wondered if his own parents were "happy to have a few moments alone," too. At the very least, he figured they were excited about a week where they wouldn't have to tell him to focus every time his thoughts drifted.

"But seriously," he muttered to Singer, "I probably *should* focus."

On one of these private walks, with the children back at the cabin, bundled up near the fire, Hildy and I stumbled into an emerald glade. There we found a babbling brook cutting its way towards a larger stream. The banks were firm and blanketed in thick moss. The riverbed itself was full of tiny pebbles that shimmered as the creek tumbled over them.

"A faerie garden," Hildy said.

She had soured on the weather of the Nehalem country but could not help her excitement at seeing this tranquil spot. I must admit that I was also taken aback. It was something stolen from a dream. The tumbling brook, the brilliant green moss, the silent, towering trees . . .

Exploring the clearing, I discovered a number of chanterelles that ringed the floor of the glade. As I plucked these golden mushrooms, Hildy began to yoik. Those not from the Nordic regions may not know this style of singing, in which tones are used to express what words cannot, but trust me when I say Hildy is quite wonderful at it. In that moment, she was trying to capture the feeling of this "faerie garden" with her voice alone.

Watching Hildy kneel on a bed of moss, braiding her silken hair, voice filling the clearing, tones

gently tumbling and twisting like the rivulets of water over the pebbles, I am not afraid to admit that my eyes filled with tears. I fell to my knees on the bank of the brook, rolled up my sleeves, and gathered cold water in my cupped hands. It tasted rich with minerals.

I splashed my face and washed the day's sweat from my neck. Once the song had finished, I laid down my wool-lined logging coat and reclined on the springy tufts of moss. Hildy leaned back into me and nuzzled her head against my shoulder.

Reading about people taking a nap while he lay curled up on the couch in front of a crackling fire with rain tapping on the roof was about as clear of an invitation to sleep as ever there was. Jake could literally feel his eyelids falling shut, as if they were weighted down somehow.

"Come on, buddy," he said, sitting up. "Just finish this chapter."

My wife woke with a start. It was dark, but the sky was clear and the moon hung full above us, like a bone-white saucer.

"Gustav, I'm cold," Hildy said. "And the children . . ."

As my senses returned to me, I peered all around us. Though the forest itself felt foreboding so late at night, our special clearing was brightly lit and

peaceful. If it was indeed a faerie garden, this moment was its witching hour.

I stepped a few feet away to look for more chanterelles and heard my wife gasp—drawing breath so sharply that I feared she had slipped into the creek. I wheeled around to see that this wasn't the case. She was standing safely on its banks, her back to me.

As I approached, Hildy remained still, save for her mouth. Her jaw was working, but she failed to form words. "Darling, what is it?" I asked.

Looking down, I saw an animal perched on a rock. A turtle, its shell no bigger than the palm of a child's hand and looking as delicate as a leaf. Its head and neck no larger than my thumb. And yet . . . here was the most magnificent creature I had ever seen. Perhaps, ever to exist.

The top of the shell was made up of diamond-shaped sections, all of them about the size of my thumbnail. Each section shone deep red in the bright moonlight. As if they were gems set directly onto the animal's back by some enchanted gnome or troll.

"Gustav, have you ever seen . . . ," Hildy hesitated. "Have you ever even heard of . . . ?"

The turtle slipped off its rock and into the water. For a moment, we could see flashes of its magnificent shell beneath the surface under the light of the moon. Then it disappeared into the shadows where the banks hung over the gurgling brook.

There could be only one possible name for this strange specimen.

"The Ruby-Backed Turtle," I whispered.

"The Ruby-Backed Turtle," Hildy replied.

US 191 North—2:19 a.m., MONDAY

Stick was flying down the road, his whole truck rattling. He'd left Scrub Pine just before 4 p.m. and already crossed the entire state of New Mexico and a little corner of Colorado. He was deep into Utah now, with a tank full of gas and a thermos full of coffee.

"I reckon I'll make Nehalem Bay by morning," he muttered. "Even if it means I don't sleep a dang wink."

Stick didn't mind driving through the night. He felt like the last desperado on earth, all alone, out on the open road, crossing the badlands. He kept his window down, wind whipping against his face. It dried out his eyes until they were bloodshot and bleary, but at least it kept him alert.

With his left hand gripping the steering wheel, Stick let his right hand slide down to rest on the bench seat. It settled on the bowie knife.

Click. Stick unbuttoned the sheath.

Click. Buttoned it back up.

The knife and its owner had seen their fair share of strange jobs before this one. Stick remembered driving a Bengal tiger from Florida to New York City in this very same truck. After delivering the 537-pound beast to the apartment of a movie producer on the thirty-second floor of a high-rise in the dead of night, he'd parked in a lot nearby and zonked out on the seat—only to be awakened by the blare of his cell phone three hours later.

"You have to take this monster back," the frantic voice on the other end of the line begged. "*Hurry!*"

"Well," Stick drawled, "I suppose I can haul it back to Florida for ya tomorrow morning. I reckon it'll cost you double, though."

"I'll pay quadruple if you're here in an hour!"

Stick smirked as he remembered returning to the movie producer's apartment to find a giant claw mark through a painting of a soup can in the entryway. He'd made a lot of money bringing that tiger back and forth to Florida. And if by some strange chance this turtle was real, he'd make twenty times more off *it*.

"Nothing will get in my way," Stick muttered.

Certainly not this woman he'd been told about, Hettle Olsson, who owned the land this "Ruby Turtle" had been seen on more than seventy years ago. He patted his bowie knife.

"My Texas toothpick will make sure of that."

10

Surprise Visitors

Jake awoke to the sound of Hettle on the stairs, steps creaking beneath her. The sound woke Singer too. He pawed at the rug a few times, smacked his lips, stretched, and trotted over to the couch to nuzzle his snout against Jake's cheek.

"I'm awake, I'm awake," Jake groaned. He rolled up into a sitting position with a yawn.

"Hallo, Jacob," Hettle said, crossing the living room and heading toward the kitchen. "I see that you decided to slumber on the couch. I hope you did not find your room uncomfortable."

"It wasn't on purpose," Jake said. "I don't remember anything after reading the Ruby-Backed Turtle chapter of your grandpa's book."

"He is your relative as well," Hettle said. "His blood is in your veins, just as it is in mine."

Jake was still too groggy to come up with any answer more clever than a nod.

"After we eat," his aunt said, "there are a few more sections of the book I might have you peruse. If nothing else, it is a fascinating window into this unique region."

Hettle made coffee and watered a giant ficus and three potted ferns while Jake rubbed the sleep out of his eyes and stretched. After letting Singer outside, he walked down the hall to the bathroom, washed his face, brushed his teeth, and went to his room to change.

He knew his parents would want him to put his clothes away. But they were on a plane to California—so Jake decided to skip it.

There was one thing he wasn't going to leave out, though. He walked back to grab *Homesteading on the Nehalem*, carried it to his room, and was just about to roll it up in the pillowcase when he decided to read one more chapter. The one his mom had talked about on their drive to Nehalem—"The Curious Fable of the Boy Who Turned into a Tree."

He found the chapter in the table of contents, crashed down on his bed, and started to read.

A few years ago, on the banks of the Nehalem, lived a family not unlike this one. The only difference was that instead of two girls and two boys, there were three boys and only one girl. The mother of these children (who was quite beautiful but not nearly as beautiful as *your* mother) had to constantly remind her children to bring coats and sweaters outside when they wanted to play.

The children, like all good children, obeyed her. All except for the youngest, called Fritz. This naughty little fellow absolutely refused to wear a coat outside.

Jake took a chunk of pages between his fingers and flipped it, landing on the start of a new chapter.

XII —The Tale of the Woodsman and the Talking Deer

In the deep dark woods at the base of the mountains, where the ferns grow large and the sun only shines seven days of the year, there lived a towering woodsman. He stood head and shoulders above even the tallest men, and the muscles in his arms tore the seams of his shirts so often that he had to pay the mountain trolls on the first day of each month to mend them.

Jake flipped some more. He skipped past a chapter on getting mildew smell out of clothes and another on how to patch roof holes during a storm. He stopped when he found a limerick.

Away on the opposite bank,
Stands a cabin whose scent is quite dank.
But it's not dust or mold,

That makes it smell old.
It's the owners whose odor is rank!

Jake was still chuckling about that when he heard Hettle let Singer back inside the cabin.

"He's probably hungry."

After digging a plastic measuring cup full of dog food out of the bag of kibble, Jake hid the book again and returned to the kitchen. He poured the food into Singer's dish and filled his water bowl at the sink.

"Help yourself," Hettle said to Jake, waving a hand toward the table. "Pancakes are best served hot."

There were two serving plates on the oak slab—one piled with pancakes and another with scrambled eggs. Hettle poured herself another cup of coffee.

Jake frowned as he looked at the place settings. "You have three plates here."

"You are quite astute," his great-aunt replied.

"Is someone else coming?"

"It is very possible that more than one person is coming," Hettle said. "However, only one is welcome to join us for a meal of pancakes and eggs."

She speared three pancakes with her fork, spread a pat of butter on top of them, and practically drowned them in maple syrup. Jake waited for his aunt to finish the thought, but Hettle's attention was turned to the front door. She suddenly looked very pleased with herself.

The blinds were drawn, but someone was stomping their shoes clean on the doormat.

"Do you mind welcoming our guest?" Hettle said, glancing at the clock above the sink. "I am eager to know if my guesses about the identity of our first visitor are correct."

Jake crossed the room and swung open the door. He was greeted by Mia, with her hand raised to knock. When Jake looked over at his aunt he could tell this was exactly who she'd expected.

"Eight o'clock on the button," Hettle said. "You are every bit as prompt as your father."

Mia wore a backpack and was dressed in a windbreaker and jeans.

"Long time no see," Jake said.

He leaned past the door to look for anyone else. He didn't see anyone, just a whole ocean of gray sky above. Mist tickled his skin.

As she stepped inside, Mia whispered to Jake. "I think we should tell your aunt everything we know so far. We might need an adult's help on this mission."

"I'm pretty sure she already knows everything we know," Jake said, following her into the kitchen. "Also, what *is* our mission?"

Mia didn't answer. She just stared down at the table with its three place settings, then up at her host.

"How did you know I was coming?"

"When I explained my eagerness to get to bed last night," Hettle said, hands folded across her body, "I also mentioned that I like to eat breakfast at eight a.m. sharp. I wondered if a keen girl like you might take note."

"So it was a test?" Jake asked.

"Yes," Hettle replied. "But not of Mia. It was a test of—"

The answer hit both Jake and Mia at the exact second that three loud knocks rang out against the stained-glass window set high in the front door. Hettle winced.

"What do we do?" Jake asked.

"We have to open it," Mia said. *"Don't we?"*

"Why?" Jake wondered

He had that same panicky feeling that he got on days when all his friends had their homework written down and he'd only written a list of the fastest land animals on the crumpled pages of his assignment notebook.

CLACK! CLACK! CLACK!

Hettle took a bite of her pancakes, chewing slowly and deliberately. "I suppose we open it because we do not want them to know that we distrust them quite yet. Also, because I would prefer they not break that precious window. However, you must tell them that I am not available. I have no patience for these smiling Swedes, they aggravate me tremendously."

Mia and Jake crept to the door side by side. Mia eased the door open just wide enough to see the Magnussons.

"Hallo!" the twins chimed, smiling and angling their heads to one side in unison.

They wore the same tracksuits from the night before. Jake noticed a few flecks of wine-colored stew grease on the chest of Ragnar's yellow jacket.

"We have brought with us muffins!" Ragnar said, holding up a giant basket wrapped in cellophane.

"Tasty pastries!" Angus added. "Blueberry. Chocolate. Poppy. An excellent selection!"

"Hettle is—" Jake began.

"Not feeling well!" Mia added.

"In the shower," Jake finished at the exact same time.

The Magnussons' identical smiles faded in unison.

"She's not feeling well but also in the shower?" Ragnar asked. "That seems quite curious."

"Not really," Mia insisted. "She hoped it might help settle her stomach."

Jake felt like he should add something. "That way if she barfs, it just goes right down the drain. Bloop!"

The "bloop" line silenced everyone. Ragnar's eyes narrowed. Angus's mustache twitched.

"Um . . . maybe visit later this afternoon," Jake said, starting to close the door.

Ragnar jammed his foot against the wood and gave Jake and Mia another toothy smile. "When this afternoon? What time, *precisely*, might we, two zoologists who have come from so very far away, hope to visit your aunt?"

Mia leaned her shoulder into the door, while still trying to look casual.

"We're all going to the opening ceremony of the Blackberry Moon Festival today," she said. "You'll see her there!"

Over by the fire, Singer noticed all the jostling at the door and gave a sharp bark. It echoed through the cabin.

"Um—my dog is hungry!" Jake said. "Bye!"

Angus and Ragnar took a half step back, and Mia practically slammed the door in their faces. Then she wrenched it right back open again to snatch the basket from Ragnar.

"We'll pass these along to Hettle, I promise!" she said, flinging the door closed a second time and flipping the deadbolt.

She turned back to Jake and lifted the basket with a smile and a shrug. "These Swedes have excellent taste in baked goods."

She set the basket on the kitchen island and started unwrapping the cellophane. Jake looked over at his great-aunt, still seated at the table. She pressed a finger to her lips, then motioned for him to peek past the blinds to see if the Magnussons were gone. He watched as they folded their long bodies into a tiny white rental car and motored off.

When Jake turned back to the table, his aunt had her last bite of pancakes poised on the tines of her fork.

"Jacob, Mia," Hettle said, "it was a lie of omission for me to pretend as if I did not know why the Magnussons—and perhaps others like them—have come to Nehalem just in time for the festival. Are you prepared to hear the truth?"

11
300 Letters

Hettle folded her hands and looked straight at Jake. "One month before you were arrested at the Saturday Market, I began receiving—"

"Wait," Mia interrupted, frowning a little at Jake, "you were arrested? For what?"

"I wasn't *arrested* . . . I was detain—"

"Later, please," Hettle said, "we do not have an excess of time."

Jake fought the need to explain by taking his first bite of pancakes. It was like eating a piece of butter-and-vanilla-flavored cloud.

"As I was saying," Hettle continued, "shortly before Jacob was arrested, I began receiving letters. They came from all over the country. Plus, eight from Finland, two from Sweden, one from Spain, and one from Uganda. Each was addressed to me, from people who knew about the Ruby-Backed Turtle, though they did not seem to know very much about it. I had never in my life received a letter about the turtle before this year, but suddenly in the span of three weeks, I received more than three hundred pieces of mail."

"All about the turtle?" Mia asked, pen and notebook at the ready.

Hettle nodded. "Each person who wrote told me about how they had come across this legend of the Ruby-Backed Turtle. Over the course of reading them, it became clear that someone had heard the story and written an article on the computer that presented the turtle as fact. The article, it seems, spread around the world."

"On what website?" Mia asked, writing notes while she ate.

Hettle drew an envelope from the pocket of her robe and slid it across the table toward Jake. Mia leaned close to his shoulder, and they read the letter together.

Dear Ms. Olsson,

A few weeks ago, I published an article on my blog for the American Society for Freshwater Turtle Conservation and Appreciation (ASFTCA) after stumbling across a mention of a specimen called the "Ruby-Backed Turtle" in an archived newspaper clipping from 1972. I wrote the post in a fit of excitement—I am a lover of turtle lore, and this tale was truly thrilling to me.

Perhaps because of my enthusiastic tone, the post created quite a commotion. Larger newspapers and websites wrote about it. It was something of a "viral sensation," as the young people say. Most of my blog posts are seen by roughly 60–70 people. This one was seen by more than 1,253,000! That same week, my little organization took in more donations than any other week this year, allowing me to support freshwater turtle conservancy worldwide.

I'm following up because I've decided to visit your quaint hamlet for the "Nehalem Blackberry Moon Festival" this year, to learn more about the turtle, and would be grateful for the chance to meet you. As the granddaughter of Gustav Olsson—who, if I'm not mistaken, wrote the book *Homesteading on the Nehalem*, the only recorded mention of the Ruby-Backed Turtle—I assume you are the best person to go to for information.

Would you be open to a visit from me? Do you have a copy of your grandfather's book that I might read and photograph for my archives? Is there any information about this tale not yet made public?

I have so many questions but wouldn't dare overwhelm you! See you in the summer. I'm sure we will be fast friends!

Sincerely,
Edna Blodgett

When Jake and Mia had finished reading, Hettle spoke again. "I sent a letter back. It said, 'There is no turtle. It is a folktale, invented by my grandfather. Do not come to Oregon. Please delete all mentions of the turtle from your website and from the rest of the internet. I have more than enough friends.'" Hettle swallowed. "The next week I received this."

She slid another envelope across the table. This time the letter was much shorter.

Dear Ms. Olsson,

My ticket is booked and the hotel is paid for! Nonrefundable! And please wait before deciding whether we will be friends—I am told I can be quite charming!

Looking eagerly forward to meeting!

Sincerely, your (soon-to-be) friend,
Edna Blodgett

P.S.: I think you may have a vital misunderstanding about how the internet works. Nothing is ever deleted! Even the most insignificant thoughts, once shared, carry on out into infinity—quite fascinating, isn't it?

P.P.S: I have taken to calling this specimen the "Ruby Turtle" rather than the "Ruby-Backed Turtle." I believe that the shorter name inspires the imagination and conjures images of adventure. Don't you agree?

Jake and Mia looked up from Edna Blodgett's second letter to see Hettle frowning in a way that seemed to change the entire shape of her face.

"I can assure you, that woman and I will not be 'fast friends,'" she said. "However, when I saw her letter I understood something of what had happened and began to feel concerned. As more and more letters arrived with the phrase 'Ruby Turtle' in them, my fears increased. How many people like this Edna Blodgett might have thought to themselves, 'Why, yes indeed! I will just go to Oregon and stomp around looking for a turtle with a ruby-colored shell'?

"I do not want them marauding over this land. I do not want them to fling the wrappers from their potato chips and granola bars into our streams. I tried to cancel the festival altogether, but then decided it would not be wise."

"Why not?" Mia asked.

"My grandfather made a promise to open this property up for one week each year. It is a longtime tradition, and I fear that closing the land or canceling the festival will perhaps make people even more curious."

Hettle looked directly at Jake now. "This is why, when your mother wrote to me and mentioned your run-in with the glassblower, I wrote back saying that perhaps you should come visit during this specific week. I did not tell her that I secretly believed I needed your help."

Jake could feel Mia's gaze on him, but he didn't really know what to say. Why had his great-aunt thought *he* could help her? Just because he knew the difference between a newt and a salamander?

As if reading his mind, Hettle spoke again. "I am not able to walk in the forests anymore, due to my leg. It seemed important to have a scout, so to speak, who might see what was going on—where people are going and what they are trampling on."

Mia nodded without looking up. "You invited Jake here to be your spy? That's awesome!"

She'd abandoned her pancakes and was scribbling notes in her journal. Every few lines, she shook her fingers out to keep them from cramping.

"So the Magnusson brothers . . . ," Jake said. "You think they came all the way from Sweden just to look for this made-up turtle?"

With an almost imperceptible shrug, Hettle stood, picked up her plate, and took it to the sink.

"There is a longtime rivalry between Finns and Swedes," she said. "Finding a turtle written about by my Finnish grandfather would certainly intrigue two young Swedes. That is only a guess, however."

She kept her back to the table, scouring the pancake griddle. Mia finished scratching out her notes, took two last bites of eggs, and brought her plate over to the sink. She stood next to Hettle and they spoke quietly.

"Say that you're sick," Mia said. "Or maybe tell everyone you're worried about people leaving trash."

"I have considered these options," Hettle replied. "I believe they will have the exact wrong effect."

Jake's brain was buzzing and the voices seemed to fade into the background. He heard Mia say "mushrooms" and Hettle offer a response, but he didn't know what was being said. He had that jittery, sort of tingly feeling he sometimes got when certain ideas were slamming into each other and linking up in his brain.

The buzzing had been kick-started by Hettle's face when she'd explained how worried she was. Then thoughts of the night before and that morning—reading different chapters of *Homesteading on the Nehalem*—surged through him. He had read snatches from seven or eight different chapters. Some sounded like made-up stories a dad might tell his kids. Some sounded like a friend giving advice.

Some were funny. Some strange. But the chapter on the Ruby-Backed Turtle was none of those. It was different from the other fables. It sounded . . .

"*Jake*? Earth to Jake." Mia was calling from over by the sink. The tone in her voice said she'd been trying to get his attention for more than a second or two. He twisted toward her.

"You were off in space," Mia said. "Like out of the solar system . . ."

The Ruby-Backed Turtle chapter is written in the first person. That's when the narrator is the main character.

Jake remembered that from school: "*I* walked. This is *my* pencil. Can you help *me*?"

None of the folklore chapters are in the first person.

But there were other first-person chapters. The ones about chores that Jake had only scanned. Chapters like the ones his mom had told him about, on keeping boots black and hearthstones red.

The practical ones. The *factual* ones.

"Jacob." Hettle said his name with some force. "Are you distracted by something? Mia was asking you if maybe you should—"

"Aunt Hettle," Jake interrupted. His chest felt tight. Goose bumps rippled down his spine. This was part of ADHD too, his doctor said—these moments when everything felt crystal clear and loaded with energy. Like he might fly off the face of the planet if something huge didn't happen right away.

"Aunt Hettle," he repeated, fighting to slow his mind down.

"Yes, Jacob?"

"The Ruby-Backed Turtle is *real*, isn't it?"

12
Gustav's Last Words

The earthenware dishes scraped against each other as Hettle slid them into the sink. She lumbered across the room and settled down in one of the chairs next to the couch. Both the woman and the recliner gave a groan.

"Please, sit."

Mia and Jake followed her and sat on the carpet, in front of the fire. It was the first time Jake had seen Mia look unsure about anything.

Hettle cleared her throat. "I sat with my grandfather, Gustav, on the final night he was alive. The rest of the family cooked and shared stories down in the living room, but Grandfather and I were especially close, perhaps because I had always been interested in his famous book."

She shifted in her seat, settling in.

"As the night wore on, he drifted in and out of consciousness. He called for his wife, Hildy, who had died years earlier. His throat was dry, and he asked for root beer. None of us had ever seen him drink root beer. My mother had to drive all the way to Cannon Beach to purchase some."

Singer wandered over and plopped down next to the fire, nuzzling his head into Jake's lap.

"In the middle of the night, Grandfather woke from a fitful sleep and started to talk again. He spoke about tasting the salt in the air when he walked along the Oregon Coast for the first time. Noticing the smell of wet earth on the day his first child was born. And then . . ."

She paused, fingers playing with the sleeves of her sweater.

"Then Gustav grasped my hands in his and said, 'In my bedside drawer . . . the turtle.' "

There was a glass of water on the table next to Hettle's recliner. Jake felt pretty sure it was his, from the night before, but his aunt drank from it anyway. She took deep gulps until it was empty, then paused for at least a minute.

"I knew precisely what he was talking about. Not the actual turtle but a carving he had made. A replica. A family relic. 'Keep it safe,' he whispered. It was only a few hours later that he died."

Hettle rose from her seat and moved a framed photo that was leaning on the mantel. She took something from behind it and carried it back to her recliner.

"This is the object he spoke of," Hettle said, holding it out.

Singer let out a long, morose moan that started deep in his throat. Jake knew it was time for a walk.

Hettle smiled sadly. "The hound is right. We must not waste our morning dwelling on the past. However, I would like you both to look at this statue, if you would."

Jake and Mia shared a look; then Mia leaned forward to take the figurine. Jake scootched close to her.

The turtle was mostly carved from cedar and looked exactly how Gustav had described the Ruby-Backed Turtle in his book. It was the size of a leaf with serrations running along the back of the shell. The head and legs of the turtle were detailed and perfectly polished, but it was the shell itself that made the piece extraordinary.

"What is this?" Mia asked. "Glass?"

She ran her fingers along a series of polished red gems set into the shell. Then she held it out for Jake to take a better look.

"That figurine was my grandfather's gift to me," Hettle said. "If you do not believe in the turtle, then it would be easy to see this object as another invention of his wild imagination. A way to enhance his lore."

"And if you *do* believe in it?" Jake asked.

"Look closely," Hettle said. "Do the red pieces look as pure as glass?"

Jake and Mia peered at the red pieces set into the shell.

"They're kind of cloudy inside," Jake said.

"Yeah . . . cloudy," Mia echoed.

Hettle reached out for the turtle, and Mia leaned

forward to hand it to her. "I have come to believe that these red slivers embedded in the figurine are not glass. They seem to be something else. They are getting ever so slightly foggier as the years pass. Changing with time. Decaying. Perhaps because of all the moisture."

Mia frowned. "Are you saying it's actually—sorry—what *are* you saying?"

"Keratin!" Jake blurted.

Hettle and Mia both looked at him, clearly waiting for him to go on.

"Like what fingernails and rhinoceros horns are made of," he said. "Turtle shells too."

Hettle nodded thoughtfully. "I cannot be sure what material makes those pieces of the shell. But with thousands of nights to ponder the subject, I have come to believe that sometime after seeing the Ruby-Backed Turtle for the first time, my grandparents returned to the glade where they had seen it and, eventually, found the shell of a deceased member of the species. And, yes, that Grandfather used the shell for this sculpture."

Mia had her journal open. "How can you be sure? Did he say that? Or write about it in his book?"

"I absolutely cannot be sure," Hettle said. "This is speculation and only that. However, I personally believe that my grandfather gave me the figurine hoping I would eventually deduce this secret and know that he was telling the truth. When he said 'keep it safe,' I do not think he meant his carving."

Jake frowned. "If Gustav really found the shell of a Ruby-Backed Turtle, he could have proven to everyone it existed. He could have died famous. It would be in every animal book ever—like the Tasmanian tiger."

Singer scratched at the front door. Hettle crossed the room to open it and the dog bounded outside, running circles around her front yard.

"What good might come of that?" she asked. "In the years after writing *Homesteading on the Nehalem*, my grandfather saw hundreds of old-growth trees—each as tall as any California redwood—cut down to their trunks. He heard stories from the Siletz about the last sea otter killed in Oregon, in 1907. The man who killed that animal had good reason to believe that it was the last of its kind and shot it dead for nine hundred dollars."

Hettle looked between Jake and Mia. Her gaze burned with intensity.

"Gustav died having little faith in humans to protect the natural world. Over time, he went from trying to convince people that his turtle story was real to regretting that he had ever written a single word about it. He feared that his tale would fall into the wrong hands and, because of my own mistakes, his fears have come to pass."

Her words seemed to suck the air from the room.

It was Mia who spoke first. "But . . . you're saying he died believing in it, right?"

"That is what I have deduced across the decades, yes."

Jake and Mia looked at each other, then back to Hettle.

After a long silence, she glanced at a cuckoo clock hanging on the wall opposite the fireplace and set the turtle on the table beside her chair.

"I have an appointment that I am legally bound to attend," she said, limping over to the door and grabbing her key ring off an iron nail. "You two meet me at the festival grounds in two hours. I am quite curious to see how many people will show up this year."

"The Magnussons will be there," Mia said. "What are you going to do when we see them? And what about this woman who wrote the article about the turtle, Edna Blodgett?"

"I am not sure what to do about the Swedish twins or this persistent Blodgett," Hettle said. "All I am certain of is that if by some chance in all the world the Ruby-Backed Turtle still lives, Grandfather would want me to protect it."

"*Us* to protect it," Mia corrected. "The three of us, right, Jake?"

"Exactly," Jake said. "We'll keep it safe. Just like Gustav wanted."

Hettle nodded at the two of them and offered a wry smile. "I have been hoping you two might say that."

13
Along the Train Tracks

Jake and Mia stepped outside and started crunching across the gravel.

"We can walk all the way to my house on the train tracks," Mia said. She zipped up her windbreaker. "Even farther, actually. The train doesn't run anymore."

"Why not?"

"The tracks kept getting washed out."

Jake, Mia, and Singer crossed Hettle's yard, passing under the shade of the giant cedar, and walked out through the gap in the hedges. They headed downstream on the tracks as they wound into the woods, trying to balance on the iron rails. Singer trotted through the tall dandelions and weeds that grew up between the railroad ties.

The long, warbled *waaaak-waaak* of a crow echoed overhead.

"So I was thinking," Jake said, "the Magnusson brothers must be—"

"Actually," Mia said, "could we just walk quietly for a few minutes? I have a lot of stuff I need to sort out in my head."

Jake's face felt flush with embarrassment. He had stuff *he* wanted to sort out too. By talking about it with Mia.

Plus, what if he was missing facts? He hadn't been writing important stuff down the way Mia did. Maybe he'd been paying attention to the wrong details and something big had just whiffed right past him?

"Yeah," Jake said, trying not to sound hurt. "Totally."

The trees that lined the southern side of the tracks were all coated in pale green moss. It dangled from the branches like long beards and grew thick on the trunks. Some of the rocks were covered with moss too, but it was a different species and brighter green.

Every few feet Jake got glimpses of a slow, wide section of the Nehalem River off on his left. A thin layer of fog drifted along the river's glassy surface. It twisted and curled in smoky tendrils, as if deciding whether to break apart or travel downstream together in one single, ghostly cloud.

Out on the highway, a pickup truck roared past, but the sound vanished almost immediately. The dense forest seemed to muffle everything. Jake could hear his own breathing, Singer's panting, and not much else. He risked a glance at Mia. She was underlining something in her notebook while balancing on a rail, like it was the easiest thing ever.

Jake tried to rewind everything they'd just learned from Hettle, but right away he found himself thinking about Mia instead. Did she believe in the turtle? Did she think Hettle was making it all up? Did she really want to spend her week with him, trying to protect a turtle that might already be extinct?

"Thanks for waiting," she said, closing her journal. "Want to try the Question Game?"

"What's that?" Jake asked.

"My dad and I play sometimes," she said. "We'll take turns asking a question while we walk, and then we'll try to figure each answer out together, using logic or science."

She was smiling as she spoke. Jake smiled back and instantly felt better.

"My biggest question is this," Mia began. "Let's say the turtle is real, and let's say the Magnusson brothers or this Edna lady found it . . . what do they want to do then? What's their motive?"

Jake had been walking beside the track; now he hopped back up on one of the rails and tried balancing again. "They want to tell people about it."

"It's a long way to travel to look for an animal just to tell people about it," she said. "They must think it's worth money."

"People go search for Bigfoot all the time in Oregon," Jake said. "Everyone wants to find something that no one else has seen."

“So you mean like for an adventure?” Mia asked, slipping off the rail and hopping right back on.

“Yeah and then maybe to get famous. And I guess then to get money somehow.”

“Like they’d be the people who rediscovered Gustav’s turtle and that would make them celebrities or something?”

Jake nodded. He was off in thought, imagining what would happen if *he* found the turtle. When you discover a new species, no one cares if you have ADHD. No one talks about “attention issues” when you’re on the cover of *National Geographic.*

They even forget about the Whole Saturday Market Fiasco.

“Is that what you’re saying?” Mia clarified.

“Yes,” Jake said. “Definitely.”

“Okay, I can buy that motive,” Mia said. “Your turn for a question.”

Jake cleared his throat. “If the Ruby-Backed Turtle *is* real—”

“Let’s just say that it’s real,” Mia said. “At least for now. Your great-great-grandfather believed in it. Your great-aunt believes in it. So I think we should too. At least for this week.”

Jake thought about that for a second. “Okay, sure. And let’s also say there are still some turtles somewhere in this forest—the grandchildren of the one Gustav saw—”

“Turtles live for a long time, right?” Mia asked, spinning on the rail to face Jake. “Like in the Galapagos and stuff.”

Jake shook his head. "Big tortoises live a long time, not small turtles. In his book, Gustav said it was the size of a child's hand."

Mia nodded, spinning away again. "I want to read that book soon. Is that your question?"

"My question is, why couldn't we just walk along every stream on Hettle's land looking for it?"

Mia pirouetted back around to face Jake, laughing.

"What?" he asked.

She sprang from one track to the other, landing without losing her balance. Now she was walking backward a few feet ahead of Jake on the same rail. "Wait until I take you into the woods; you'll know why I laughed."

Mia spun back around. Jake stopped walking and watched the back of her head, her braids bouncing a little with each step.

"I thought the point of the game is that we actually *answer* each other's questions. Isn't that what you said?"

"Do you know how much rain Nehalem gets?" Mia asked over her shoulder.

"I actually do," Jake said. "One hundred twenty inches a year."

"And this deep in the valley it's even rainier," Mia said. "A lot rainier, actually. Where do you think all that rain goes?"

Jake looked off into the woods but didn't answer.

"It runs together into little—my dad calls them 'rivulets'—which are as thin as your finger," Mia said.

"Then those run together to become brooks, and the brooks flow into streams, and the streams crash together and dump into the river."

Jake thought he understood what Mia was getting at, but she wasn't done.

"Look," she said, stopping to point through a clearing at the densely forested hills across the road. "That forest goes all the way back to the highway you came in on. Between here and there you could probably find a few hundred thousand rivulets, which turn into a few thousand different brooks, that lead to hundreds of streams. And they all change every winter, when the rain is really heavy and they run over their banks. Or if there's a landslide or a tree falls. And who's to say that the turtle would have stayed in the same area over the years?"

Jake was starting to understand. "So you could never actually search all the streams," he said. "Because you'd have to keep starting over."

"Dad always says it would take a thousand years before he could see every inch of this valley. He says the only way to know it all would be to become a mushroom and use his mycelium to learn about it from all the other mushrooms."

"Your dad has a funny way of saying things," Jake said. He saw Mia's body go rigid and finished the thought. "I like it."

"He's right too. Even the trails behind our house change every year."

They stared across the road into the wild tangles of the fog-shrouded forest, pierced only by towering evergreens. Jake tried to envision all those rivulets leading to brooks leading to streams; he imagined trying to trace them all for days upon days only to have them change course when the rain was heavy. Just thinking about it made him feel overwhelmed.

Mia had stopped walking to look into the endless forest; now she started moving again. It was her turn to ask a question, but she didn't seem to be in any rush. In the long silence, Jake started to notice the smell of the Nehalem Valley. It smelled *green*, if it was possible for the air to smell like a color.

Alive. Like everything's wet and covered in dirt and growing all the time. Which . . . I guess is exactly right.

"Next question," Mia finally said. "Your aunt said you were arrested—what was it for?"

Jake was so taken aback that he fell off the rail he was balancing on and started walking in the tall grass instead. Singer trotted beside him, clearly hoping for a scratch behind the ears or a forgotten treat found deep in his jeans pocket.

"I wasn't arrested," Jake said. "I was just sort of . . . *detained* for a few hours."

"What for?"

Mia was walking the rails, not looking at Jake, so it was hard to read what she was thinking.

"You have to answer," she said. "That's the game."

"I knocked over a bunch of blown glass figurines," Jake said.

"How many?"

"Six hundred and ninety-two dollars' worth," Jake said. He paused before adding, "I was trying to do a handstand."

Mia slowed down enough for Jake to catch up. They walked side by side. Once, she got unsteady and put her hand on Jake's shoulder for balance. He liked that. It made him feel like she didn't think he was weird because of the Whole Saturday Market Fiasco.

"That's not a great reason to get arrested," Mia said after a few more steps.

"Detained."

"Especially compared to your aunt."

"Yeah," Jake said without thinking.

It took a few seconds for him to register what Mia had said. He stopped cold.

"Wait . . . what?" he asked.

Mia hopped off the train track and motioned Jake to follow her with a jerk of the head. They veered toward the road, walking along a rutted car path. Singer trotted behind them.

"Your aunt was arrested last spring," Mia said. "It was in the local newspaper. I think it even made the news in Portland."

The road was quiet and Mia jogged across it. She unlatched a white picket fence and swung it open onto a large property that sloped uphill toward a two-story house situated about a hundred yards off the road. Off to the left of the home was a garden dominated by a long greenhouse and two planter boxes running next to each other.

"Is this where you live?" Jake asked when he and Singer caught up.

"Yep," Mia said, closing the gate behind them, "so if your next question is going to be about your aunt getting arrested, hang on to it until we know if my dad is home."

She motioned Jake and Singer to follow her uphill, toward the house.

"I was thinking we could look for the turtle for a while before we meet Hettle," Jake said. "I know it's hard to know where to start, but still . . ."

Mia turned. "Your aunt said that she got more than three hundred letters, all because of some article on the internet, right?"

Jake nodded.

"Have you ever written someone a letter about an article on the internet?"

"I only wrote one letter ever—the author of my favorite book."

"Exactly," Mia said, "your *favorite* book. So if three hundred people wrote to Hettle about one article they saw online . . . ?"

She flared her eyebrows and Jake caught her drift.

"It must've been one heck of an article," he said.

Nehalem, Oregon—10:37 a.m., MONDAY

The door of Stick's truck swung open and its weary driver slid out. His first step was right into a rain-filled pothole.

"Dang it," Stick grunted, looking down at the muddy water sheeting off his left boot.

Stick walked to the bed of the pickup and unwound the tarp that had kept his gear from scattering across the highway. He spotted a black duffel bag, jerked it toward him, and started to rummage through its contents. He'd decided on the right disguise for this job about halfway through his drive—he'd pretend to be a Texas State park ranger, hoping to relocate in Oregon.

That would explain his accent and license plates.

"A real friendly sort of character in a tan uniform," Stick muttered.

He grabbed for a fake beard, got out his spirit gum, and applied it to his face, peering at himself in the side-view mirror to make sure all the edges were pressed down.

"I'll say all the sorts of things that people in Oree-gone think Texans say," he said. "Stuff like 'Giddyup!' and "Yes-siree!' and 'Well, howdy, pard!'"

He found the outfit he wanted in the duffel bag and changed clothes in the cab of the truck. The park ranger uniform was tan and stiff. It felt a little tighter around the midsection than Stick remembered.

He swapped the belt from the jeans he'd been wearing on to the tan shorts, sliding the sheath with his bowie knife over to its spot on his right hip.

Click. Stick undid the button of his Texas toothpick.

Click. Snapped it down again.

After swapping his cowboy boots for a pair of hiking boots, he started walking through Nehalem's block-long downtown. When he got to the Nehalem Food Mart, he stopped. The sign above the door was yellowed plastic but had big patches of green lichen growing on it.

Stick wondered just how much it must rain in Nehalem for something to grow on plastic.

A bell on the door jangled as he stepped inside the store. A stack of metal baskets rested on the floor. Stick grabbed one and started picking out things he could cook over a fire. Two bags of rice, four cans of baked beans, and the hottest hot sauce they had.

Near the register was a corkboard with wrinkled advertisements pinned to it. There were tractors for sale, a flyer for "Barb's in-home hairdressing," and a man offering fresh razor clams delivered to your doorstep. In the middle of the bulletin board, half hidden by business cards and Post-its, Stick saw what he was looking for.

A flyer announcing the Nehalem Blackberry Moon Festival.

He tore it down, folded it up, and stuffed it in his shorts pocket.

"You in town for the festival?" the teenaged clerk behind the register asked. "Gonna look for the Ruby Turtle?"

Stick wrote her a check from the El Paso First National Bank to pay for his groceries, then looked up from under his mirrored sunglasses.

"Well, howdy, pard!" he said with a smile. "Yesiree, that's exactly why I'm here."

14
Telephone

Just like Hettle's cabin, the walls of Myron's house were wood and lined with books, but the similarities ended there. Instead of a hodgepodge of colors and wall hangings, everything was some shade of either brown or green. There was *lots* of green—from the avocado-colored chairs to the forest-green kitchen counters to the emerald-green posters on the walls. The carpet looked like a mint milkshake and was so thick that Jake and Mia's footsteps didn't make a sound.

Also, the plants were green and they were *everywhere*. Their tendrils dripped out of clay pots that hung from the ceiling and snaked across the exposed wooden rafters. There were five or six growing in each corner—their spreading leaves overlapping and reaching toward the ceiling.

It made the whole house feel steamy. Pulsing with life. Jake felt sort of like he was in an aquarium.

Mia went to the fridge to grab two cups of water. A few seconds later, she came out of the kitchen, ice clinking in the green pebbled glasses, and motioned Jake to the stairs with a jerk of her head. They walked downstairs to the basement, which was quiet and dim enough to feel a tad creepy.

"My dad is probably just over in the greenhouse," she said. "We can work in my office."

The room was barely big enough for the two of them to stand shoulder to shoulder. It had one small, square window, set high in the wall. Jake wondered if it had been a closet once.

"This is where I get my best thinking done," Mia said. "When Evie lived here, she'd take up the whole kitchen table with her books, so I'd come down here."

"Evie is your sister?" Jake asked.

Mia pointed to a photo on the bulletin board that hung above the desk. It was framed by pushpins and little star stickers and showed Mia standing on a running track with an older teen girl. It looked like it'd been taken a few years earlier.

"She was supposed to be home to hang out with me this summer, but she met some guy with a camper van, so I had to spend the summer here with Dad all alone." She paused, then added, "My mom lives in Portland."

"You probably have lots of friends, though," Jake said.

"She *promised* she was coming home," was Mia's only response.

Jake nodded.

Mia flipped open a laptop. “Okay, let’s see . . . I’m just going to search . . .‘Ruby Turtle’ . . . and . . .”

Her fingers scurried across the keyboard.

“Wow.”

Jake leaned close as results unfurled down the page. A lot of websites had written about the turtle, not just one.

“Is ‘Blodgett’ with two *t*’s or one?” Mia asked, adding the name to her search.

They tried it with one *t*, and even though the spelling was wrong, the top result was the one they wanted—from the American Society for Freshwater Turtle Conservation and Appreciation. The link read:

“DID A TURTLE WITH A RUBY SHELL ONCE LIVE IN THE OREGON WILDERNESS?!?!”

Mia clicked the story. “You want to read or take notes?”

In school, Jake had always liked reading in front of the class. It was the one time he felt locked in—when another kid fiddling with something or tapping their foot wouldn’t grab his attention. He motioned to the spot at the computer, sat down, and scrolled to where the article started.

Greetings you leatherbacks, loggerheads, and all fellow lovers of chelonians, Testudines, terrapins, tortoises, and turtles!

"Oh, this lady is a *lot*, huh?" Mia said, scratching a few words in her notebook. "Are those all just different names for turtles?"

Jake nodded, though he wasn't actually sure about chelonians and Testudines.

As my loyal readers (all 47 of you!) know, besides being the founder, president, treasurer, and only employee of the ASFTCA, I am a collector of turtle-themed antiques, memorabilia, trinkets, relics, whatsits, odds, ends, and ephemera.

It's safe to say that if it features turtles, especially my beloved "freshies," I know something about it!

UNTIL TODAY, FRIENDS! UNTIL TODAY!

It's a mystery how this little gem (*we'll get to that!*) of a story escaped my knowledge for decades, but it's swiftly become one of my favorite pieces of turtle lore EVER.

It was early January of this year when a journalist pal in Oregon sent me a newspaper clipping he had stumbled across (while working the local crime beat, of all things!). The clipping dated back to 1972, when I was a 19-year-old biology major at the University of Vermont, and told of a strange old curmudgeon from Finland who had moved his family to that wet, wooly West Coast wilderness in the early 1930s.

"She means Gustav moving to Oregon, right?" Mia asked, interrupting Jake's reading.

Jake nodded. "Gotta be."

Well apparently, this man, named Olsson, wrote a book, called *Homesteading on the Nehalem*, in which he claimed to have seen a turtle with a ruby shell—meaning that the segments of the carapace seemed to be made of a deep red gemstone. And I will say, his description of the animal was quite lovely. I'll quote—from the article, which quoted from the original book:

Looking down, I saw an animal perched on a rock. A turtle, its shell no bigger than the palm of a child's hand and looking as delicate as a leaf. Its head and neck no larger than my thumb. And yet . . . here was the most magnificent creature I had ever seen. Perhaps, ever to exist.

"Yeah, I definitely need to borrow the book," Mia said.

"Sure," Jake said. "But it doesn't really tell much."

He kept reading.

Sadly, that was the only section of the book quoted in the article and no copies of the book itself can be found online. And yet! It was enough to make my entire spine tingle! I tell you, my arms got actual goose pimples!

Can you imagine? An undiscovered turtle species! Could it be true?

To my dismay, the newspaper clipping from the *Oregonian* was not focused on the turtle at all. In fact, the writer treated this part of the story as a simple side note. Instead, the article focused on a quaint shindig that had sprung up around the turtle tale. A chance for Oregon's bead-wearing hippies and country yokels to mingle together, called the Nehalem Blackberry Moon Festival.

By the 1970s, it seems this festival had already been going on in some way or another for decades, featuring a craft market and several small events. Apparently, it culminates with a contest among the locals to see who can design the best "Ruby-Backed Turtle" from rocks, flotsam, and plants (Dear Reader, I will be calling it the Ruby Turtle henceforth, because I find that name far more charming).

This was all quite interesting on its own, of course, but nothing compared to the dream that a real turtle might actually exist. What a wonder that would be!

To cut my meandering short, let me say simply: I was eager for the chance to learn more about this story. Maybe even to search the area for this mystical cryptid for a week with these rain-sodden "Nehalemites." So I booked a ticket. And even though it sounds like the festival has lost some steam since the roaring '70s, I'm excited for the adventure.

Stay tuned for more updates! It ought to be one *shell* of a time!

"Yikes," Jake said. "Now *that's* a bad pun."

"Get up real quick," Mia said. "I want to check something—"

Jake popped up, and Mia crashed into the chair. She went back to their first search and started clicking links from other websites. Some quoted the post from the turtle conservancy. Others just quoted the later posts written *about* the original post. Mia and Jake skimmed more than ten articles altogether, each with wilder and wilder headlines.

One read, “Check Out This INSANE Story about a Lost Turtle with Rubies on Its Back!”

Another was, “‘The Bigfoot of Turtles’???—Is There Really a Turtle Covered with Rubies Hiding in Oregon?”

And, “Someone Discovered a Ruby Turtle in the 1930s. You’ll Never Guess What Happened Next!”

“They’re treating it like it’s one hundred percent real,” Mia said after skimming the text. “Like it’s not even in doubt.”

“And it’s just getting more and more tangled up,” Jake said. “Click on that one.” He leaned over her shoulder and pointed to an article headline that read, “There’s a Turtle with a Ruby Shell Hiding in Oregon and Now Our Minds Are Absolutely Blown!”

“It doesn’t mention *Homesteading on the Nehalem* or the article in the *Oregonian*,” Jake said, as they both skimmed the page. “Or even that turtle conservation lady! It just talks about a whole *other* article based on her original post.”

Mia shook her head in disbelief. “We’re looking at an article about a different article, which was written about a newspaper clipping that was focused on a festival based on a chapter in a book.”

Jake shook his head, bewildered. “A book that Gustav wrote almost eighty years ago and none of these people have ever seen.”

"That Blodgett lady has one thing right. 'Ruby Turtle' sounds better than 'Ruby-Backed Turtle' for sure."

"Uh-huh," Jake muttered. "And that's part of the problem. It's the sort of name that makes people curious."

"Mia," a voice boomed from upstairs, "you down there?"

She quickly slapped the computer shut and popped to her feet. Jake jumped up too.

"How much are we going to tell your dad?" he asked.

Mia rolled her bottom lip between her teeth a few times. "For now? Right this second? With the information we have?" She drew a tight breath. "Exactly and precisely nothing."

15
Opening Ceremony

Jake watched Mia from the back seat of Myron's station wagon as they rolled up to the festival grounds. She was leaning toward the windshield, staring at the crowd gathered for the opening ceremony. Her mouth gaped and her eyes were wide.

Myron gave a low, rumbling chuckle. "I drove by an hour ago and couldn't believe it. There's even more folks now."

The sun had punched holes in the clouds, and the park's grassy lawn was covered with picnic blankets. Cars clogged every inch of the gravel lot. A few locals had even arrived by boat, coming upstream from different sections of the river and tying off to tree branches that hung out over the water.

"Is this more people than usually come?" Jake asked, leaning into the gap between the front two seats.

Mia looked over at him. "Dude, last year the opening

ceremony was like . . . *maybe* ten people. And three of those were friends of my sister's from U of O who were getting extra credit for a journalism class. There are other things people come to—like the tube float—but everyone usually skips the opening ceremony except us and your aunt."

"Now you see why I said we should leave Singer back at our place?" Myron said to Jake. "It's a zoo."

Myron crunched to the far end of the gravel lot and parked in a spot that wasn't really a spot, angled in front of the boat ramp. The trio got out of the car and started toward the crowd.

"Where do you think my aunt will be?" Jake asked Mia.

"About that," Myron said. "Your aunt called me from the Food Mart on her way through town. She said she can't make it—she's not feeling great—but she said she's excited to hear all about it from you two."

Jake and Mia exchanged a long look.

"Myron!" called a woman as she rushed toward them. She looked a few years younger than Jake's parents and wore her long black hair in a bun, piled high on her head. "Hey Mia! Yu-Jun is down at the river somewhere with his friends—mostly kids you know. He'd love to see you!"

The woman gave Jake a wide smile. Her eyes twinkled as she spoke.

"Jake, this is Ms. Choi," Myron said. "She was Mia's teacher in third grade and has a son Mia's age. Keona, this is Jake, ah . . . actually, Jake, I don't know your last name."

"Rizzi," Jake said, smiling at the stranger.

Keona Choi wore a flowing, pale-blue sundress. She had a tattoo of an evergreen running down her entire forearm.

"So, Myron," she said, smiling up at Mia's dad, "this is the year I want to learn how to forage mushrooms. Officially! Is it still too early?"

Myron passed a hand across his beard. "We had a lot of rain the first half of the month; I actually found a few lobster mushrooms yesterday. We've got a good chance of finding something tomorrow."

As Keona started to reply, Jake felt a tug at his elbow. It was Mia, guiding him away from the adults. They slid through the crowd until they got to the opposite end of the park, where there were fewer people.

Mia scrabbled up the trunk of a spreading oak tree, and Jake followed her lead. The second branch was maybe six feet up and so wide you could sit on it without the slightest fear of falling. It felt like they were high above the crowd now.

"So here's my idea," Mia said. "I think we should write down everything strange we see today. Anyone who looks out of place."

She took her notebook out of the pocket of her windbreaker and flattened it on her thighs.

"If there were only ten people here last year," Jake said, "that means that practically everyone came because they read one of those articles on the internet about the turtle, right?"

"Bingo," Mia said. "Some might just be here for fun, and some might be ready to tear this forest top to bottom to find the turtle."

Jake looked over at her. "Even though it hasn't been seen for so long?"

Mia tilted her head side to side. "People believe what they read on the internet. They don't always worry if it's true." She paused, tapping her pencil to the cleft of her upper lip. "Although, I guess in this case they're technically right to believe it . . . even though we don't *want* them to believe it and they don't have any proof."

"No one has any proof," Jake said. "Even us. Unless you count that figurine of Hettle's."

Mia thought about that for a second, then flipped her journal open. "We agreed to trust Hettle, and she trusted Gustav, right?"

"Yeah," Jake said.

"That's enough for me," she said.

With that, Mia began scratching out little half sentences about what she saw. The sun had barely been out for an hour, but it was enough to remind Jake that this was still summer. He swept his hair to one side.

"Okay, anything strange," Jake said, repeating Mia's word. "There's a man over there with a long gray beard, and he's really skinny. He looks kind of weird."

Mia looked up and saw who Jake was motioning toward. "Oh, that's Old Zane Kesey. He actually has a sheep farm near here."

"I thought he was like a gold miner from the eighteen hundreds or something," Jake said with a little chuckle.

Mia smirked. "Dad says he used to be a pro surfer back in the day. I actually go to his farm every spring to help him shear his sheep. It's super cool to watch."

Jake felt bad that the first person he mentioned was a friend of Mia's. He wanted his next pick to be a good one.

"Okay, over there by the water, that lady looks like she—"

"Actually, this 'anyone who looks out of place' idea might not be my best," Mia said.

"Why?" Jake asked. "I was just getting warmed up."

"Well, if someone else did this, they might name me and my dad."

Jake frowned. "No they wouldn't. *Why*?"

Mia raised her eyebrow. "Look around. Not a whole ton of Black people in Nehalem."

It was a fair point.

"Okay," Jake said, "maybe just things they're *doing* that are weird?"

"That's better, yeah," Mia agreed. "Like that guy with the patchwork pants is trying to play with a hacky sack. It's like 'come on, dude, there's no space for that here!'"

"He just stepped on someone's sandwich," Jake added, pointing.

Mia giggled. "No one wants those dusty feet in their egg salad! What else you got?"

Jake saw a man turn his body in their direction. He

had a huge camera and seemed to be taking photos of the crowd.

"There's a guy over there taking pictures," Jake said. "You think maybe he works for the *Oregonian*?"

Mia nodded and wrote it down in her notebook.

They kept on like this for fifteen minutes. Jake was having fun noticing the little quirks he saw. It was the exact opposite of being told to focus—he didn't have to try to block anything out. Every stray movement or sound that caught his attention was called out; Mia wrote them all down.

Soon they'd filled a whole page of her journal.

- Tall, bony-looking man with binoculars around his neck.
- High school kids kicking up dirt and leaves, like the turtle might be hiding right there in front of them.
- Family with matching "Oregon Caves" shirts; definitely on a statewide road trip.

A loud blare of feedback rang out and everyone turned to look toward the noise. Myron stood next to a PA system, taller than everyone in the crowd, microphone in hand. He waved for people to quiet down and they all fell silent.

Mia wrote a note in her journal.

"Why'd you write that down?" Jake whispered.

"When's the last time you heard someone ask this many people to be quiet and they actually *got* quiet?" she said. "People must really be hoping Dad is going to say something about the turtle."

"Hey, folks, welcome to the Blackberry Moon Festival," Myron began. There was some scattered clapping. "My name is Myron Davis, but most people call me Myron the Mycologist. I'm the one leading the nature walk tomorrow to show folks how to walk these forests without damaging them, and while we're at it, we'll look for summer chanterelles, too. Anyone be interested in that?"

Hands shot up, and there was a ripple of applause. Jake let his eyes fall on random faces. The crowd hung on Myron's every word.

"Sounds like it's going to be a big group!" he went on, the microphone crackling with static. "Boy, I'm glad Rick Collins had this mic setup in his truck. We haven't needed a mic for the opening ceremony in all my years living in the Nehalem Valley. Rick's in a band, by the way; they're called the Fifty Dollar Crab, and they're a ton of fun. They're playing the music for the Maypole dance, later this week. And they're going to be playing a few songs today, setting up under the tree over there."

Myron pointed to the tree that Mia and Jake were sitting in, and every head turned to look at them.

"Ha! Hey, there!" Myron boomed into the mic from across a sea of strangers. "That's my girl in that tree, Mia, and her new friend, Jake Rizzi. Jake is the great-nephew of Hettle Olsson, whose grandfather wrote the book that started this whole tradition. So, I guess, Jake, that makes Gustav Olsson your great-great-grandfather? Or great-great-uncle? I'm not sure, but round of applause for Jake—he's said to be quite the animal expert himself!"

Jake could feel his face going hot. The entire crowd was focused on him, clapping as if he'd done something special. He forced a little smile and half wave.

Why does everyone keep saying I'm an animal expert? I'm just a kid who always seems to end up looking at animal stuff when I'm supposed to be doing math.

Myron continued. "Ever since I've lived here, Hettle Olsson is the one who gives this little speech to kick off the ceremony. But she's under the weather and won't be able to make it today. She gave me notes though . . ."

Myron unlocked his phone and started to read.

"First," he announced, "Hettle says . . . 'I want to remind everyone that we are on Tillamook Indigenous ancestral land and all of us are visitors here, myself and my grandparents included. The land is also shared by all sorts of insects, animals, and plant species—which explains why my grandfather fell in love with it and moved his family here from Finland in the first place. Let us please tread lightly.'"

Myron read the next line to himself, then spoke into the microphone again. "Okay she also says, 'I have heard that there are quite a few people in town for our quaint festival. While I am confused by so many people suddenly finding themselves interested in Gustav Olsson's myth of the Ruby-Backed Turtle, I do think it would have made him proud to hear that his tall tales inspired curiosity. His only concern would be that in searching for his made-up turtle, we would trample real habitats.'"

Myron leaned into the microphone. "And I'll just add fungi to that—let's not trample the fungi."

He looked back at his phone, reading the notes Hettle had given him. Jake glanced over at Mia.

"Is this speech normal?" he asked.

"Your aunt always says something to welcome people," she whispered. "But it's usually just the stuff about appreciating nature and protecting the forests. I don't remember her calling the Ruby-Backed Turtle story a myth last year."

She held her journal out to Jake; he could see she'd already written that note down.

"That's smart of her," Jake said. "Maybe it convinces a few people not to look as hard."

"Okay," Myron finished, "that's pretty much it. She thanks you all for coming, and she's sorry she couldn't make it, and she hopes to be feeling better by the time the jam-making contest comes around. She's the judge for that, for those of you who haven't been here before—which must be . . . almost all of you."

Myron pushed a thick loc out of his face and looked at the crowd. "Okay, this is just me talking now. There are little events all week in town and along the river. There's a tube float. Also, Buttercup Ice Creams and Chowders released all their summer flavors at their shop, including their 'Ruby-Backed Fudge Ripple'—I've tried it; it's delicious."

The mic squealed again.

"That's all from me," Myron said. "Have a great festival, everyone!"

The second her dad was done talking, Mia flipped to a new page in her journal. Jake noticed people grumbling about something near the mic and speaker. At first there were just a few murmurs from the crowd; soon the voices grew louder.

"You might want to write down that your dad is doing that eyebrow thing that you both do," he said.

"What eyebrow thing?" Mia asked.

"You're doing it right now," Jake said, "when you're questioning something. It's not a bad thing . . . I think it looks cool. Like a detective."

"So you want me to write 'Dad doing detective eyebrow thing'?"

"Now you're *really* doing it," Jake said.

Mia opened her mouth with a comeback but the murmurs from the crowd were getting too loud to ignore. Myron had set down the microphone; now he snatched it up again.

"Okay, we have a lot of people up here asking if I'm going to read the chapter from *Homesteading on the*

Nehalem that talks about the Ruby-Backed Turtle," he said. "It sounds like many of you were expecting that. But Hettle didn't say anything to me about it, and, of course, I don't have the book, so . . . that settles that! Anyway, have fun, everybody!"

The crowd didn't go anywhere. Mostly people just milled around, chatting with one another. A juggler started tossing bowling pins into the air and old friends called to each other across the sea of people.

"What now?" Jake asked.

Mia shrugged. "Last year there was only a few of us. Everyone joined up for a group hike, then went out for pizza."

Jake was distracted by a strange sound.

Click. Click.

Click. Click.

He looked around to see where the noise was coming from.

Click. Click.

Jake glanced over his left shoulder and spotted a park ranger in a tan uniform a few feet away, leaning against the trunk of a tree. He had mirrored aviator sunglasses on and was chewing on a toothpick.

But that wasn't where the sound came from.

Click.

Click.

Jake's eyes caught on the man's left hip. A leather sheath hung from his belt with a very serious-looking knife inside. He figured the blade alone must've been a foot long—reaching down to the hem of the man's tan shorts. A leather strap came across the handle of the knife and buttoned to the front of the sheath, to hold it in place.

The man flicked that button open and closed, open and closed, with his left hand. Jake noticed that the sounds were actually ever so slightly different.

Click and it was open. *Cleck* and it was closed.

"Here's a good one for the notebook," Jake muttered to Mia. "Why does that park ranger carry such a huge knife?"

He looked to his right. Mia was gone. She'd swung to the ground and stood on the outskirts of the crowd with a cluster of kids her age. Jake saw her smiling and fist-bumping a boy whose black hair was tied up in a bun on his head and shaved on the sides. A few other kids started talking to Mia, too. But by the time Jake scrambled to the ground, the whole cluster had moved off, closer to the riverbank.

Mia waved Jake over. He started toward them when he heard someone else calling his name.

"Jake! Excuse me! Jake Rizzi, was it?"

A very short woman with tight gray curls hustled over to the oak tree, waving both hands. Jake's first thought was to signal Mia, but she hadn't noticed and there was no time to get her attention. The stranger might have been small, but she moved like lightning.

"Hello, to you, my boy!" the woman said, thrusting a hand out. "My name is Edna Blodgett, and you're the young lad who's related to Hettle Olsson!"

The woman waited for an answer, eyes twinkling.

"You wrote the blog post about the Ruby-Backed Turtle," Jake said.

"I did indeed," Edna said, standing up a little straighter. She was wearing a corduroy suit and brushed a bit of fuzz off the sleeves of her jacket. "Though I have officially dubbed it the 'Ruby Turtle'—much better ring to it, don'tcha think? Truthfully, I was surprised the gentleman, Myron, didn't mention my article. It seems to me I deserve a nice slice of the credit for this tremendous turnout. I was hoping I'd be welcomed to free frostees all week!"

"Frostees?"

"That's how we Vermonters say 'ice cream,'" Edna said. "Wouldn't you agree I'm a bit of a hero, after all? A good bit of tourism I've brought to this rainy region!"

Jake gave one more look toward Mia. Her back was to him, and she was chatting with a few girls. The whole group had started wandering down to the river.

"You told everyone the turtle is real," Jake said.

Edna looked like she'd been slapped. "I simply shared my excitement! What's wrong with a little excitement in this old broken-down world of ours, Jake m'boy?"

"I'm going to see my fri—"

"Now say, kiddo," Edna said, stepping closer. "I promised to look in on your aunt when I got to town; when do you think a good time to visit might be?"

"She's very private," Jake said.

"Understood, understood," Edna said, "but I promised her we'd be comrades and I thought I might . . ."

She trailed off, distracted by something over Jake's shoulder. Jake turned to look, too. The park ranger he'd just been watching, the man with the knife on his hip, approached them with long strides. In one smooth movement he took the toothpick from his mouth and flicked it into the dirt.

"Now, little lady," he said, "the boy said his aunt is private. Did you fail to hear him?"

"I heard . . . but I . . ." Edna's eyes caught on the knife that the man kept fiddling with.

Click. Open.

Cleck. Closed.

"Well then, ma'am," the park ranger said. "I reckon you should respect his answer."

16

Edna and the Park Ranger

Edna recoiled, palms raised, like she was pulling back from a flame. When she had some distance from the park ranger, she turned to Jake.

"Sorry if I pressed you, m'boy! Just an eager beaver, is all. I'm a renowned lover of turtles, and a *protector* of turtles, I should say."

Jake looked past the park ranger at Mia. He wished she'd come over and write some of this stuff down—it felt important. But she didn't glance in Jake's direction at all.

Edna studied the park ranger warily. "And what did you say your name was, Park Ranger?"

The man stepped forward, slowly took off his sunglasses, and slid them into the chest pocket of his starchy brown shirt. He broke into a crooked smile.

"Well, gee pard, I guess that came off a smidge unfriendly!" he said, giving his beard a scratch. "Howdy! Name is Hank Stamper, but folks always call me 'Stick'—on account of me having been a skinny kid."

Edna beamed back at him.

"Not quite so skinny anymore, hey, Stick?" she said, with a wink and a cheery laugh. "Now, are you a *national* park ranger?"

Stick's nostrils flared but his smile never faded.

"Why, little lady, aren't *you* a keen observer?" he drawled. "Since you asked, I'm actually in State Parks, down Texas way. I've been thinking of transferring up here, though. What about you, ancient one; what brings your brittle bones to Oree-gone?"

Jake winced. He hated when people mispronounced "Oregon."

"*Brittle bones*?" Edna scoffed. "Why, you're not exactly a spring chicken, now are you, Ranger? And what brings me to Oree-gone isn't much of your business, is it?"

With the two adults throwing sly insults at each other and saying "Oregon" wrong, Jake saw a chance to sneak away. He looked for Mia but didn't see her anywhere on the riverbank or the now-thinning crowd of people. He *did* see Myron, though—walking his direction, thirty feet from the oak tree—helping a musician carry his amplifier with one hand and holding part of a drum kit in the other.

Jake slipped between Hank Stamper and Edna Blodgett and hustled up to the mycologist before either of them could try to stop him. "Myron, hey! Is Mia around?"

Keona Choi stepped out from behind him and chirped, "Oh, she and my son, Yu-Jun, and some of their other classmates just went on a hike."

Myron frowned. "Sorry, Jake, when she asked me, I figured you were with them. Didn't she invite you?"

"Oh . . . I think maybe she didn't know where I was," he lied. "But, um . . . I'm actually feeling a little sick. I probably have the same thing as Aunt Hettle. I'm just gonna walk home on the train tracks."

Myron set down the kick drum he'd been holding and looked at Jake curiously. Then he motioned him aside with a wave of his hand. They ducked off a few feet from the growing cluster of people under the oak tree.

"You okay, buddy?" Myron asked. He took a knee in the grass in front of Jake and used an elastic band to pull his locs together behind his head.

Jake nodded. "Like I said, I think I just have whatever Aunt Hettle—"

Myron smirked. "Jake, I don't think you have what your aunt has because she's not really sick. She just didn't want to deal with all these people."

Jake nodded. "Do you mind if I walk back to her cabin anyway? I can't get lost along the tracks."

Myron drew a long breath, staring off in the direction of Hettle's house. "It's gonna take you a solid twenty minutes of walking to get to our house to grab your dog and another fifteen minutes after that to get to your aunt's. I'll drive you. I just have to do one or two quick things . . ."

"I can wait," Jake said.

Myron brightened and patted Jake's shoulder. "You sure? It's just that I'm supposed to introduce the band. It won't be too long. I'm also going to have a talk with Mia about leaving you, just so you know."

Jake didn't want to talk about Mia ditching him. But also . . . why *had* Mia ditched him? He knew he'd gotten on people's nerves before when his thoughts bounced around too much or if he interrupted them a lot. But he hadn't interrupted Mia . . . *had he*?

Keona Choi tapped Myron on the shoulder and said that the band was ready to start.

"We'll leave in a few minutes, I promise," Myron said, giving him a squeeze on the shoulder. "I actually have a little section where I sing the harmonies in one of Fifty Dollar Crab's songs—I expect a full review."

As Myron wheeled back to grab the microphone, Jake could feel his attention getting stretched thin. He couldn't spot Edna Blodgett in the crowd and wondered if she'd already gone to Hettle's cabin. Plus, there was the way that park ranger buttoned and unbuttoned his knife sheath, which gave Jake the creeps. He also hadn't spotted the Magnusson twins all day.

Have they been off looking for the turtle this whole time?

He pictured them finding it and getting famous. He imagined their faces staring out from magazines and viral articles online. Then his mind bounced back to Mia.

Does she think I'm annoying?

Or not good at paying attention?

Is it because I told her about the Whole Saturday Market Fiasco and now she thinks I'm a criminal?

What Jake really wanted at that exact moment was

Singer. Walking his dog always helped him calm down if he felt like he had too many thoughts to keep track of. Even petting him helped. He looked over at Myron, who was chatting with the band members.

"I was feeling overwhelmed and needed my dog." That's a solid excuse.

It was the truth, too. Hettle would understand; Jake was sure of it.

As the band began to play, he faded into the crowd.

Mom and Dad wouldn't want me to leave without permission.

Jake glanced over his shoulder to make sure Myron hadn't noticed him go. Then he scrambled up the incline and onto the road, jogging until he was out of sight of the oak tree.

But Mom and Dad aren't here.

17

"The One Good Thing about ADHD . . ."

After collecting Singer from Mia's yard, Jake walked along the train tracks toward Hettle's cabin. The clouds had thickened overhead, making it darker between the towering pine, spruce, and cedar trees. The abandoned, overgrown tracks held a strange sense of danger.

Jake shivered. And not because he was cold.

The sound of rushing water grabbed his attention. He saw a storm drain up ahead that ran under the road, opened into a creek for twenty feet or so, and then disappeared into a second storm drain cutting under the train tracks before emptying into the river. He remembered passing it with Mia, but they'd been talking about the Whole Saturday Market Fiasco and he hadn't stopped to check it out. This time, he paused and looked uphill, following the line of the creek until it disappeared into the undergrowth.

Mia had said it would take a thousand years to find the

turtle by walking up the creeks one at a time, but Jake couldn't help but be curious. He made a "coo-eee," and Singer's ears snapped up, alert.

"You feel like a hike, buddy?"

Jake and Singer scrambled up the embankment, jogged across the road, and bounded back down into the creek bed. The wilderness that lay before him reminded Jake of photos from the Amazon rain forest—with brilliant green creepers and vines splayed wildly beneath the dense canopy of trees. The only time he knew he was in Oregon was when he tipped his head back to see all the giant evergreens.

"We'll walk right along the bank," he said. "That way we can't get lost."

The plan worked for about ten steps. Right until Jake tried to step over a blackberry bramble, got his leg tangled, slipped on some pale-green lichen, fell off the rock he was on, and splashed down into the creek. He popped up and waited for something to hurt.

It never came.

"Well . . . I guess I'll just walk straight upstream," he said to Singer with a laugh.

The rushing water was the same mild temperature as the lightly falling rain. Jake started to trudge forward against the current, with the sound of tumbling water blocking out everything else. Every twenty feet or so, he would stop to make sure he could see his dog. Sometimes Singer trotted up the creek bed; other times he disappeared into the dense undergrowth.

Wet but not cold, Jake fell into a steady rhythm. He'd lift a foot, look for a place to set it, step down, make sure he was stable, lift the next foot, and so on. The rocks alongside the banks of the stream were smooth and slick. The wood of the fallen trees was so mushy that the branches wouldn't even snap when he grabbed them—they just sort of collapsed into soggy fibers. Strange mushrooms clung to the bigger downed logs. To Jake they looked like misshapen troll ears sprouting from blankets of emerald moss. He thought about plucking a few and bringing them to Myron.

Ferns grew out of the dead trees, too. And even smaller ferns seemed to sprout right from the faces of rocks in some places. Everything, everywhere around him was wet.

As Jake neared a giant tree trunk that had fallen across the creek bed, he felt the strange impulse to press his face against the thick, shimmering matt of moss growing on its bark. It was cool and soft on his cheek and smelled of wet earth.

He crouched under the downed tree and saw that it had come up by the roots. The base of the tree blocked most of the water from running that direction and formed a little hideaway. Jake ducked into this tight cubby. His eyes caught on something moving in a shadowy overhang.

The turtle?

He leaned closer to see a rough-skinned newt the size

of his pinkie. It plodded forward on tiny legs, like it was wandering over to visit a neighbor. Its orange belly was so bright that the slick pebbles reflected it.

"They really are enchanting," Jake whispered, thinking back to his conversation with Hettle in Portland.

Soon he noticed a second newt following the first. Then two more—even smaller than the others.

After marveling at the newt family for a few silent minutes, Jake doubled back, climbed around the fallen tree trunk, and cut a path along the banks of the creek. There was a giant blackberry bramble and he stopped to pick a few berries, popping them in his mouth. They gushed with juice.

Singer leapt out of the bushes up ahead, right where two creeks turned into one. Suddenly, Jake got what Mia had been saying about all the creeks. The forest was so big, and he'd already passed five or six tiny brooks that fed into the stream he was tracing.

What if the only remaining family of Ruby-Backed Turtles was in one of those and he'd already passed it without realizing? Or, even worse, what if he wasn't looking and stepped on the last baby of the species with his big, soggy shoe?

"But I noticed the newts," Jake said aloud. "That's the one good thing about ADHD—I notice things. Too many things, sometimes, but still . . ."

Jake realized he'd never thought that there was *any* "good thing" about ADHD before. Not since he was diagnosed two years earlier and definitely not since the Whole Saturday Market Fiasco. His only thought about his "attention issues" had been to try and do whatever he could to be like the other kids.

I wonder if all the other kids would have noticed the newts?

Singer's tags clinked and Jake looked up.

"A little farther," he called.

They kept walking upstream. It had stopped raining; the sun fought to drive off the clouds. The water rushed so loudly that it somehow seemed to make Jake's mind quiet. All he had to do was walk, look around, and let his thoughts slip along, just like the current. He didn't feel like he had to fight to pay attention to anything, but he wasn't fighting *not* to pay attention to anything either.

He was . . . calm. Which felt really, really nice.

After climbing over a mossy boulder, Jake imagined finding the turtle. Walking out of the forest with it. Delivering it to the Oregon Zoo.

Would I just walk in and hand a turtle in a box to Valerie, that woman who runs the reptile den?

Then there would be pictures taken. He'd be famous. Maybe even get to be on Animal Planet. Or a late-night talk show.

If Edna's story about the turtle made international news, actually finding it would be huge. They might even make a movie! After that, people would call him the "Ruby-Backed Turtle kid."

Which is way better than being the "knocked over hundreds

of dollars' worth of glass figurines kid" or the "gets extra time on all his tests because of ADHD kid."

Jake realized that he'd been smiling just imagining it all. Wading through the tangled, wet vines, smiling as wide as could be.

18
Stick

After more than an hour of trudging upstream against the current, Jake noticed he was shivering and decided to turn back. Hiking downstream took half the time—he sloshed through the pools with more confidence and less fear about missing a chance to spot the turtle. When he and Singer got to the culvert that ran under the road, Jake decided they should crawl through it, instead of crossing up on the tarmac.

Navigating this tight tunnel on his hands and knees felt like something out of his favorite TV show, *Extinct or Alive*. Up on the road, a car rumbled past. Jake paused to wonder who it was. There weren't many houses between Mia's and Hettle's.

Probably Myron driving to the cabin to look for me. I'd better get back.

Singer let out a long moan, and it echoed three times as loud as normal.

"Just a little farther," Jake said.

He scampered out of the culvert to see a faded blue truck, covered in dust, parked a few feet away. "Stick" Stamper, the park ranger, leaned against the passenger door. He was peeling an apple with his bowie knife.

Stick smiled and sort of shook the apple at Jake in place of a wave.

"Well, howdy there, pard," he said. "Mighty kind of you to just pop up like that."

Jake stepped back. "Oh . . . hey. My dog and I were just . . . on a hike."

"That so?" Stick asked. "Why, I'd bet you were looking for that . . . what do they call it? *Ruby Turtle*?"

Jake shrugged.

"Every trail along this road is thick with people looking for that critter this afternoon," Stick said. "But you're smart; you just walked straight up a stream. No crowded trail for you."

The apple peel fell at his feet, like a corkscrew-shaped snake. He wiped the knife on his shirt, slipped it into its sheath, and buttoned it closed.

Cleck.

"I call that knife my Texas toothpick," Stick said, pushing off his truck, skidding down a little hill, and splashing right into the creek.

Jake didn't like standing this close to the park ranger. He made a soft "coo-eee" for Singer and started toward the railroad tracks. A hand on his shoulder wrenched him back, spinning his body completely.

"Now wait one second, fella," Stick said, taking a big,

dramatic bite of his apple. "You're related to the woman whose grandfather first wrote about the turtle, ain't that right?"

"Yeah," Jake said. He felt his pulse starting to race as his eyes caught on the knife again. Stick chewed with his mouth open, swallowed, and gave a big smile. Jake noticed that his teeth were backed with silver fillings.

"Do you think she'd let me come by to read that book? I'm mighty interested."

"She's sick," Jake said.

"Nothing serious, I hope." Stick let go of Jake's shoulder and dusted him off, like they were old pals. "It's a shame when someone gets sick. Or hurt. Or terribly injured."

The park ranger smiled, as friendly as could be. One hand held the apple, and the other fiddled with his knife sheath.

Click. Cleck. Open. Shut.

"See you around," Jake said, starting toward the railroad tracks.

Stick let him go. "That sounds like a plan! We'll see one another around! Heck, I might even see you when you don't know it! Until then, I reckon I'll hike this same trail and have a look-see for that turtle."

Jake got a little farther down the track and turned. Stick was waving at him, mouth chomping down on another big bite of apple.

"Good luck!" Jake called, walking backward along

the railroad ties. "My aunt says it's all a made-up story. But if it *was* real, it would be the coolest amphibian ever, right?"

Stick chewed and swallowed before cupping his hands around his mouth to be heard over the rushing stream.

"Actually, pard, a turtle isn't an amphibian. It's a rep-*tile*!"

19

Anyway . . . Sorry

By the time he arrived back at the cabin, Jake was chilled down to his bones. The sight of a fire crackling away in the fireplace made him want to cheer. Then he noticed Mia on the couch.

She offered a weak smile and a half wave.

"We were beginning to feel concerned," his aunt called from her recliner near the hearth. "Myron told us you agreed to stay with him and then quite immediately disappeared."

Jake stepped out of his shoes and tugged off his sopping wet socks. "I . . . went for a hike. Up one of the creeks."

"Did you discover anything of interest?" Hettle asked.

Jake stayed on the doormat so that he wouldn't drip on the floor. "Just a family of newts."

"I have also had an intriguing afternoon," Hettle said. "Those towering oafs the Magnussons dropped by uninvited for a second time, as did Edna Blodgett, who tried three times to hug me and insisted quite adamantly that you two have already begun to form a wonderful friendship."

"I didn't even say two words to her," Jake said. "I was too busy trying to figure out where Mia went."

Mia opened her mouth, hesitated, then seemed to stop herself.

"They both appear very keen to read *Homesteading on the Nehalem*," Hettle said.

Jake was too wet to sit, even on the carpet. "Is it okay if I take a shower to warm up?"

Hettle turned toward him a little and nodded, with her hands folded in her lap. Singer settled down next to the fire, and Jake tiptoed toward the bathroom, hoping that he wasn't leaving a trail of water.

The showerhead was the size of a tennis racket, and the water thrummed down on Jake's shoulders as if he were standing under a waterfall. Way better than his shower back in Portland. The heat left him feeling drowsy, and he could have easily taken a long nap. His little nook bed was cozier than his bed at home. The blankets were all faded and soft from decades of wear.

But Jake knew he had to go back to the living room to face Mia.

Her dad probably made her come to apologize for ditching me.

He threw on some jeans and a T-shirt and shuffled

back to the living room. Hettle was in the kitchen now, but Mia still sat on the couch, writing something in her journal. He crashed down on the floor and started scratching under Singer's collar.

"Jacob, I purchased a frozen pizza that looks both distinctly horrible and incredibly delicious," Hettle called. "When it is done baking, we can talk about an idea that Mia has for how to take action against this Blodgett woman and those towering twins. Remind me, Mia, what do you call it?"

"Phase one," Mia said. She was distracted, scratching out something in her notebook as fast as her hand could move.

"Yes," Hettle said. "Phase one of our plan."

So we're all in this together again? Not just going our separate ways while one of us has to deal with Edna Blodgett and some park ranger guy with a giant knife?

Hettle stepped out of the kitchen to look at Jake.

"Sure, that sounds good."

His thoughts were interrupted by something landing on his lap. Mia's notebook. She motioned for him to read.

I didn't live here during the last school year. I was in Portland, with my mom. And the year before that, I was sad a lot of the time. So I sometimes feel a little weird around all my old friends.

I haven't really been hanging out with anyone besides Dad this summer.

Mia waved Jake on, and he flipped to the next page.

Everyone has had stuff going on and vacation plans and . . . I've just kind of been keeping to myself.

Anyway, today I was in a good mood. So when I saw everyone and they were happy to see me and wanted to hike and look for the turtle, I said "yes" instead of making a big thing out of it.

Which is good!

But I didn't slow down to grab you.

Which is . . . not so great.

I DID WAVE YOU OVER TO US!

. . . not sure if you saw.

Jake flipped the page again.

I should have told them to wait for you.

They would have said yes.

I just saw you talking to those two people and got caught up in feeling glad that everyone was acting cool with me.

Because I'm not really part of the group anymore.

Another page turn.

So I guess I figured we'd both gather intel and share it now. But even if that was the plan, I should have told you.

Okay, this is getting long and you just got back from your shower. What I'm saying is that I'm sorry I ditched you.

Not my best moment.

Jake looked down at the page for a second. Then he motioned Mia for a pen, and she tossed it to him. He wrote:

What made you so sad two years ago?

He slid the pen into the spirals of the notebook and tossed it up to her on the couch. Mia read it as Hettle clanked a few pans in the kitchen. She thought a long time before writing something and tossing the journal and pen back.

My parents split up. And Evie was getting ready for college. Then I was going back and forth to Portland all the time.

I couldn't shake out of it and just feel normal.

That sounds hard. Sorry.

It is what it is. I just wanted to explain.

Did you tell your friends what we know so far?

NO!!!

We can't tell anyone about the turtle.

Plus, Phase I of our plan is just for you and me.

Got it. Sooooo . . . What's Phase I?

20
Phase I

"This is a little wild, right?" Jake asked.

"More than a little," Mia whispered.

They were flat on their stomachs, peering out of a bamboo grove. In a clearing, twenty feet upstream from their hiding spot, stood a dome-shaped tent. There was a lantern glowing inside—making the tent light up like a plump firefly.

"Dad says no one knows how bamboo started growing in Nehalem," Mia whispered. "Probably from someone's home garden. Makes it feel like we're in a real jungle, right?"

Jake didn't answer. His thoughts were zeroed in on the tent and the two bodies shifting around inside it—Angus and Ragnar Magnusson. They'd just settled down after a long dinner and what seemed like a lot of loud arguing in Swedish.

The seconds trickled by as Jake and Mia waited for the lantern to go out. Once the brothers were asleep, the plan was for Jake to creep into their camp and disconnect a few pieces of their tent, so that it collapsed. Meanwhile, Mia would open up their cooler so that all the ice inside melted and they had to make a run into town the next day. She might decide on some other mischief too, if inspiration struck.

They'd already sabotaged the brothers' rental car, using butter knives to press down the inflation valves and let the air out of the tires.

"Anything to slow them down," Mia had whispered as the air hissed from a tire. "And make them want to leave Nehalem."

Her idea for Phase I of their plan had been just that simple. Make the Magnussons miserable. Hope that it left them less time for walking the creeks and forests. Which would also mean less chance of finding the turtle.

"Not a perfect solution," Hettle had said while chewing a piece of pizza crust. "Nevertheless, the idea of it delights me."

The light in the tent faded, then died completely. It only took a minute or so for Jake's eyes to adjust. There were clouds overhead but they were thin and smoky, allowing the brighter stars to poke through. The bamboo grove cast them in darkness, but once Jake and Mia started to creep up toward the Magnussons' camp, they'd have plenty of light to see by.

The moon was just a few days from being full. It hung low in the sky, glowing hazily behind the clouds.

They waited for a few minutes, then rose to their feet and started to advance forward, inch by inch. The Magnussons had set camp close to Nehalem Falls—which Mia told Jake weren't really waterfalls at all but more like big rapids—and the sound of the river tumbling over the rocks was loud enough to drown out the sound of stones shifting underfoot.

Jake's heart raced. He wondered if what they were doing was officially illegal. That thought was swallowed by his next one: What would the Magnussons do if they caught them? They didn't look like the sort of people you wanted to tangle with.

Mia touched Jake's elbow. "Meet you on the road."

The Magnussons' campfire and cooler were on the upstream side of their camp—she started in that direction. Their tent was on the downstream side—Jake veered that way. He figured he was thirty feet from the nearest tent stake.

Jake tried to breathe as quietly as possible. His left shoe, still wet from his hike, slipped, and made two rocks clack together. He recovered and stayed frozen, waiting for a flashlight to flick inside the tent.

Twenty feet left.

Thwap. Thwap.

Jake recognized the sound of latches on a cooler flipping open. Mia was ahead of him—already starting to sabotage the Magnussons' food.

Ten steps.

Someone's snoring in the tent. That's good.

Five steps.

Or is the snorer keeping the non-snorer awake?

Two.

If anyone moves, I run for the road, just like we agreed. Hide in the bushes and wait for a chance to get to the train tracks.

Jake crouched and wriggled a tent stake from the ground. The earth was hard-packed, and he had to really tug at the stake before it came free. He slid the first stake into his hoodie pocket and moved to the next corner. It came free a little easier.

He crept around to the third corner. This stake must have been driven next to a buried rock.

Sheeenk!

The sound of stone scraping against metal rang loud in his ears.

Jake froze. He felt like he could hear the blood whooshing in his head. He looked across the camp, past the smoldering embers of the fire pit, for Mia. He could see her by the cooler, frozen and waiting for the Magnussons to stir.

Neither did.

Jake felt tuned into the snoring sounds now. It was actually two separate snores on ever so slightly different rhythms. He slowly rose to his feet. He'd seen the tent from enough angles to know that it wouldn't fall apart just from the stakes getting pulled.

He breathed slow and steady, feet locked in place, then

bent his body along the curve of the dome so that he could get close enough to see the pieces that held the tent frame together. Jake peered at where two of the interlocking metal tubes connected. If he separated the poles, the whole thing would collapse while he was right there.

Too risky.

But if he left them the way they were, it would stay up all night.

"When in doubt, don't risk getting caught." That's what we agreed.

Suddenly, the river seemed like it was booming along louder than ever. Like someone had turned its volume up and lowered the sound of the screeching cicadas and the snoring inside the tent. Jake felt a certain calm. Clarity.

Like . . . the *opposite* of how he usually felt at school.

All his attention was in one single place. His senses seemed heightened.

He bent down and took one of the poles out of its grommet and drove it a half inch into the dirt. This way, the tent stayed up because of the pressure of the pole on the dirt. But as soon as someone rustled inside, it would slip free and the rest of the tent would collapse.

After doing the same thing to another pole, just to be sure, Jake crept through the camp and up a short path. He breathed easier with each step. Mia was waiting, crouched behind a bush, just a few feet off the gravel road.

"How'd it go?" she asked breathlessly.

Jake reached into the pocket of his hoodie and drew out three tent stakes. He grinned.

"I heard one of them get pulled out from over by the cooler," Mia said. "I can't believe they didn't wake up. Or that you didn't run away."

A jolt of pride ran through Jake like a full body shiver. "How did you do?"

He saw the bright white of Mia's teeth as her face broke into a broad smile. "I tore open a pack of bacon, so some animal should smell that before too long. Hopefully it's skunks. I also dumped out all their milk. And I turned on the gas to their little propane grill. By morning, they won't have any way to make coffee or what's left of their breakfast."

"They could just make it over the fire though," Jake said without thinking.

Immediately, he felt the heat of Mia's glare. "Yeah, but it would take longer."

"Definitely," Jake said, feeling bad for bursting Mia's bubble. "Want to see if the tent falls down?"

She nodded. He lifted up on his toes, then slammed the stakes down on a stone. They clanged noisily, bouncing off into the undergrowth. A flashlight popped on in the Magnusson tent.

Jake and Mia had a direct view as one side of the tent fell. The other three corners collapsed next. Finally, the whole dome deflated like a popped balloon.

As the friends snuck back up the path and onto the road,

they got one final glimpse of the camp—with the outlines of two giant Swedes tangled up and wrestling inside the tent, yelling at each other, and searching desperately for the zipper.

"Nice work," Mia whispered, slapping Jake's shoulder. "Now, *run!*"

21
Phase II

Jake and Mia didn't break stride until they hit the bridge. When the gravel road turned to tarmac, Jake sucked down a few deep breaths. The third exhale brought a big laugh from somewhere deep in his chest.

"Phase one complete!" he cheered.

As the last word left his mouth, Jake felt Mia freeze. He immediately saw what had caught her attention. Two headlights down the gravel road.

The Magnussons were in their car.

"Can you drive on flat tires?" he asked.

Mia pulled his elbow and started sprinting again. "Let's not find out!"

Jake's shoes slapped against the road in rhythm. He followed Mia as she veered left off the end of the bridge, dove into the bushes, and skidded down a muddy embankment. They came to a stop ten feet from the train tracks and ducked into a tangle of vines—waiting for the Magnussons' headlights to shine from the road above.

“We’d hear them clunking down the road if they drove with the lights off,” Mia panted.

“I think you’re right.”

After ten minutes, the two friends emerged from their hiding spot. When they didn’t see or hear anything, Mia led the way down the train tracks toward Hettle’s house; Jake trotted to catch up. It was too dark to try balancing on the rails, so they walked side by side through the thick weeds that grew up in the middle of the tracks.

The crackle of a fire made Jake freeze. He grabbed Mia’s arm, stopping them both. Up ahead, shaded from the moonlight by a towering pine, a sagging one-man pup tent sat nestled right along the track next to a small circle of coals.

Together, the two friends crept forward. There was no light coming from the tent. No movement either. After a few steps, the profile of a hulking truck came into view—parked on the steep dirt grade between the road and the train track, beside another culvert.

“That’s the park ranger’s truck,” Jake whispered to Mia. “He’s from Texas.”

“He’s here to hunt for the turtle, too?” Mia asked.

Jake nodded before realizing that Mia probably couldn’t see him. The tall evergreens that lined the train tracks blocked the moonlight.

“Ready for phase two of our plan?” he asked her. “The more people we can slow down, the better, right? And I don’t get a good feeling from this park ranger.”

Without waiting for Mia to say anything, Jake stepped over the rails of the track and started toward Stick's tent. He was still fifteen feet away but feeling bold. This would be easier than sneaking up on the Magnussons had been—there were two Swedes and only one park ranger.

Just past the campsite, the stream emptied out of one culvert, gurgled along for fifteen feet, and disappeared into a second culvert that ran under the train tracks. It looked almost identical to the stream where Jake had taken his hike. He wondered how many streams and culverts there were along this fork of the river.

As he closed in on the tent, it dawned on Jake that this gurgling brook was quieter than the booming river up by Nehalem Falls. And quieter wasn't a good thing.

Maybe I should—

Too late. A light snapped on inside the tent. Jake froze.

"What you are doing is"—the park ranger took a long time picking his next words—"*ill-advised*."

The Texas drawl was harder and colder than it had been at the opening ceremony or when Jake and Stick chatted that afternoon. Jake stayed stock-still.

Maybe the ranger's a sleep talker? Or reading something aloud? Or maybe—

"Whoever you are, I've got one hand on the tent zipper and one hand on a very large knife," the voice announced. "And I did not come all the way here from Scrub Pine, Texas, to have someone get the jump on me in the middle of the night."

Jake's heart was racing. You could hear the seriousness in the man's voice.

"I'll give you ten seconds to get moving. But I don't reckon you want to waste a single one."

Mia must've agreed with the ranger—she' d already crept up behind Jake. Now she jerked the collar of his shirt back toward the track. They were racing toward Hettle's house before Stick even started to count.

Nehalem, Oregon—6:12 a.m., TUESDAY

It was 5:02 a.m. when Stick crawled out of his soaking tent and into the cab of his truck. And it was precisely 5:07 a.m. when he decided he didn't like Nehalem. In fact, he hated it. Too wet. Too misty. Soaked and sodden right down to its rotten core.

Moss everywhere. And he'd never seen so many slugs.

"I just gotta find that old lady," Stick grumbled. He was drenched from a night in a tent with no rainfly. Down in Scrub Pine, Texas, it didn't rain enough to bother keeping one handy.

"The Olsson lady is the only one who knows about the turtle," he said. "Her and maybe that nephew of hers."

Stick grunted thinking about the nephew. He hoped that wasn't who he'd had to scare off the night before. It would hurt his chances of seeming like a friendly park ranger. But no, there had been two people—he knew by their footfalls.

"Maybe I'm in the clear."

By 5:45 a.m., Stick was busy trying to get a fire going. He figured eating a whole pound of bacon and drinking roughly a gallon of coffee would go a long way toward making him feel better. He got some newspaper off the floor of his truck and lit it, then slapped the bacon in the frying pan.

But there was no other fuel that wasn't soaked. In a few minutes, he was left with a wet, smoldering fire and a pound of pink, curled, half-cooked bacon. Stick spat angrily at a charred log in the center of his fire pit.

The spit didn't even sizzle. The rain had already killed the coals.

Click. Click. Click. Click.

By 6:12 a.m., Stick decided it was time to leave camp. No need to waste a minute staring at his dead fire or drooping tent.

"Find the old lady," he said aloud. "Get her book. Find the turtle. Get paid. Get dry. Get the heck back to Texas."

22
Four Is a Crowd

Jake woke up to the smell of bad breath. Not his but Singer's. The hound was literally panting right on his face. His tongue was hanging out, and he was whining for a walk.

"Morning to you, too," Jake grunted.

He sat up in his bunk and took Singer's head into his lap, scratching the dog behind both ears at once. Visions of the night before came flooding back—walking upriver to find the Magnussons' camp, sabotaging their tent and supplies, running away with an electric feeling coursing through his veins. Then trying the whole thing all over again when they saw the park ranger's tent by the train tracks.

That cold, hard Texas twang, warning him to get away.

The threat of a knife.

When they'd arrived back at the cabin, Jake and Mia hadn't talked about their encounter with Stick. They'd been too busy laughing about how they snuck up to the

Magnusson camp. Hettle's eyes glowed through the whole story, and she'd laughed out loud when she heard about the two Swedes tangled in their collapsed tent.

"It will take those oafs half the day to get their camp set up again," Hettle had said with a dry chuckle.

"And that's half a day they can't spend looking for the turtle," Mia added.

Jake looked at his pillow. *Homesteading on the Nehalem* was resting open, in a little pool of morning light that trickled past the window curtains. He'd been rereading it before bed, and there was a little drool mark on the page where he'd fallen asleep.

Jake stopped petting Singer and started to read a few lines:

> **Looking down, I saw an animal perched on a rock. A turtle, its shell no bigger than the palm of a child's hand and looking as delicate as a leaf. Its head and neck no larger than my thumb. And yet . . . here was the most magnificent creature I had ever seen. Perhaps, ever to exist.**
>
> **The top of the shell was made up of diamond-shaped sections, all of them about the size of my thumbnail. Each section shone deep red in the bright moonlight. As if they were gems set directly onto the animal's back by some enchanted gnome or troll.**

"The bright moonlight," Jake mouthed. "The . . . *bright* moonlight."

A thought struck him. A big thought.

Could the Ruby-Backed Turtle be nocturnal? Is there a chance that it only comes out at night?

Singer let out a long yawn. Jake hopped to his feet and padded out toward the living room with the dog at his heels, eager to run his idea past Mia and Hettle. Mia had spent the night, and she was sitting up on the couch, reading a note.

"Hey," Jake said, "I have this theory about the—"

He stopped midsentence. Mia reached over the back of the couch and thrust the note toward him. "Found this when I woke up."

Jake took it. Hettle's handwriting was far more delicate than he would've expected.

Jacob and Mia,

Congratulations once again on your clandestine operation at the Magnusson camp. You have inspired me to take action of my own this morning. Look for me to return in a few hours, hopefully with positive news about yet another "phase" of our plan.

Obviously, you are quite welcome to anything you would like to eat. There is a key on the table, please lock the door if you leave. We have to be careful about unwanted guests.

Yours,
Hettle

Jake read the note twice. It was a trick his school resource teacher had taught him. After he passed it back to Mia, she folded it neatly and tucked it between two pages of her notebook.

"What do you think she's up to?" she asked, pulling her feet up under her so that Jake had room to sit on the couch.

He shrugged, plopping down. "No idea. I sorta think she likes it that way."

"Being mysterious?"

"A little."

They both fell silent for a moment, lost in their separate thoughts.

"Speaking of mysteries," Mia said after a minute, "what were you about to say?"

Jake remembered, and he turned to fully face Mia. "Have you ever heard of a turtle species that's nocturnal?"

Mia considered it. "I guess I haven't really paid much attention to turtles at all before this."

"When Gustav writes about seeing the turtle, it was night. A clear night. He mentions how bright the moon was a couple of times. I was just wondering if maybe the Ruby-Backed Turtle is a species that's more active at night."

Mia wrote it down in her journal. "We could go to my house and look around for nocturnal turtles on the internet. I want to do name searches for the Magnusson brothers, Edna Blodgett, and . . . what was that park ranger's name again?"

"Hank Stamper. But he said everyone calls him 'Stick.'"

All four names went into Mia's notebook.

Jake rummaged the kitchen for something to eat. At home, he liked making food for himself, but his aunt didn't have pancake mix or instant oatmeal or toaster waffles. He found some eggs and some cheese in the fridge that looked like Swiss.

"Do you like omelets?"

"Sure," Mia said. "Hey, I was wondering if I could spend some time today reading *Homesteading on the Nehalem*."

Jake hesitated just long enough for Mia to glance up at him. "Yeah. Yeah, of course."

Singer was pawing at the doorknob, and Mia crossed the room to let him out. As Jake went back to the fridge to look for bacon, he heard her open the door. But before the hound could slip outside, she slammed it shut again and flipped the lock.

Jake wheeled around and saw Mia with her mouth open and her back pressed against the wall. Singer stared up at her, head tilted curiously.

"Speak of the devils," she said, drawing deep breaths.

"What do you mean?"

"Those four names I just wrote down in my journal . . ." She motioned outside.

Jake crossed the room, stood on his tiptoes, and peeked out through the stained glass. "All of them? Here?"

"Look," Mia said.

She dragged a chair over from the kitchen table, and they stood on it together—hunched so that anyone outside wouldn't see their outlines through the lighter-colored panes of the stained glass window. By peering through a dark blue section at the bottom of the windowpane, they could see Stick's truck parked across the road, lined up with the gap in the hedges. They could even make out his outline at the wheel.

Edna Blodgett was sitting on a stump in Hettle's yard, just ten feet from the giant cedar, twirling an umbrella with a satisfied little smirk on her face. The Magnusson brothers were there too. They stood defiantly right in the middle of the gravel driveway, glowering at the house and wearing garbage bags to keep the rain off.

Whether it was true or not, Jake felt like they could see him. He pulled Mia off the chair and out of sight.

"Why do you think they're all here?" he asked.

"To talk to Hettle?" Mia wondered. "Talk her into showing them Gustav's book?"

"It doesn't look like any of them are here together, though," Jake said. "You think they just all had the same idea?"

Mia bit her lip in thought. "The Magnussons and that Stick guy could suspect us—you know, from last night. But we didn't do anything to Edna Blodgett." She shook her head decisively. "They all must think it's imperative that they see the chapter on the Ruby-Backed Turtle."

Jake couldn't remember hearing the word "imperative" before. Still, the meaning was clear.

"Well then," he said, "it's *imperative* that we don't let them."

23
The Strangest Chase

The stairs leading to Hettle's bedroom creaked dramatically. Even with a good reason to sneak up to the second floor and into his aunt's bedroom, it seemed wrong to Jake on some level. Like an invasion of her privacy.

He tried not to look around too much to balance out the feeling that he was snooping. Mia wasn't as worried. She inspected the pictures lining the stairway one by one. When Jake entered the bedroom, she followed, holding a frame with a piece of paper inside.

"Look at this," Mia said. She held the frame out toward Jake. "It says 'The Last Chapter' on it. Do you think it was supposed to be the last chapter of Gustav's book?"

Jake didn't answer. He was trying to open the river-facing window, using a little metal crank he'd found on the sill. Seeing the Magnussons, Edna Blodgett, and Stick Stamper all loitering outside the cabin had sent nervous energy coursing through his veins. His brain was flooded with ideas, and he felt like he was scrambling to keep up.

Gotta get out of here.

Gotta get them *out of here.*

Gotta make sure they don't follow us.

Gotta make sure they don't stay at the house . . .

"Whoa, this writing is kind of depressing," Mia said. "Listen to this . . .'I have come to believe that modern people are destroyers of the natural world. Species die out by our hands. Habitats crumble beneath us. Colonies collapse. We think of ourselves as great creators, without ever asking: "What is broken so that we might build?"' That's heavy."

Jake tried to focus on one thing at a time, just like the resource teacher always said: "Focus on getting one task all the way done. Then you can move on."

The window.

He gave the window crank a final few turns and looked over at her. "Let's get out of here."

Mia returned the framed piece of writing to its hook in the hall. Jake threw one leg over the sill.

"Wait, so . . . what's your plan?" Mia asked.

She was beside him now, looking down at Hettle's backyard.

"We can't just be trapped here until Hettle gets back," Jake said. "And we can't leave them all here either. What if they break in?"

He swung his other leg over the sill, stepping onto the

shingles of the slanted roof that hung over Hettle's porch. He whistled, and Singer bounded up the stairs and into the bedroom.

Mia frowned. "Dude, have you looked down there? It's gotta be fifteen feet."

Jake could feel the world whooshing a little too fast. He was ramping up. Just like the Whole Saturday Market Fiasco.

Mia paced. "You're right though; this is a multistep operation. We have to get away from the house. And then we have to get *them* away from the house. We want them to follow us but not *catch* us. Because who knows what they're all capable of. It requires a detailed plan with—"

She stopped when Jake leaned back over the window-sill and hoisted Singer onto the roof. The hound squirmed in his arms, feet pedaling in the air.

"Hold up," Mia said. "Are you—*and the dog*—about to jump?"

Jake had already edged his way across the moss-slicked shingles and was looking down at Hettle's back lawn. It was mostly just an overgrown field of ferns, tufts of grass, and blackberry brambles spreading out in front of the river. There were a *lot* of blackberry brambles.

"We can't let them see us up here," Jake said. "So we have to be quick."

For a moment, Mia seemed to agree. She climbed out onto the overhang and pulled the window shut behind her.

"Are you noticing how high this is?" she muttered, shuffling toward Jake.

He didn't register her words, just handed Singer to her and sat down on the ledge, legs dangling. Then he rolled over so that he was facing her. With his hands pressing the shingles for traction, he slid down as slowly as he could, lowering himself inch by inch.

"It's definitely fifteen feet," Mia said. "If not a little more."

Jake gripped the edge of the roof tight, looking down at his dangling legs and the ground below.

It does seem pretty high.

He felt his arms tremble.

Really high, actually.

His fingers were slipping.

Too high.

Finally, it registered to Jake that his plan was impulsive. But by then he could already feel his grip slipping.

I just have to hope—

Jake felt Mia's fingers encircle his wrist. He looked up into her face. She'd set down Singer and was holding him tight.

"It's too far! You'll break an arm!"

She hoisted Jake up, and he managed to throw one knee up onto the mossy roof tiles. Then another. When he was safely on the roof, he stood, panting.

"Okay, that was a bad idea," he admitted. But he was still ramped up. "Maybe we could make a rope ladder. Or maybe there's one in Hettle's attic. Or we could tie a sheet to the roof and then—"

"Couldn't we just go out the back door?" Mia asked. "I'm not sure it helps for us to go off the roof, does it? We'll just lock the door behind us, right?"

Jake stopped panting. He stared at her. Then at Singer.

"I mean . . . ," Mia said. "If you have the back door key."

He did have the key. His aunt had showed him where it was hidden. He felt embarrassed for not thinking to use it.

Jake peeked over the edge of the overhang again. There was a dense thicket of blackberry brambles right where he would have landed.

"Back door," he said, catching his breath. "Good idea."

"You have the book hidden? Just in case they break in."

Jake nodded. "We can't take it with us, right? What if they stop us?"

"Yeah, I think it's safest here. In the dog food bag."

It was only a few minutes before Jake, Mia, and Singer were in Hettle's backyard with the back door locked. They managed it without being seen and ran along the banks of the river before cutting back through the undergrowth until they got to the road. Then they walked down the tarmac, toward the cabin.

"Now we have to figure out how to get *them* away from the house," Mia said. "Because they all definitely seem shady enough to break in."

“We can’t just yell, ‘Hey, guys, follow us!’ ” Jake said. “They’ll figure out what we’re trying to do.”

“But we *need* them to follow us,” Mia said.

They both looked up and down the road, as if Hettle’s truck might just come jerking and jolting along at that exact minute. It was raining and the road shone like a long oil slick.

“What if we walk close enough for them to see us?” Jake said to Mia. “Then whisper to each other and try to look nonchalant—so they get paranoid and think we’re talking about them.”

“You think they’ll follow us just because of some whispering?”

“Trust me, no one likes to have secrets told about them,” Jake said.

Ever since his ADHD diagnosis and especially since the Whole Saturday Market Fiasco, he’d noticed a lot of people whispering and spent way too much time thinking about what they might be saying.

Jake and Mia kept walking toward Hettle’s cabin, until they saw where Stick was parked. From there, they crept forward a little farther along the hedge that lined the driveway.

“Okay, how are we going to get their attention?” Mia asked.

“Hmmm . . . ,” Jake said. “I can make myself sneeze.”

“What good will that do?”

“Want to see?”

He pinched the bridge of his nose and let out a rattling sneeze. Even with all the sounds of the forest and the pattering of the rain, it stood out—seeming to ring through the valley. A few seconds later, there was movement on the other side of the hedge.

Jake sneezed again. This time he practically screamed, "AHHH-*CHOO*!"

Thirty feet away, Stick flung open the door of his truck and stepped onto the road.

"AHHH-*CHOO*!"

The Magnusson brothers came jogging past the hedges next, just a few feet from where Stick stood. Edna Blodgett hustled behind them.

"Three sneezes for the win," Mia said. She leaned over to Jake. "Okay, I'm whispering something in your ear so that they think it's about them. This better wor—"

"Jacob! Mia!" Angus called with a bright, friendly shark smile.

Jake leaned toward Mia. "Now walk away, but not too fast."

"Hey there, you kids!" Stick called, taking a step forward. "Can I have a word? Is your auntie coming home soon?"

Jake looked over his shoulder. Stick was looking at the Magnussons, who were looking at Edna, who was looking back at Stick. None of them had started following Jake, Mia, and Singer yet.

"They're not coming," Mia said under her breath.

They were more than a hundred feet ahead of the four adults now. Edna, Stick, and the Magnussons were all just standing there, trying to figure out what to do.

"Give me your notebook," Jake said.

Mia hesitated.

"I won't look."

She handed him the notebook and Jake stopped in his tracks. He turned to face the adults who were still watching from the middle of the road and opened the notebook to a blank page near the end. He pretended to pull out a pen, then scribbled some imaginary notes.

"Okay, act like you're reading it, then look at them," Jake said, passing the notebook back to Mia. "Now, keep walking."

They'd gone another twenty feet before Jake risked looking back again. When he did, he had to fight to keep from smiling. All four adults were headed after them.

"How'd you know that would work?" Mia asked.

"When I saw you writing the night we met, I would have given anything to read what was on the page. I figured they were the same."

Mia chuckled. "That's a way better idea than jumping off the roof."

Soon, the whole group was practically speed walking away from Hettle's cabin. Before long, they passed over a culvert and Jake knew they were close to Mia's house. With the four adults drawing closer, Mia raced ahead to her front gate. She swung it open, and Jake and Singer dashed into the yard. Then she pulled it shut.

They hurried up the sloped lawn toward the side door of the house.

"What now?" Jake called.

"What do you mean 'what now'?" came a deep voice.

Myron.

The mycologist wore hiking boots and a navy-blue rain slicker.

"You two came for my nature hike?" he called. "You gotta go inside and get rain jackets though. Then check out how many people came—it's packed!"

Jake and Mia looked at each other, eyes wide, both out of breath.

"Everyone else is waiting at the trailhead," Myron said, clapping his hands to get them moving. "Let's see some hustle."

Jake noticed Mia's eyebrows pinch together and turned to follow her sight line. The Magnussons, Stick, and Edna had all arrived at the gate. They stood shoulder to shoulder, elbowing for room.

"You four stragglers here for the mushroom hunt?" Myron yelled, waving them toward him.

Stick's eyes lit up and he took a few steps toward the gate. "Yes, siree! That's exactly why *I* came! I am excited to learn more about this verdant ecosystem! I thought we were supposed to meet down the road a spell. I must've been fouled up!"

Ragnar stepped up next. "Hallo, Myron! We are wanting to come also! We love to learn about mushrooms!"

"Yes, exactly as my brother says!" Angus added.

“And me!” Edna said. “You’ll see that I move faster than you might expect!”

“Love to hear it!” Myron boomed. Then he turned to Mia and Jake. “Can you two go open the gate?”

24
The Mushroom Hunt

Once they had rain slickers on, Jake and Mia ran to the back of the property to find thirty people at the trailhead. Myron stood facing everyone, standing on a clover-covered stump. Beyond him, the forest looked dark and ominous. Long tendrils of moss dripped off the branches.

Jake didn't know most of the people, but he recognized Keona Choi beaming up at Myron. Her son, Yu-Jun, was next to her—though he didn't seem particularly thrilled about it. As the Magnussons, Edna, and Stick crowded toward the front of the group, Jake, Mia, and Singer drifted to the back.

"Well," said Mia, pulling on the hood of her slicker, "we wanted to get them away from your aunt's house, so . . . I guess congratulations to us?"

Jake started to respond when Myron held up his hand to speak. A hush fell over the crowd.

"I *love* mushrooms," he said, in that booming voice.

A few people giggled. "In fact, I love *all* fungi. And trust me, my daughter reminds me how weird that sounds almost every day!"

His deep laugh was contagious, and the whole group giggled along. Myron looked at a few of the younger kids near the front of the group.

"Has anyone ever heard of a fairy circle?"

Jake's attention had been wandering a little. He'd been gazing around at the faces of some of the other people gathered for the hike, trying to figure out which people were interested in mushrooms, which were just tourists, and which hoped Myron might have a secret that would help them find the Ruby-Backed Turtle. But the mention of a fairy circle made his focus snap into place.

The phrase was a lot like "faerie garden"—the words Gustav's wife, Hildy, used to describe the spot where they'd seen the turtle.

"Anyone?" Myron asked.

A kindergarten-aged girl in the front raised her hand. Myron called on her, but her voice was too quiet to hear from where Jake and Mia stood. Myron leaned close to listen to her answer, then grinned. A few people near him chuckled.

"She said it's 'a ring of mushrooms where fairies live and dance and play!'" Myron repeated. "I can't speak to the last part, but she's right about the first bit. It's a perfect ring of mushrooms—and those mushrooms are all connected in ways you can't see, under the ground, working together. Thanks to a network of . . . well, they're sort of like veins in your body, called *mycelium*."

Someone's cell phone rang, and a boy just a few years younger than Jake whined, "I'm getting wet!" loud enough for everyone to hear.

"We're getting moving right now," Myron said. "I just want to say: *that's* why I love fungi—because of the unseen connections it makes throughout these forests. In fact, there's mycelium under all of you right now. And I just want to say, before we set off, I wish humans honored *our* unseen connections to the forest—and to one another—a little more."

There was a smattering of applause, but mostly the group seemed antsy to walk. Myron quickly explained to everyone where lobster mushrooms and summer chanterelles like to hide. He told everyone to look for a "rise in the duff"—a spot where a mushroom pushed up underneath fallen leaves and pine needles. Then he hopped off the stump and legged it up the trail, deeper into the dense forest.

Jake noticed that Stick was close on Myron's heels, chatting eagerly. The Magnussons skulked along together a few feet behind them, and Edna Blodgett fell back to the middle of the pack, twirling her umbrella.

"Should we sneak back to my aunt's house?" Jake asked.

"I think it's better to keep an eye on the four of them," Mia said. "If they see us leave, they might just follow us. Then we're right back where we started."

It was still sprinkling, but the forest canopy kept most of the rain out.

"Who might follow you?" came a voice.

The voice belonged to Mia's friend, Yu-Jun, who'd stepped off the trail to wait for them. The hair on the sides of his head was buzzed and he wore the hair on top in a bun, but a few tendrils had fallen in front of his face.

Mia put her hand on Jake's forearm and squeezed, as if to tell him not to answer.

"Yu-Jun, this is Jake," she said. "Hettle Olsson's nephew."

"Really?" the boy asked.

"Grandnephew," Jake said.

"Cool," he said, blowing a wisp of hair out of his eyes. "You'll be here all week then, right?"

Jake nodded. He wanted to be alone with Mia so they could talk about Stick, Edna, and the Magnussons. More importantly they needed to figure out the third phase of their plan.

"My mom had promised to take me surfing at Short Sands today," Yu-Jun muttered, kicking some soggy leaves. "I was gonna catch waves and then get some footage with my drone."

He blew the hair out of his eyes again.

"I've always wanted to try surfing," Jake said absently.

The words made Yu-Jun's face light up. Once he started talking about the sport, it was hard to get him to stop. He described how heavy the waves had been the week before and how he'd seen some pros visiting from Hawaii get barreled. Jake didn't know exactly what "barreled" meant, but it seemed to be something Yu-Jun *really* wanted to do. In the span of about thirty seconds, he also called it "shacked," "getting tubed," "tunnel gliding," and "slipping into the green room."

By the time Yu-Jun started breaking down the different boards he rode on different days, Jake was back to thinking about the Ruby-Backed Turtle. The idea of trying to keep people from finding a small turtle in the colossal Nehalem wilderness made his brain ache.

"Actually," Yu-Jun said, "I'd be super stoked to teach you guys to surf. And I could get drone footage of you, too."

"That sounds cool!" Mia said. She nudged Jake. "This could be your chance!"

"For sure," Jake said, only half paying attention.

"I'll talk to my mom about it. I bet we can come pick you up tomorrow or the next day."

After that, Mia and Yu-Jun started talking about kids from their school, and Jake's pace sped up. He didn't want to be at the end of the line, last to see everything. Even if the chance of the turtle walking along the path on its little stubby legs was very, very close to impossible, the least he could do for his aunt was try to find some mushrooms.

He whistled for Singer, then looked down at a mound of rotting leaves, using the toe of his sneaker to peer underneath them.

"You know," came a voice, "certain turtles live in fallen leaves, just like mushrooms."

Jake swung around to see Edna Blodgett, offering a friendly smile.

"What?" Jake asked.

Edna walked closer and started poking at the same leaf pile with the point of her umbrella.

"In Southeast Asia, there are turtles that don't have to always be in the water—"

"I think you mean tortoises," Jake interrupted. "Tortoises are on land, but turtles—"

"No, these are turtles, thank you kindly," Edna said, her voice crisp. "They don't need to live in the water because the fallen leaves in the jungles where they're found hold so much moisture. The Ruby Turtle could be like that, don'tcha think?"

Jake didn't answer. The path led up a small rise through a dense section of forest, completely shaded by trees.

"My aunt wrote to tell you the turtle was a myth," he finally said.

Edna started to huff a little and slapped a bug on her neck. "Maybe so . . . But I haven't decided if I believe her. Ought I to?"

Jake didn't hesitate. "Yes. Definitely."

Edna looked around to make sure the coast was clear, then leaned closer. "People say you know about animals, so let's just pretend there *was* a turtle. Just pretend, sonny. And let's think about what we know about other types of turtles living in a similar habitat."

Jake felt strange talking about this. He looked back

again. Yu-Jun was blowing the hair out of his eyes for what must've been the fiftieth time, Mia was smiling at something he'd said, and Singer was trotting beside them with his tail snapping left and right.

My own dog ditched me!

Up at the front of the group, Stick and Keona Choi were walking on either side of Myron—peppering him with questions. Jake had questions too. But they weren't for Myron.

Where are the Magnussons? Did they go ahead? Did they double back and break into Hettle's house to look for the book?

Then his thoughts skipped further.

Is Hettle home yet? Where has she been all morning? Why is she being so secretive?

His thoughts began to bounce around. His resource teacher at school called it "ping-ponging."

Are my parents having fun? Are they making cool pottery? Are they happy for some time away from me?

Jake could feel Edna studying him. "I'm sure you've heard of the Sulawesi forest turtle?"

Jake was distracted.

"Or the black-breasted leaf turtle?"

That name grabbed him. "The one from Vietnam, right?"

"Bingo bango," Edna said. "Both of those turtles live in tropical forests—one in Indonesia and the other, as you said, in Vietnam."

"So?"

Jake turned back, and his eyes met Mia's. She motioned him toward where she and Yu-Jun were walking, but he wanted to hear where Edna was going with this. It might help them come up with a plan.

"Those two turtle populations are incredibly small," Edna continued.

Her shoulder bumped Jake's side, and he realized she was actually shorter than him. Her tight gray curls bobbed as she walked.

"The Sulawesi turtle loses a lot of eggs to lizards," she continued, "and the black-breasted leaf turtle babies often get swept downstream when the rains are too heavy. Then the eggs or the babies are drowned or eaten by fish when they reach the river."

Edna waved her hand out across the Nehalem wilderness. "Either of those things could happen here. Rodents could eat the eggs or the rain could pull eggs into the river. So the population *could* stay incredibly small. And this is a mighty bit of wilderness for a highly endangered species to hide out in. A whole monstrous lot of it."

Jake found himself looking at Edna again. She had a cheery face and small, clever eyes—sort of like how he imagined a hobbit might look. He'd already caught the Magnussons in a lie and was feeling more and more sure that Stick's whole "friendly park ranger" thing was fake, but this woman seemed to actually care about wildlife. Sure, she'd been pushy with Hettle in her letters, but there was no denying that she loved turtles.

She's even wearing turtle earrings.

"If there *was* a Ruby Turtle," Edna huffed as the incline of the path got steeper, "it would need to be protected. My conservation society could do that." She glanced directly at Jake for the first time all conversation. "But the turtle doesn't exist, of course. Don't worry, sonny, you don't have to remind me!"

Jake was thinking of what to say back when the whole line of hikers stopped, then spread out in a half circle around Myron. He was holding up a massive brown mushroom with a whole bunch of floppy, ear-shaped pieces attached to a thick base.

"Anyone know what this is?" Myron asked.

A dad yelled, "A mushroom?" and his kid added, "A *super weird* mushroom?"

Myron boomed out a laugh. "Well, it's both of those. This is called a 'hen of the woods,' and it's definitely weird looking. It *is* tasty though. I'll cook this one up with some roasted garlic and browned butter at my demonstration later in the week, and you can all try it!"

A few adults murmured in excitement while some of the younger kids scrunched up their faces at the thought of eating such a strange-looking thing.

"The good news for us," Myron continued, "is that hens of the woods and summer chanterelles are often found near one another. So I say we all poke around this area a little—remember to look for a rise in the duff."

Jake decided to go find Mia and Yu-Jun and look for

chanterelles and lobster mushrooms with them. He'd read about pigs sniffing out certain types of mushrooms in Italy; maybe Singer could do that. But before he left, he turned to Edna Blodgett. She was clearly a turtle expert, and he did have one question for her that he'd been stewing on all morning.

He scratched the tip of his nose. "Since you know a lot about turtles . . . are there any species . . . ?"

He hesitated. Something told him to slow down but Jake had the strange feeling he got sometimes when he got an impulse to say something he worried he shouldn't. It was as if the question had already been asked and he was too late to stop it.

"Go ahead, sonny," Edna said. "We're just talking in the hypothetical."

"Yeah . . . ," Jake said. He glanced back at the others. He wanted to have something new to tell Mia. Some reason to pull her aside.

"Are there any turtles you know of that are . . . *nocturnal*?"

Edna hitched up. "Nocturnal, eh?"

Jake shrugged one shoulder. "It means—"

Edna smiled a tight little smile. "Oh, I know what nocturnal means, sonny."

Without warning the woman veered off the trail a little farther, poking around with the tip of her umbrella for chanterelles and humming a little tune. As she did, she chuckled to herself.

"But my," she said, "isn't *that* a very specific question from someone who keeps saying the Ruby Turtle doesn't exist? A very precise question. Even for a hypothetical."

Jake opened his mouth to tell her that he was just curious and that it didn't *mean* anything, but Edna had already wandered farther into the undergrowth, and now she was out of earshot.

Say something! You can't just let her think—

"I've just always been curious about that," he said, dodging under a tree to follow Edna. His heart raced and his face felt flush. "Not because it has anything to do with the Ruby-Backed Turtle, but just because—"

Edna snickered without looking at Jake. "Fascinating how sometimes the questions people ask are far more revealing than the answers could ever be."

25
A Nasty Bump

Later that afternoon, when the time came to tell Aunt Hettle exactly when things had gone wrong on the hike, Jake knew he should start at the beginning. Right after Edna Blodgett walked away from him, whistling as if she'd just found a four-leafed clover. The moment he realized that his question about turtles being nocturnal had been the very thing to convince her that maybe the Ruby-Backed Turtle *was* real.

He wanted to come clean with his aunt and describe how the embarrassment he felt over his question seemed to bring on a wave of noise. How it buzzed in his ears and wouldn't let him block anything out. How the noise and embarrassment and the leftover adrenaline from that morning had somehow multiplied each other. And how every conversation and flash of movement started fighting for his attention.

He would tell her that all of the fuzz and static made it

seem like the world was speeding up. As if he were running downhill, right on the verge of losing his footing. And that at the same time all this was happening, a cry went up in the crowd and he'd turned to see Yu-Jun with a fist thrust high in the air and a giant lobster mushroom clutched in his grasp—which sent everyone else into a frenzy.

Maybe he could even explain how at this point his attention felt like it was being pulled apart, strand by strand. Like the very worst days at school, when they took the standardized tests. When everyone seemed to be prepared with four sharpened pencils and all Jake had was one with a cracked tip and an eraser that'd been chewed down to a nub.

If he got that far, Jake probably would've managed to keep talking. He'd tell Hettle how he had wanted to stay near Edna so that he could see what she was going to do next. But he also wanted to find a mushroom. Not just because Yu-Jun had found one, but also *sort of* for that reason. Because having Mia's full attention and sharing this adventure had been fun, so if the cool surfer kid with the great hair took *some* of her attention, then Jake would have . . . *less of it*?

That was basic math.

"How could this other boy finding a mushroom *possibly* make Mia want to be your friend any less?" Jake imagined Hettle asking.

He knew there was no good answer. He also knew that

in that moment the static and energy and noise surging inside him had become way too much to even *try* to block out. He was too ramped up to even think of slowing down. Breathing was the last thing on his mind.

So while Edna Blodgett whistled and Myron clapped Yu-Jun on the back, Jake had started racing around the undergrowth, beside a surging stream, looking for chanterelles or lobster mushrooms or maybe, by some wild miracle, the Ruby-Backed Turtle, all while racking his brain for ways to convince Edna that his question about turtles being nocturnal had actually been meaningless.

None of it felt like it could wait; it had to be "now."

Right now. Right now. Right now.

At least that was how it felt. Like a million things had to happen, all at once, and there was no slowing down until they were all done. He was hungry and wet and agitated and . . .

Jake knew that if he really took the time to lay that all out, piece by piece, his aunt might have understood what happened next. How he had come to a ledge and seen the Magnusson brothers standing below him, both knee-deep in the creek, smiling those giant toothy grins at each other and clearly looking for the turtle.

They were recording each other with cell phones, too.

Why were they doing that? Had they already found it?

Jake didn't wait for the answer. The buzzing and whirring overtook him. He walked close to the edge of the bank, looked down to where the creek curled past a fallen log and formed the pool that the Magnussons were standing in.

He could jump into the pool. And if the turtle was there, it would dart away and hide. If they'd already found it, he could knock it out of their hands and back into the water. And so, when he got to the edge of the embankment, without warning or even really deciding to do so, Jake stepped forward, drew a tight breath, and leapt . . .

From that point on, the story wouldn't be Jake's to tell anymore. Because he didn't remember it. According to Yu-Jun, who saw the whole thing, he landed right between the two towering Magnusson brothers—splashing into the pool with a whole lot of momentum. His legs buckled at the force, and he jolted forward, slamming chin-first into a rock. A rock that was covered with moss, like everything else in Nehalem, but not *so* covered in moss that it couldn't leave him with a nasty bump.

After that, Jake's memories got fuzzy. He'd learned later that afternoon that the Magnussons carried him down the trail. That Myron seemed worried and Edna Blodgett seemed worried and Mia seemed *extra* worried. Also, that no one understood exactly what he'd done. Or why.

As they rushed him to his aunt's house, everyone had wanted him to explain himself. Luckily, his chin hurt too much for him to open his mouth.

"Why in the world . . . ?" Mia had said, as soon as they got a second alone.

Jake just shrugged and swallowed down the lump in his throat. He didn't want to explain himself to her right then. He *did* want to explain things to his aunt . . . sort of . . . but he couldn't do that either. Because while he lay on the couch thinking about how he would tell the story to Hettle, Stick stood just a few feet away. He had his elbow up on the mantel as if he owned the place and wore a crooked grin on his face.

"Yep," he drawled, "the young fella gave us quite a scare. He was out cold for a few seconds there. But I reckon he'll be fine. As long as he gets plenty of rest. And maybe no more going out in the woods for a few days, hey, pal?" He narrowed his eyes and his voice hardened just enough for Jake to take notice.

"Yessiree, pard. It seems like a mighty dangerous time for you to go wandering around in the wild. A mighty dangerous time indeed."

26
Hettle's Secret

"Hallo, Jacob." Hettle passed Jake a plate of French toast and sat down across from him at the kitchen table. "It looks as if you have grown a second chin on your chin. Are you in tremendous pain?"

"I'll be fine," Jake said, forcing a swollen smile. He was distracted by the smell of his breakfast.

He'd seen his face in the bathroom mirror a few minutes earlier. His chin was bruised midnight blue, and there was a bump the size of a plum. It didn't hurt too much, except when his forearm grazed it while putting his shirt on. Then it throbbed enough to make him yelp.

"I am still unclear about what happened yesterday," Hettle said. "But I gather that you were trying to help our cause in some way that is evident only to you."

Jake knew he should say something. Tell his aunt everything he'd wanted to say the day before. But he hesitated so long that Hettle seemed to move on.

“Well,” she said, “perhaps I will cheer you up by showing you one piece of what I have been doing with my time.”

Hettle brought a worn canvas knapsack up from the chair beside her and dropped it on the table. She motioned with her eyes for Jake to look inside. He hooked his finger on one of the bag’s straps, dragged it toward him, and unzipped it. Inside was *Homesteading on the Nehalem*.

Beneath that was another copy. And another.

There were five copies of Gustav’s book altogether. Two were in better shape than Hettle’s own copy, two were worse, and one looked like it’d been left in the rain for a month.

Jake’s eyes snapped up to meet his great-aunt’s. “What’s this?”

Hettle folded her hands in front of her on the table.

“When he finished his book, my grandfather was so proud that he paid to make copies for his friends and neighbors,” she said. “Over the years, various people in the area have mentioned to me that their own grandparents handed down a copy or perhaps that they found one at a garage sale. With this latest surge in interest in the turtle, I decided it was important to make sure that those copies were no longer floating about.”

“Did you *steal* them?” Jake asked.

“I did not steal,” Hettle said. “I bartered. In some cases, I paid money. In others I traded. Speaking of which, we have forty-five jars of blackberry jam to make by tomorrow—that was my primary bargaining tool.”

"This way," Jake began, "we can be sure—"

"Not sure," Hettle interrupted. "But we may rest more easily believing that anyone looking for my grandfather's book will not find it."

"So you don't have *all* the copies?" Jake asked.

Hettle's glistening eyes studied him closely while he ate a big, puffy corner bite of his French toast. It dripped with melted butter and tasted even better than the pancakes from two mornings before. Jake cut another piece with his fork while he waited on an answer. He was trying to save the middle bite for last, since that was always the best.

"Almost, but not quite," Hettle said. "There is one more copy that I know of. The man who owns it rejected my generous offer to buy it back. I will admit that this troubles me."

"There's no way to convince him to give it to us?" Jake asked.

Hettle had a steaming teacup in front of her. She took a long, noisy sip.

"I cannot try again," she finally said. "He was quite clear about that. I believe that perhaps you and your friend Mia could, however."

Jake wondered where Mia was. He remembered the look she gave him when she and her dad left Hettle's house the day before. Part of it was worry for him, like a friend. But there was something else, too. Like maybe she was worried *about* him.

"Why are you always trying to jump off things, dude?" she'd asked before she left. She'd been smiling at the time, but Jake caught her studying his face—like she really wanted to know the answer and understand. It reminded Jake of the look his mom gave him on the way home from the Whole Saturday Market Fiasco.

Like they didn't get how his brain worked.

"When do you want us to try to talk to this person?" Jake asked.

Hettle took another sip of her tea. "I assume that by this point you have heard about my arrest last fall?"

Jake nodded.

"It does not bother me that you know," Hettle said. "Do you know why I was arrested?"

"No." Jake waited for her to continue.

"I was caught on a surveillance camera while pouring sand into the gas tank of a large excavator."

Jake couldn't help but laugh, even though it made the bruise on his chin ache. "Sand?"

"And water. Also, one sack of sugar."

Hettle said all of this as if it were the most normal thing in the world.

"Why?" Jake asked.

Hettle finished her tea and reached for the kettle. "I did it to sabotage a limestone mine three miles down the road," Hettle said. "I do not like to see that scar in the forest every time I drive to town, and I do not like to imagine how far their diggers and earthmovers might spread."

Jake had noticed the giant gash cut out of the forest when he was driving with his parents, not long before they'd arrived at his great-aunt's cabin.

"Did it work?" he asked, sawing a bite of French toast with his fork.

"Not particularly well," Hettle said. "I was arrested, and the mining company filed a lawsuit for damages. Meanwhile, their equipment was up and running the next day."

"It was brave of you to try to stop them," Jake said.

"As you know, bravery and recklessness are close associates," Hettle said. "My actions led to ramifications that I did not expect. Today, I need to drive to Cannon Beach to meet with a lawyer in hopes of handling those ramifications."

Jake took his last bite. He really didn't think he'd ever tasted better French toast, even in a restaurant.

"I promise to make a swift return," Hettle went on. "Then I thought we could make some jam. As I mentioned, we have quite a bit to prepare. You are welcome to have Mia join us."

Jake nodded. His aunt went to the door, pulled on her heavy fisherman's sweater, and stepped outside.

"Speaking of Mia," Hettle said, "she has mentioned a number of times that she is eager to read *Homesteading on the Nehalem*. Be sure to give her a copy, then please hide the others. If you depart, please go out the front door and be sure that it is locked."

Hettle clambered into her truck, started the engine,

and crunched across the gravel drive. Before pulling onto the road, she jolted the engine into reverse, swung the driver's side toward Jake, and rolled down her window.

"Jacob," she called, "remind me again of your middle name?"

Jake frowned. "Um . . . Antrei."

"Ah, yes, it is my brother's name. Your grandfather. You remind me of him in many ways."

"Why do you need my middle name?" Jake asked.

Hettle's lips curled into a thin smile. "We will have to discuss this topic later, Jacob Antrei Rizzi."

27
Exploring the House

Once Hettle was gone, Jake bolted the door and turned to face the empty cabin. Singer was staring at him longingly from beside the fire. A moan began to boil deep in the hound's throat.

"Gimme a minute," Jake said.

He'd always liked being home alone. It was filled with possibility and there was a sort of nervous energy to it. At his parents' house, he'd go up into the attic and poke around or explore his dad's woodshop in the basement. Sometimes he'd make extra cheesy mac and cheese on the stove and eat it in his room, surrounded by stacks of animal books.

No one ever told him to focus when he was home alone.

At Hettle's cabin, that feeling of excitement about being alone was heightened. There were no neighbors close by. It was just Jake, Singer, and miles of dense forest.

He felt like he was the star of the sort of scary movie his parents didn't let him watch.

Jake grabbed the knapsack with the five copies of *Homesteading on the Nehalem* off the kitchen table. With Hettle telling him to hide the books, he didn't feel strange anymore about poking around her house. He'd already wondered what might be inside the storage closet under the stairs, the engraved wooden chest in the living room, and the shed next to the house that was shrouded in blackberry brambles.

But the attic was the first place he wanted to explore. Mostly because it had one of those ladders that retracted into the ceiling. Jake had always wanted to climb into an attic on one of those rickety ladders.

As he started up the stairs toward the second floor, Jake listened to the creaks and groans of each step. He looked at the photos he hadn't slowed down to check out the day before. The first picture was almost the same as the one he'd seen in the hall the day he arrived. It showed the same two men, but instead of standing beside the giant tree, the tree was cut down and they were puffing their chests out atop its colossal stump.

The next step brought a photo of a woman. It was a strange portrait, like it had been taken in black and white and then painted with watercolors. The woman was tall, with blond hair, and her painted-blue eyes stared right at the camera. Under the picture, there was cursive handwriting—"Hildy, 1936."

Every step brought a new image. There was one of the house. One of the river. There was a black-and-white family portrait full of people with his mom's same nose. Jake reminded himself to go back and study it later.

As he took the last step, he saw the frame Mia had been holding the day before. The one with writing titled "The Last Chapter." He'd been too ramped up to listen then, but now he took it down and brought it into Hettle's bedroom to read where there was more light.

Jake creaked the door open and sat down in the wooden rocking chair near the window.

The Last Chapter . . .

I have come to believe that modern people are destroyers of the natural world.

Species die out by our hands. Habitats crumble beneath us. Colonies collapse.

We think of ourselves as great creators, without ever asking: "What is broken so that we might build?"

The delicate robin's egg is crushed when the branch that held its nest is chopped for timber. The boundless spirit of the deer twitches in terror at the crack of the rifle. Nature's oddest creation vanishes from the creeks, never to be seen again.

Peering closely through the glass of the frame, Jake mouthed the words "nature's oddest creation." That was what Gustav called the turtle in *Homesteading on the Nehalem*.

This must be something he wrote.

But Jake hadn't read any writing in the book that was like this. It was so . . . What had Mia called it?

Heavy.

Jake put the frame on the floor and looked around the bedroom. Should he maybe hide one of the copies of *Homesteading on the Nehalem* in here? The bed and dresser drawers were out. Maybe a closet? His attention locked on a window on the far wall, with the shades drawn.

It faced upstream. The same direction he, Mia, and Singer had walked that first night at the cabin. He remembered looking up at the second story as they walked back for dessert.

Was there a window there?

Jake frowned. His attention had been bouncing around that night—hoping to make friends with Mia, racing to figure out what the Magnusson brothers were doing, and fighting to understand what the whole turtle thing was all about. But he remembered looking up at the house.

I don't think . . .

The floor creaked as Jake crossed the room. When he reached the far wall, he grabbed both the curtains, drew a breath, and flung them apart.

There was no window.

But there was a map.

28
The Map

The map covered a huge section of the wall, just like the ones they had at school. But Jake could see right away that it didn't show the world, the United States, or even the state of Oregon. It was zoomed in—with a giant curve of faded blue across the bottom half.

Leaning close, he saw the words "Nehalem River" printed in the blue section. Most of the map was centered on the forest northeast of the river.

"I think this shows all of Hettle's property," Jake muttered to himself. He thought of how his aunt would react to him calling it her property and felt the need to correct himself. "Or . . . y'know . . . whatever."

The map was topographical—representing various elevation levels in odd-shaped rings. It looked old to Jake. The green hills were faded; the edges of the paper were yellowed and brittle looking. In the bottom right-hand corner was a stamp:

Charted by the Oregon Department of Forestry: 1972

Then Jake noticed something else. The map was marked. Someone had drawn on it in faint pencil. And not just a little, either. The entire map was divided into a grid, with most of the squares shaded with diagonal lines. Some sections were crosshatched with two sets of lines.

The more he looked, the more Jake realized that most of the map was marked up like this. By following the lines, he saw that there were tiny dates written on each of the sections, too—most in the 1970s and 1980s, with fewer in the 1990s. The best Jake could tell, the first date on the map was October 24, 1972, and the last date was April 29, 2002.

What do these little shaded sections mean? Why do they have dates on them? Why are some sections shaded twice?

Jake stepped so close to the map that his nose almost touched it. Then he backed up a foot. Now two. He kept taking steps backward, trying to unlock what the shaded sections of the map meant.

As he took one last step backward, the floor creaked again. It was noisier than usual, and almost immediately Jake could hear Singer racing upstairs. When the dog spotted Jake through the open door, he practically dove into the boy's arms—paws on his chest, licking his face, and nuzzling into his neck.

"I didn't forget you!" Jake said. "I'm just trying to figure out what this is."

Singer let out a long, low moan.

"Okay, maybe I forgot you for a minute."

Singer nuzzled his leg.

"Maybe if we go for a walk, I can make sense of this— "

But Jake didn't have to wait. The answer hit him like a thunderbolt.

The shaded sections with dates next to them; some of the sections shaded twice with two sets of dates . . . He thought back to his mom's story on the drive to Nehalem. Of how the kids would search the forests and the adults would smile and wink at one another but also how Hettle took them seriously and wrote down exactly where they searched.

The map—Jake was so sure of it that his skin rippled with goose bumps—must show all of the places where his aunt had tried to find the "faerie garden" Gustav wrote about. It was her record of where she or her relatives had searched for the turtle, only to come home disappointed and shade in a new section on the map.

"And she double-shaded sections where people searched twice!"

Jake felt jittery. He wanted to tell someone right away.

"Why can't Hettle have a phone?" he said aloud.

He settled for talking to Singer. "So if the shaded spaces are where people looked for the turtle, then the unshaded space is where *no one* has looked yet."

Singer moaned again.

"We're going, we're going," Jake said, walking back toward the map. "I promise we're taking a very big hike—just as soon as I find someplace to look for the turtle that hasn't been explored yet."

He traced his finger across the grid, looking for unshaded spots. At first, there didn't seem to be any. The spots that looked unshaded upon first glance always seemed to have faint pencil marks on them that had faded over the decades.

Then Jake saw it, a block of four open sections on the map. By his best guess, by looking at the legend in the lower right corner, each empty section was about one square mile. They were in a valley with hills on either side—upstream, maybe a half mile past the falls.

Gustav had hiked to the glade where he saw the turtle from the cabin. The empty squares looked like an hour's hike; maybe a tad more. The distances made sense.

Energy surged through Jake. Visions of finding the turtle flashed in front of his eyes. He imagined microphones in his face and flashbulbs all around. He saw the same kids who looked at him funny after the Whole Saturday Market Fiasco asking him to retell the story again and again at lunch.

"Okay, we're walking all right," Jake said to Singer, voice trilling with excitement, energy flooding his body. "We're walking straight to this blank area!"

29
The Second Hike

As Jake strode along the oxidized, rust-flecked railroad tracks, he was overcome by a strange sensation. A certain crawling feeling. Like someone was spying on him.

The giant trees lining the train tracks blocked the light and made the woods feel lonely, enchanted almost. Moss dangled from the branches and the wind rustled the pine needles. Singer's head snapped left and right with every creak of branches or distant birdcall.

It wouldn't be so scary if Mia were here.

Jake knew his aunt had wanted him to go to Mia's house that morning. He imagined sitting in her tiny office and telling her about Hettle's hidden map, watching over her shoulder as she read the turtle chapter in *Homesteading on the Nehalem*. But that also meant getting asked about jumping off the ridge the day before. And the bruise on his chin.

It meant having to explain his ADHD and how it

wasn't *just* about getting distracted. Which filled Jake with dread.

"She might not even *want* to see me."

He remembered how certain friendships changed after the Whole Saturday Market Fiasco. Some kids talked to him less; others wanted to know the sorts of details he didn't want to share—like how much money it had cost his parents and what his punishment was. And then in July, when he went to Oaks Park with his younger cousins, Jake spotted a bunch of kids from his class in line at the roller-skating rink.

"Lexi's mom planned it," his friend Tyler had said with a shrug when they saw each other in line for a corn dog. "Maybe she forgot to invite you."

For days, Jake wondered if Lexi's mom had forgotten to invite any other kids.

Singer gave a strange snort that snapped Jake out of his thoughts.

"Let's just walk a while, buddy, you and me," he said. "Mia will be the first person I tell if we find the clearing that Gustav wrote about."

Jake and Singer walked another twenty minutes down the train track. Soon, the trees started thinning out. The weeds that grew up between the railroad ties were taller here. Massive dandelions and mustard plants shot up to shoulder level. For the first time all week, the sun shone brightly.

Jake arched his back and soaked it in with his eyes closed.

“I’d forgotten it’s still summer,” he said to Singer.

He stood like that until the strange feeling of being watched returned. His eyes snapped open—nothing there. He made a full circle to make sure no one was following them.

Jake didn’t see anything. Still, he couldn’t help being creeped out.

There was a sandy dune twenty steps away, next to the river, with nothing growing on it. Jake scrambled up to get a better view of the valley. From that spot, he spied the big wedge-shaped hill that he’d seen on Hettle’s map. It was still farther away than he’d expected, covered in dense forest and shrouded in fog.

This can’t still be Gustav’s homestead . . . can it?

As Singer scampered up to join him, Jake looked to his right and saw the river plunging along—splashing up on protruding gray boulders and sweeping toward the falls. Turning further, he saw a tiny coil of smoke and a green, dome-shaped tent. It took a second to recognize it from this side of the river.

The Magnusson camp.

From his spot on the hill, Jake could just make the brothers out, hunched over a fire. He dove to the ground, to keep from being seen. Singer growled.

“It’s fine,” Jake hissed. “I just don’t want them to see us.”

The hound’s hackles rippled along his spine. He growled again. Jake realized that Singer wasn’t facing the Magnusson camp—he was staring back the way they’d come, down the path. His teeth were bared.

"What?" Jake asked.

Singer ignored him. His attention was locked on something in the distance.

A mountain lion? A bear? Are there bears this close to the coast?

Jake rolled up into a crouch. He wanted to be on his feet in case he had to run from a charging predator.

"If it's a bear, you're supposed to play dead," he reminded himself.

Singer let out a bark. Not one of his deep, low redbone moans, but a fierce warning bark. Jake had only ever heard him bark like that a few other times.

The sound echoed through the river basin. Jake peered down the train tracks but still couldn't see anything. Then he turned back toward the Magnusson camp.

The brothers were both standing tall now, facing upstream toward the sound, squinting into the sun.

Maybe they won't see me. Maybe they'll—

"HALLOOOOOO, JACOB, OUR GOOD FRIEND!" Angus called, with his hands cupped around his mouth.

"WAIT RIGHT THERE!" Ragnar boomed. "WE WILL WADE OVER AND VISIT YOU!"

30
Sprint

Jake didn't start running the second he saw Angus and Ragnar wade into the Nehalem River. He didn't bolt as they waved at him and grinned their wide, shark-toothed smiles, with the water sloshing up against their thighs. The adrenaline was firing but his energy felt focused and unfragmented.

You could talk to them, act like everything's normal . . . But then they might force you to tell everything you know about the turtle.

"WHAT ARE YOU DOING SO FAR UPSTREAM, JACOB?" Angus called. The Magnussons were halfway through the river now.

You could run back to Hettle's cabin . . . But then they might chase you and make you show them the book.

Ragnar cupped his hands around his mouth. "JACOB, ARE YOU LOOKING FOR THE RUBY TURTLE AT THIS VERY MOMENT?"

Or you could run and hide . . . And . . . They might chase you.

"STAY THERE!" Angus boomed, waving both arms. "WE WILL LOOK FOR THIS SPECIMEN TOGETHER!"

But if they chase you, there's no guarantee they'll find you.

Finally, Jake did start to run—scrambling downhill, and tearing upstream along the train track, chest heaving, trying not to trip on the railroad ties. As he sprinted, he imagined how long it would take the towering Swedish twins to clamber up on the banks of the river, sopping wet, and give chase.

Mid-stride, Jake forced out a "coo-eee." As if by magic, Singer was at his side, bounding through the weeds. They ran side by side for more than two hundred feet, until Jake slowed to risk a look over his shoulder.

No sign of the Magnuss—

"OOF!"

He went down with a thud.

Before Jake could even draw a breath, Singer was on him. The dog's nose pressed hard into his ribs, prodding him back to his feet. Rising to his knees, Jake could see a twisted piece of steel poking out of the earth where he'd fallen.

The rest of the track was gone—buried under a massive mound of dirt.

This is what Mia talked about. Rain washing out the tracks.

Jake turned and scrambled uphill, following the path

made by the mudslide. The ground was soft, and he dug his feet in, like he'd seen mountain climbers do. Singer panted beside him.

As the incline grew steeper, Jake started to scramble on all fours. He felt like his lungs might burst and his head was pounding—his bruised chin seemed to radiate heat across his whole face. Just when he thought he couldn't take another step, he looked ahead and saw where the path of the mudslide crested and flattened out. He scampered the last few feet and fell to his knees.

Chest heaving, Jake realized that the Magnussons would still be able to see him from down by the train tracks. He needed to hide. There was thick forest beyond the little plateau he was on but that meant going farther uphill. He didn't think he could do any more climbing.

Jake looked to his right. The incline there was less steep, but it was still uphill.

"JACOB! WHY ARE YOU RUNNING? IT IS US, ANGUS AND RAGNAR!"

Jake looked down toward the river. He couldn't see anyone.

Can the Magnussons see me?

"JACOB, DO NOT RUN FROM US! WE ARE YOUR PALS!"

To the left, the hill fell away, sloping down into a ravine.

"JACOB! WAIT THERE! PERHAPS YOU HAVE A CONCUSSION!"

Jake's hand shot out to grab Singer's collar and he dove left into the gulch, sliding down the loamy soil, dodging trees and bumping over ferns. Singer's legs pedaled forward, losing and regaining footing over and over. When a rotting log blocked their path, Jake let go of Singer's collar and they both leapt over it.

It took less than a minute for them to skid to a halt at the bottom of the ravine. Jake looked back the way they'd come and saw no one. The valley seemed to suck up all the noise of the river. The forest felt still again.

The only sound was his ragged breath, Singer's panting, leaves tapping and swaying against each other in the breeze, and the light *tinkle-plop-clink* of water flowing over rocks. The sun filtered through the forest canopy and cast strange, dancing shadows on the ground.

It seemed strangely peaceful.

"Let's keep moving," Jake said to Singer.

In front of him stood a wall of ferns and spreading emerald creepers. In the gaps between them, Jake spied a thin brook.

I can follow that creek back to the Nehalem River anytime I want. Then I can walk downstream back to the cabin. Just as soon as it's safe.

Looking back up the ravine, Jake didn't see the Magnussons. Yet. But he wasn't about to take any chances either. If he circled back to the tracks too soon, they might be waiting for him. Plus, there were two of them—they could have one brother wait at the path while the other tried to track him through the forest.

Jake clicked his tongue for Singer and stepped past the wall of ferns. They plunged into the creek and started wading upstream, away from the big river—eyes flashing left and right for any sign of danger.

Hettle's Cabin—3:12 p.m., WEDNESDAY

Stick had been staking out Hettle's house when he saw Hettle Olsson's nephew, Jake, and his dog start walking upriver. He'd been following the boy at a distance but doubled back to the house the second the coonhound spotted him and started barking. The last thing he needed was to get bit by a dog.

"Time to find this book," Stick said, hustling back to the cabin. "I'll tear that dang house to shreds if I have to."

The lock on the back door of the cabin was a pin tumbler from the 1950s. It was the first type of lock Stick had ever learned to pick and still the easiest for him. He flipped the bolt in less than a minute.

The door hinges creaked as they swung open—long and low and spooky sounding. Stick stepped inside and looked down at his watch. He gave himself ten minutes, max, to explore the house. Not that he thought the old woman or the boy would be back quite so soon, but he worried about some neighbor, like the mushroom hunter's daughter, dropping by.

There was a room near the back door of the cabin, and Stick peered in. The bed was strewn with clothes. Animal books were piled on the desk.

"This is where the kid sleeps," he said aloud.

Stick tossed the clothes and checked under the mattress. He opened the dresser drawers. No luck. He knew sometimes people hid precious things right in their pillowcases, but the pillow on this bed didn't even have a case on it.

His gaze fell on the bag of kibble beside the bed. There was a photo of a golden retriever on the front and next to it the words **NIBBLE KIBBLE DOG FOOD.**

"Spill it, pup," he said to the photo, "where are they hiding this dang book?"

He surveyed the room again—looking for any nook or cranny he might have missed—until his eyes settled on the photo of the dog again.

"What do you say, boy? Is it up in the old lady's room?"

Stick stepped back into the hall, then took the stairs toward Hettle's room two at a time. The door was open. The furnishings were spare—a rocking chair, a few trinkets lining the shelves, a closet, and . . .

There was a framed piece of paper on the floor. Stick picked it up off the ground.

"The Last Chapter."

It was some sort of poem. He took photos of it with his phone and put it back where he'd found it. When he rose to his feet, he looked across the room.

Stick's mouth fell wide open.

"Well, this must be my lucky day after all," he muttered.

31
Cornered

Jake didn't know for sure if he was being followed, but he wasn't about to take any chances. He unfastened Singer's collar so it wouldn't jangle, slipped it in his pocket, and traced the creek uphill. It took a full twenty minutes before he started to feel safe again.

Stopping to unwind a vine from his ankle, he realized that he ought to be keeping his eye out for more than just the Magnusson brothers.

"This must be close to the unshaded part of the map," he said to Singer. "I mean . . . it couldn't be too far off."

Jake began peering into the pools formed by fallen logs and mossy rocks wedged tight together. He tried to imagine what it would feel like to see the deep-red hue of the Ruby-Backed Turtle's shell flashing underwater. Would he definitely recognize it?

And . . . then what?

Jake could see himself holding the turtle in the flat of

his palm, its ruby-red shell practically glowing in the flash of cameras.

And then . . . And then . . .

After his diagnosis, Jake's dad had showed him a list of famous people with ADHD. Now he envisioned himself on that list, right next to the Olympians, movie stars, and authors.

There was a flicker of movement in Jake's periphery, somewhere uphill, and he jerked his head around to look.

"Must've been a bird," he said aloud when he didn't see anything.

Singer looked ready to lunge. Jake grabbed for the hound's collar, but he'd taken it off. Instead, he wrapped his arms around Singer's body.

"Calm down," he whispered. "I can't have you running off right now."

After a minute or two standing in a little pool of water, arms wrapped around his dog, Jake let go. It seemed like the coast was clear. He turned his attention back upstream again and was just figuring out how to get past an overhang made by a log and a giant rock slab when he heard yelling far off to his right.

"HEY, GUYS, IT IS ANGUS AND RAGNAR AGAIN!"

The Magnussons! How did they . . . ? How could they . . . ?

"YOU WILL NOT BELIEVE THE INFORMATION WE HAVE FOR YOU ABOUT THE RUBY TURTLE!"

Who are they talking to?

"OUR TRIP TO OREE-GONE HAS BEEN A NONSTOP ADVENTURE!"

Jake spun to his right, the direction the sound had come from, and looked up the ravine. The rim of the rock overhang blocked his line of sight. On the chance that the Swedish brothers had crossed to the other side of the gulch and the sound had carried strangely, he looked that way next.

Nothing.

"NOW WE ARE SEARCHING A DARK, ENCHANTED RAIN FOREST!"

Jake thought that sounded like Ragnar.

"WE'VE BEEN LOOKING FOR THE FAMOUS RUBY TURTLE FOR THREE DAYS NOW!"

And that had to be Angus.

But where are they?

Jake bent down and scooped up Singer in his arms, then crab walked back to the far corner of the little cave made by the protruding rock. When the cave ceiling sloped to meet the waterline, he crouched as low as he could go, slowly lowering himself so that he and Singer were sitting in a few inches of water, facing out, and hidden by the giant slab. There was the sound of crashing through the forest. Jake's mind flashed to the image of an elk, but he quickly realized it was the Magnusson brothers headed down into the gully.

"JACOB!" one of the brothers yelled. "ARE YOU DOWN HERE?"

Even though the voice was partially drowned out by

the echoing of the stream in Jake's little cave, it wasn't hard to hear. It sounded like it was somewhere close.

If I popped my head past the ledge, they might be right there looking at me.

Jake held Singer tight—one moan, bark, or even growl would give their hiding place away. He stayed as still as he could, ears tuned to any unfamiliar sound. The seconds seemed to drag, and the minutes stretched on endlessly.

Then the Magnusson brothers started talking again. It was almost as if they were right on top of his rock—speaking in Swedish to each other. Singer squirmed, and Jake squeezed him tight. He nuzzled his face into the hound's neck to calm him down.

After some back-and-forth in Swedish, Angus started to speak in English again.

"Hello, everyone! We are the Swedish Adventure Bros—still in Oree-gone of the USA, looking for the Ruby Turtle. On our last video, we told you about our camp being sabotaged and our cooler raided—maybe by a Big Foot? Crazy, right, bros? Press the Subscribe button for more of our adventures!"

There was a pause and more talking. Jake felt tuned into every sound around him. The voices of the Magnussons, the babbling creek, Singer's breathing, the birds in the distance, and the echoes that all those noises seemed to make as they filtered into his little cave. He did his best to stay focused by imagining the towering Swedes standing right above him.

Who is Angus talking to?

After more discussion in Swedish, Angus started in English again. The words were almost the same, but they were louder and more energetic this time.

"Hey, everyone! It is Angus Magnusson—one half of the SWEDISH ADVENTURE BROS! My brother and I are still in Oree-gone! USA! And we are looking for the incredible Ruby Turtle! If you saw our last super-cool video, you know about our camp being ATTACKED by what probably was a Big Foot! CRAZY, right, guys? Make sure you subscribe to our channel to follow our adventures!"

Jake frowned. Was Angus shooting . . . a YouTube video?

Is that why the Magnussons came to Nehalem?

The whole speech started again. "Hey, GUYS! It is Angus Magnusson—one half of the SWEDISH ADVENTURE BROS!" Jake rolled his eyes. "My brother and I hope you LOVE all our videos and subscribe! Click it now!"

Now Ragnar's voice came in. "After our camp got ATTACKED BY A SASQUATCH, we have ventured back into the forest looking for a boy who knows about the Ruby Turtle! So smash that Like button and follow us into THIS SPOOKY, HAUNTED RAIN FOREST!"

From his nook, Jake could hear the brothers arguing in Swedish again before Angus started the speech for the fourth time. And a fifth. Soon, every single word was practically screamed before Ragnar ended with "SMASH SUBSCRIBE, BROS! HIT LIKE! SHARE OUR VIDEO, ADVENTURE TEAM!"

Finally, both brothers seemed satisfied. For a minute

or two, the only sound Jake heard was the tinkle of the creek and the chirps of far-off birds. Then a new sound—sort of like static on a TV—began echoing through Jake's tiny alcove. Softly at first, but getting stronger in a hurry.

Is that the Magnussons again? Are they walking upstream?

In an instant, Jake realized what the sound actually was. Rain. And not a light sprinkle like he'd seen so many times since arriving in Nehalem. This was a downpour. It slapped against the leaves of trees—sounding less like a rainy day in Portland and more like the videos he'd seen of the Amazon rain forest.

The Magnussons called a few sentences back and forth to each other and started bounding downstream—with Angus filming as they went. They waded right past Jake's hiding spot and were out of sight seconds later.

As the rain continued to spatter against rocks and slap the leaves of trees, Jake waited, stone-still.

"Let's get back to Hettle's, then go get Mia," he whispered to Singer once the coast was finally clear. "I can't *wait* to see the look on her face when she hears about this."

32
The Break-In

Jake approached Hettle's cabin from the back, creeping along the riverbank to keep out of sight. He had all sorts of things he wanted to ask his aunt, but his plan vanished the second he saw the deep scowl on her face after tapping on the windowpane. And it skipped even further out of mind when he saw Mia at her side, holding the fire poker as if she might have to swing it at someone.

Hettle flicked the bolt on the lock; the door swung wide.

"Jacob, did you go out the back door when you left?"

The force of her voice surprised Jake.

"You told me not to," he said. "I went out the front. I locked it, too. I double-checked."

Hettle held up a small, folded piece of paper. "I had this tucked into the back door when I departed this morning. It's an old tactic to see if someone enters a home unwanted. It was on the floor when I returned."

"Meaning someone came in this door," Mia said.

Singer nudged past Jake to slip into the house.

"Quick, Jacob," Hettle said, "where did you hide the copies of Gustav's book?"

"*Copies?*" Mia asked, arching an eyebrow.

Jake rushed inside his tiny room. In his hurry to explore the unshaded area on the map, he'd hidden all five extra copies of the book—plus Hettle's original copy—inside the pillowcase. Sweat beaded on his forehead as he unrolled the kibble bag.

Please let them be here.

He could feel Mia and Hettle staring as he felt around inside the bag. The pillowcase was there. He hefted it. It felt full.

Jake dropped the pillowcase on his mattress, then reached inside and took out the books, one by one.

"Six books?" Mia said. "You guys have *six* copies of Gustav's book now?"

"It seems quite obvious that you did not bring a copy to Mia, as we had discussed," Hettle said. "Which leads me to a question—where have you been these past hours?"

Jake dusted off the copies of the book, tossing them on the bed.

"Jacob?" Hettle pressed.

Jake looked at his aunt. "I found your map when I was looking for a good hiding place, and I wanted to see if I could find the unshaded part. But the Magnussons saw me and I had to ditch them in the forest."

Hettle's face had begun to relax. Now the mask of panic returned. She wheeled around and limped down the hall, faster than Jake had ever seen her move. Her feet thudded up each step, with Mia at her heels and Jake trailing behind them.

The curtains!

Hettle burst through her bedroom door. Jake watched her giant frame sag before he even set foot inside. His face and neck went hot.

"Aunt Hettle, I think I closed . . ." He turned to Mia. "All this time she's had this map of all the places people have looked for the . . ."

Hettle drew deep breaths. She kept her eyes focused on the map. She didn't look at Jake or even Mia.

"I really think I closed the curtains," Jake insisted. There was a lump in his throat that he couldn't swallow down.

I know I was going to close them. Then Singer barked. I thought he was going to pee on the floor . . .

Hettle turned to face Jake and Mia. "Whoever broke into my home came looking for Gustav's book. By a stroke of good fortune, they did not find it. But surely they came into this room and just as surely they saw this map."

Jake's mind was racing, trying to think of something to say to convince Hettle that he had closed the curtain.

But did you? Are you sure?

Jake realized Hettle and Mia were talking, but there was so much noise in his head that he couldn't focus on them. He tried breathing. Tried closing his eyes to reset.

"So the map shows where the turtle lives?" Mia asked. "You know for sure? You've seen it?"

"No," Hettle said. Her voice was distant. "I did not show you two the map because finding the Ruby-Backed Turtle is not what interests me." Now she looked at Jake. "I did not bring you here to look for the turtle, Jacob. I brought you to help me make sure it does *not* get found. There is quite a significant difference."

Jake frowned.

"The map shows the location of the one spot that has never been searched," Hettle continued. "If the turtle or its descendants are alive, I believe it is most likely found there. However, that does not mean that I care to find it. My only interest is in protecting it. Now I fear I have failed."

"So you figured out the turtle's habitat through process of elimination?" Mia asked, stepping close to the map to study it.

Hettle nodded. "A process of elimination undertaken across decades." She paused. "We must now assume that someone has seen the product of all that searching."

"That woman Edna Blodgett came by our house today to ask my dad about the forest," Mia said. "So it couldn't have been her. Maybe the Magnussons?"

"No," Jake said, without looking up. "They saw me on my hike and chased me. I hid and could hear them talking. It couldn't be them."

It was silent for a long time. Jake still felt anxious and jittery. He wanted to say something to fill the quiet.

Mia faced Hettle. "I have to go. *I'm going to see a friend.*"

The words were loaded with meaning. Jake knew she was talking about Yu-Jun, of course. He was supposed to go surfing with them; he'd been excited about that.

Mia turned to leave. "Hettle, can I take home one of the books on my way out?"

"I think that is a good idea."

"Thank you, *Hettle*," Mia said. "It's so nice when real friends share things, *Hettle*. Instead of keeping them to themselves, *Hettle*."

She stomped out of the room. Hettle stayed right where she was, with her back to Jake. For the very first time, he thought of her as old. Her body looked worn down as she stared despondently at the map.

"I really don't think I left it open," Jake said. "I just . . . I get overwhelmed sometimes and forget."

"It does not matter," Hettle said. "It will soon be your problem far more than it is mine."

Jake didn't understand and wondered if he'd misheard her. "Yeah, I'll fix it. Is that what you mean?"

"That is not what I mean," Hettle said, her voice almost a whisper. She walked to the map, ran her fingers along its shaded sections for a moment, and dragged the curtain shut.

"Jacob, I would like some time alone. We can speak again this evening."

33
Midnight Jam

Jake shuffled downstairs to his room, peeled off his wet clothes, and curled into bed. By the time he woke up again, the nighttime sounds of the Nehalem Valley could be heard outside—creaking branches and strange, distant hoots. Rain slatted against the cabin.

He hadn't eaten since breakfast. His stomach felt like it was folding in on itself. He slipped out from under his covers and crept out of the room to find something to eat.

The house felt spooky this late, especially after the break-in. The living room was cast in darkness, the fire was burnt down to coals, and the shades were drawn on all the front windows. Jake could hear Singer snoring in front of the fire and make out the dog's general shape, but not much else. He had a sense of where the couch was and tried to avoid banging into it on his way to the kitchen.

There was a tinkle of a pull chain. A lamp snapped on.

"GAH!" Jake yelled.

It was Hettle. She'd been sitting in the dark, in her recliner. Jake's voice startled Singer enough for the dog to stir, but he was snoring again in seconds.

Thanks for your concern, old buddy.

"Did I alarm you, Jacob?" Hettle said.

"No—or . . . I mean, yes . . . I guess," Jake stammered. "I was just hungry."

"I did not want to wake you. Perhaps I should have," Hettle said. "Let us go to the kitchen to fetch your plate."

She grunted as she stood up from her recliner and lumbered into the kitchen, where she flipped on a light. Jake followed her.

The butcher block was covered with hundreds—maybe more than a thousand—blackberries in woven baskets. They spilled over their brims and clustered in little piles.

"You can see that I have had quite a productive afternoon," Hettle said.

"You picked all these since I came back?" Jake asked.

"We have a very significant amount of jam to make."

There was a plate covered with a cloth napkin on the counter, and Hettle handed it to Jake. He pulled off the napkin to find a BLT—bacon, lettuce, and tomato—with a thick chicken breast inside, cut down the middle.

"BLT with chicken is my favorite," Jake said.

"Your mother mentioned that to me."

Jake picked the sandwich up and took a bite. He couldn't help but smile.

“I think this is the juiciest chicken I’ve ever had,” Jake said, mid-chew.

Hettle nodded. “Bertha was well fed.”

Bertha? Was this one of the chickens from Hettle’s yard?

Jake gulped.

“All food comes from somewhere,” Hettle said with a shrug.

Jake hesitated. Then took another bite.

“Gustav once wrote that ‘life is a dance, and the natural world—’ ”

“ ‘Is the human being’s eternal partner,’ ” Jake finished.

“Yes,” Hettle said. “Fascinating that you remember that.”

“I liked how that sentence sounded,” Jake said.

“As do I. However, I am quite sure I did not yet notice it when I was your age.”

“That’s the thing about my brain,” Jake said between bites of his BLT. “Sometimes it loses things, and sometimes it grabs on to them.” He paused, thinking of the map and the open curtain. “The problem is I’m not really great about telling my brain what to grab on to and what to let go of.”

“I wish that more people on this planet had brains that remembered nice sentences.”

Hettle smiled. Jake had seen her smirk a few times now. And the skin around her eyes would crinkle when she poked fun at someone. But this was the first time he could remember seeing her teeth. For the first time, he could imagine his great aunt as a little girl.

"Now," she said, "about these blackberries."

Hettle took two lemons from the basket that hung above the sink. Then she piled all the blackberries into a strainer to wash them.

"Jacob, are you prepared to learn the special ingredient in my famous blackberry jam?" she asked.

"Is it the lemons?"

Hettle went to the refrigerator and drew out two giant silver pitchers. She set them on the center island and motioned for Jake to look. He stood on his tiptoes to peer inside. The liquid was clear.

"What's in there?"

"Water," Hettle replied. "Water drawn from these creeks. Water filtered through moss, not machines. This water is the secret to my jam. And to all my cooking, to be honest . . . Though pork lard and butter are also often helpful."

"You collect it?" Jake asked, nodding at the water pitchers.

"When my hip allows and there is jam to be made, I venture to a nearby creek."

Hettle poured a pitcher of water into a giant pot waiting on the stove and turned the burner on. The pilot light crackled and the blue flame glowed to life. She dumped hundreds of berries into the pot, along with a heaping bowl of sugar.

"Jacob," Hettle said, slicing the lemons in half and squeezing their juice into the pot next. "It is time for you to understand why I brought you here. Are you prepared for the full truth?"

Without waiting for an answer, Hettle turned the burner to a simmer, crossed the kitchen, and started toward the back door. Jake hurried after her.

"Where are we going?"

"You will see."

Jake followed his aunt as she limped along a path cut through the blackberry brambles. At the banks of the Nehalem sat a bench, roughly carved from one giant piece of wood. Hettle eased herself down and patted the space beside her.

Jake sat. They watched the river—the moonlight bouncing off its surface like one giant sheet of reflective metal.

"On the occasions that I visit the local library, I often check out books for people closer to your age than mine," Hettle said. "I have always liked these sorts of stories—fantasies full of wizards and strange lore."

Jake wanted to know which books exactly, but he fought the urge to interrupt.

"In many of these books, the adults are the same. They pretend to be helpful only to hide information, in the name of protecting children. It bothers me immensely." Hettle paused. "And yet I have done exactly that to you."

Jake had been focused on the slick-looking surface of the river. Now he turned to his aunt.

"There was a very important conversation that led me to invite you here," Hettle said.

"With my mom, right?"

Hettle shook her head. "With my lawyer. The same one I went to see this morning."

Jake wanted to listen but felt his attention racing in a new direction. There were thoughts connecting in his head. About the Magnussons. About Stick. About Edna Blodgett.

Just hold on to it. Just hold on. Just . . .

"What the lawyer told me," Hettle continued, "is that—"

"Sorry, Aunt Hettle," Jake interrupted. "I know it's rude, but I had this thought—I think I'll keep getting distracted if I—"

"Go ahead, Jacob."

"Edna Blodgett went to Mia's house and the Magnussons were in the valley looking for me, and . . . I think they're hosting some sort of video series on the internet . . . So if someone broke into the house—someone we already *know* is looking for the turtle—then it has to be Stick Stamper."

"The park ranger," Hettle said. "Sitting in the dark, I came to a similar conclusion."

"I guess it could be someone else. But those are the four most likely people, and three of them couldn't have done it. But Stick, the way he looks at me, and that knife he carries . . . who else could it be?"

Hettle nodded. Jake was getting excited now, but he didn't feel out of control.

"So let's say he knows where you think the turtle is. He

still doesn't know anything about it. He's never read Gustav's book."

"You must admit, the name 'Ruby-Backed Turtle' is quite descriptive itself," Hettle said.

"Fine," Jake agreed. "Maybe he has an idea what it looks like, but he's not sure. And he probably doesn't know that the turtle doesn't always have to live in water."

By the moonlight, Jake could see confusion register on his aunt's face.

"There are turtles in Vietnam that live in the leaf litter near creeks in the rain forest. They're not tortoises, they're turtles, but there's enough moisture in the leaves for them to survive. Edna Blodgett—the turtle foundation lady—said that if the Ruby-Backed Turtle *was* real, it might be like that."

Hettle nodded slowly. "It is an interesting theory."

"Yeah," Jake said, "and here's another thing the park ranger doesn't know."

He drew a breath.

"He doesn't know the turtle is nocturnal. Not even the article on the internet mentions that."

Hettle's face registered her surprise. "Jacob, you did not tell me you knew that the turtle is nocturnal. When did you deduce that fact?"

"The morning after I got here," Jake said. "There are a lot of nocturnal reptiles in my different books."

"It took me much longer," Hettle said. She raised a heavy hand and put it on Jake's shoulder. It felt good to have part of her weight on him like that.

"Very astute of you to notice such a thing so quickly. Does anyone else know that the turtle is nocturnal?"

"Only Mia."

And Edna Blodgett. You have to tell her that.

"I don't think anyone else," Jake said, racing to the end of the sentence.

"Jacob," Hettle replied, "you are quite a clever boy . . ."

"Yeah, so what I was saying was as long as no one has the book—"

"But you are not much of a liar. Perhaps the worst I have seen."

Jake winced.

"I will ask again, who else knows that the turtle is nocturnal?"

Jake's eyes snapped to his aunt's face. She was facing forward, focused on the smooth movement of the river.

"No one. I . . . I just asked Edna Blodgett if there are any nocturnal turtles that she's heard of. I just wanted to get information from her, but . . ." He swallowed. "I think she could tell it was important."

Hettle nodded.

"So Stick Stamper knows the turtle's location and Edna Blodgett knows it is nocturnal," she said. "Then our task is simple—we must keep them apart for three days. After that, anyone on our property will be trespassing."

Jake turned fully in his seat to look at his aunt this time.

"Did you just say *our* property?"

"I misspoke," Hettle said. "It is raining, let us walk inside."

Jake looked up. The moon had gradually been blotted out by clouds, but there was no rain at the moment. Not even that fine Nehalem mist.

"Um, Aunt Hettle . . . it's actually not rain—"

Hettle had pushed herself off the bench and was already plodding up the path back toward the house. Jake trotted after her.

"Not raining here and not raining yet," she said. "But downstream it is raining, and that rain will reach us momentarily."

"How could yugggg—" Jake stepped on a pinecone with his bare heel and hopped on one foot until the pain passed.

"I have lived in this forest quite some time," Hettle said. "Now as to the matter of our land, I believe I misspoke. Which returns us to the point I was making before we got sidetracked."

They were weaving a path between the hulking blackberry brambles now.

"I was telling you what the lawyer told me. Which is that if I had been any more effective in disabling the mining company's vehicles, it could have led to a much larger lawsuit."

"Because you poured sand into the gas tank of their tractor?" Jake asked.

"Sand in one, water in another. I spread a full jar of

blackberry jam across the electrical panel of a brand-new conveyor belt."

"Wow," Jake said. "That's pretty extreme."

"When I saw the holes they were gouging into the forest, I imagined a day when I could no longer collect drinking water from our streams. A day when these towering trees and emerald forests no longer exist."

"Still . . . ," Jake muttered. "You really went all in."

"You are not the only impulsive person on the planet, Jacob."

Jake couldn't help but chuckle when she said that.

"What the lawyer asked me," Hettle continued, "was if I could be trusted not to do anything so reckless in the years to come, as the mine widens and I grow less patient in my old age."

Jake felt a drop of water land right on the ridge of his ear. Another hit the back of his neck. Hettle had been right about the rain.

"My answer was 'I highly doubt it.' In fact, I find myself getting angry every time I pass that scar in the forest. Every time I notice its continued expansion."

They were crossing the yard now and Jake could see better by the back porch light.

Hettle was huffing, and her limp was more pronounced. "At which point the lawyer gave me a piece of very interesting advice."

"What advice?" Jake asked.

Hettle took the three steps onto the back porch and

stopped. She gripped the handrail and caught her breath. There wasn't room on the porch for two people, so Jake didn't follow her up the steps. He waited on a patch of grass.

When Hettle turned around, she looked massive under the porch light. Jake saw a triumphant look in her eyes. She was basking in some private victory that he couldn't understand quite yet.

"He advised me on strategies for passing on the deed to the land. So that no future actions of mine might lead to it being taken."

"Passing on the deed?"

She swallowed.

"In short, he told me to sign the land over to someone else, someone who I hope will know how to protect it."

Jake was standing just under the roof overhang so he wasn't getting rained on. He wasn't cold either. He felt as patient as he ever had in his whole life. He knew the feeling that went with the look in his aunt's eyes—when you're saying something so important you can feel your blood wooshing in your veins.

"I had a few people to choose from, but only two blood relatives living in Oregon."

What is she saying?

"Your mother is a kind woman. But I do not know if she loves the wild, far, far in, deep down."

She can't mean . . .

"I was wrong earlier to say 'our' land," Hettle continued. "Because, in fact, according to the State of Oregon, this is technically *your* land, Jacob Antrei Rizzi. Although you won't be in complete control of it for a few years."

"You're . . ." Jake was stunned. "You're giving all this to *me*?"

"Remember that I believe very little in the right of humans to own the earth. Also, that I am of the opinion that many living things might lay a better claim to the property than you or I. But for all technical purposes—yes, I am giving you this land, set up in what is called a trust."

Jake asked the first question that came to mind. "*Why?*"

The way Hettle's eyes glistened made Jake realize that, somewhere overhead, the moon had shaken free of the clouds for just a moment.

"It was actually our conversation about newts and salamanders," she said. "Do you happen to recall it?"

Jake frowned. "You're giving me your land because I knew the difference between newts and salamanders?"

"Of course not," Hettle said, chuckling. "That would be quite absurd."

"Yeah," Jake agreed. "I was gonna say."

"In fact, it was because you said they were both enchanting. That moment made a tremendous impact on me."

Now Jake felt like laughing.

"That you could be enchanted by such things," Hettle continued, "the small creatures of the natural world—that is what gave me hope that the Ruby-Backed Turtle, and if it one day is proven extinct, then the salamanders and newts, the trees and the moss and the chanterelles all have their best chance at survival in the years to come with you."

Jake felt flooded by a wave of guilt. "Do you still think that . . . after I forgot to cover the map and accidentally said the thing about the turtle maybe being nocturnal to Edna Blodgett?"

"Yes, Jacob," Hettle said. "I most certainly do,"

34
The Last Book

After Jake and Hettle finished making blackberry jam, he lay awake for hours, thinking about the fact that his great-aunt was putting him in control of her homestead, the cabin . . . *everything*. What was he supposed to do with it? He'd never owned anything bigger than a bike!

Once sleep did come, it was fitful. By 7 a.m., he was dressed, ready to venture into the forest to look for Stick Stamper. Where else would the park ranger be than in the foggy, moss-filled woods, searching the unshaded part of the map?

And then what?

"I'll come up with something," Jake muttered to Singer as he laced up his still-soggy shoes. "If ADHD is good for anything, it's good at coming up with lots of ideas, so . . . I'll do that."

But when Jake got to the kitchen, Hettle was already awake.

"We must eat briskly," she announced, motioning to the plates of eggs, sausage, and biscuits on the table. "Today is the day of the jam-making contest."

Jake grabbed a piece of sausage off a plate and ate it standing up.

"I was thinking I should go straight to the forest to look for Stick. Or maybe do something to keep him from talking to Edna Blodgett?"

Hettle crossed from the stove to the table and used her fork to spear her own piece of sausage.

"It is wise to keep an eye on Stick," she said, mid-chew. "As well as this other woman, Blodgett. Also, I am still distrustful of the Magnussons, even if you feel convinced that they are making some sort of entertainment to be seen on the internet."

Jake spread jam on a biscuit. "So why would we go to the festival then?"

Hettle set down her fork. "Stick, Blodgett, and the Magnussons are all quite aware that this is their only chance to learn about the turtle from me, the one person who they know for certain has seen Gustav's original book. They will all be at the park hoping to meet me there, I assure you."

Jake opened his mouth to argue but stopped. She was absolutely right.

"So why even go?" he tried. "We could say you're still sick. Myron could judge."

Hettle shook her head. "That will create suspicion all through town. I am known as a hermit, and this jam-making contest is the one social event I enjoy. I missed the opening ceremony, but if I do not go today, people will talk. When they talk, it is quite possible that they will talk about how I spent the spring tracking down almost every known copy of *Homesteading on the Nehalem*."

"All but one, right?" Jake asked.

"Which brings us to our next item of business," Hettle replied. "Now please, we must hurry."

Exactly twelve minutes later, Hettle's rusted-out truck was crunching up onto the main road. Forty jars of blackberry jam stacked in two cardboard boxes jangled and clinked against one another near Jake's feet. Singer stayed behind to guard the house.

The drive was a quiet one. Jake had been looking forward to time alone in the woods. It would be a chance to pull his thoughts together about everything that had happened the day before.

Especially what had happened with Mia.

When they passed the park where the festival was held, there were just a few people, setting up tents. The truck rumbled past a long estuary, then a craggy, rocky beach. At some point, Hettle pressed a cassette into the open mouth of her car's old tape deck.

Jake had never heard a tape before. His parents had a record player, but a tape was different. The songs sounded sort of curved and wobbly in a way that he liked.

"You fill up my senses, like a night in the forest . . ." a voice sang.

Jake knew the song but couldn't place it. His parents had played it before.

Was it on the way home from Mount Hood?

The voice was soaring now.

Or maybe Prineville?

Each line felt loaded with meaning.

Or on the way home from the Deschutes?

It was beautiful—like a lullaby.

Maybe it was . . .

And with the voice on the tape and the truck trundling steadily beneath him, Jake drifted off. The next thing he knew, the car was easing into a parking spot.

"We have arrived at our destination," Hettle announced.

Jake opened his eyes and yawned. His face was slick with condensation from leaning against the window. His aunt turned her body toward him.

"The man inside this building has the last copy of *Homesteading on the Nehalem* that I know exists for certain."

Jake was disoriented and groggy after his nap. "Wait—you're coming with me, right?"

"He will be nicer to you if I do not come inside. We were once quite close but that is not the case anymore."

Jake took this in with a nod.

"You are naturally friendly," Hettle continued. "Do your best to see that he likes you."

Jake opened the truck door and stepped into the parking lot. It was mostly empty, just two other trucks parked at opposite ends of the lot. Hettle motioned toward a door on a big gray building, then remembered something and waved him back toward the car.

"This will help you make an impression on him," she said, reaching under her seat and fishing out an oversize jar of jam. "His name is Robert Bobb, and he is a member of the Siletz nation."

"Robert Bobb?" Jake asked. "His name is Rob Bobb?"

"Indeed. His family has been prominent along the Oregon Coast for hundreds of years."

How is she expecting me to get this book? I don't even know what this place is.

The answer to the second question revealed itself quickly. As Jake crossed the parking lot, he saw a sign that read "Siletz Tribal Cultural Center & Museum." With a quick glance back at the truck, he swung open the door and stepped inside.

The door echoed when it closed behind Jake. He'd been to a ton of museums with his class but still didn't know exactly what to expect. Would there be paintings? Statues? Mannequins in reenactment displays?

Nope. Baskets.

The room Jake entered was *full* of baskets. Rows and rows of them. Most looked tightly woven, though some were looser. Some had simple lines and diagonals while others had diamond shapes and even more complicated patterns.

As he walked deeper into the museum, holding the jam

jar with two hands, Jake also noticed jewelry in glass cases. He recognized artifacts that he'd seen in other museums in Oregon—like an elk hide robe with carved shell pendants dangling from leather laces.

On a wall above a display case was a frame with a newspaper in it. It was from the *Oregonian*. Seeing it made Jake think of whatever article had been written about Hettle's vandalism of the mining camp. And how one article on a website had led someone to the old newspaper article that mentioned the turtle, which had been read by Edna Blodgett and posted on her site, which was then posted by a whole bunch of other sites and spread around the entire world.

"You're interested in that, hey?" came a low, rumbling voice.

A tall man with broad features, tightly clipped hair, and a graying goatee ambled slowly in Jake's direction from the other end of the room. Jake decided this must be Hettle's onetime friend Robert Bobb.

"That article is about a teacher on the Siletz reservation in the early 1900s," Robert said, without any introduction. "She taught at the reservation school for twenty-five years, and when she retired, they gave her this basket."

He pointed to the display case, which held a woven basket inside.

"I like it," Jake said.

He didn't know much about baskets, but clearly this was a nice one—the pattern of different-colored reeds was more complicated than some of the others he'd seen so far. There were red diamonds in a ring around the lip that made him think of the Ruby-Backed Turtle. Under the diamonds was a row of zigzags in black.

"The teacher was well liked, and her basket was always talked about as one of the best ever made in this region. It was meant to honor her."

Jake nodded. "Is that what the article is about?"

"Nope," Robert said. "The article is about her granddaughter giving the basket back to the Siletz, about thirty years ago."

"Why'd she give it back?" Jake asked, all too happy to keep the conversation going.

Robert passed a hand through his goatee. "She thought her family had enjoyed it long enough. She thought we would take the best care of it."

"But it was a gift, right?" Jake said. "She didn't have to do that."

"It was a gift when it was given to her grandma," Robert said; he looked down at Jake now. "And a gift when she gave it back to us."

The story seemed to fit almost too perfectly. It was exactly why Jake had come—to get Gustav's book back after all these years. To ask for its return as a gift.

"I see what you're thinking, kid," Robert grumbled before Jake could form a single word. "But it's not gonna work. Not even close."

Jake frowned. "What do you—"

"That's Hettle Olsson's truck out front. She's probably the one who told you to ask me about that article in the first place. She's tried that reasoning on me before."

"I didn't ask you about the article," Jake said, "you just started talk—"

"I was down at the opening ceremony of the Blackberry Moon Festival," Robert continued. "I saw the stuff on the internet, too. I understand why she wants Gustav's book back."

Jake didn't know what to say, and Robert wasn't leaving any room to speak even if he did. Instead, he handed over the jam jar.

"Ha! She sent you in with her famous jam!" Robert exploded. "Why, that's a cheap trick! Of all the sneaky, low-down—"

"Sorry!" Jake said, scrambling to make peace. "I'll take it back."

Robert's face cracked into a mischievous smile. "Let's not go that far, kid. I'm keeping the jam." There was a lilt to his voice that sounded playful. "But you're not getting that book."

Robert held the jam jar toward the light, and it lit up, deep purple. Then he looked back down at Jake.

"Listen," he said, "I wouldn't want people poking around my property either." He paused and gave a sort of gravelly chuckle. "Of course, the Siletz haven't had a choice in that matter. Neither has any other tribe in this country."

Robert walked away to set the jam jar on a shelf, then

pivoted back to Jake. He was smiling, and his hands were folded in front of his stomach, like he was on a stroll in the park.

"It was a good try though, I'll give you that. Asking me about that article was clever."

"But I didn't ask—"

"Just take the compliment, kid," Robert said with a wink.

Jake searched for something else to say. "So you . . . and my great-aunt . . ."

"Were close friends once," Robert said. "I was the one who bailed her out of jail when she got arrested."

"Seriously?"

"Quite."

"But she still can't have the book back?"

"Certainly not."

"Can you tell me why? Since we both know she's going to ask."

Robert's face tightened, and his brow furrowed. "She knows why, but I'm happy to tell you. First, there's an interesting retelling of one of the Thunderbird stories of this region. Have you read that bit yet?"

Jake shook his head.

"Beyond that, well . . . I don't exactly love the idea of the descendants of European homesteaders asking for things *back* from the Siletz, no matter how many years have passed. Why should we give more than we already have?" He stroked his goatee. "Nor do I feel much need to help Hettle Olsson protect land that her grandfather 'homesteaded,' turtle or not."

It was clear that Robert had his mind made up.

"Got it," Jake said. "Well . . . thanks anyway."

As he walked toward the exit, Jake glanced at a clock mounted to the wall—he'd only been in the museum for seven minutes. They had time. And he was in no great rush to get to the festival.

Hettle won't mind.

Jake wheeled around. "Last question."

"Better make it a good one then," Robert said, grinning.

"Can you show me around before I go? These baskets seem pretty cool."

Robert smiled. "Now *that*, I can do."

35
The Mining Camp

Hettle was hunched forward, pressing the old truck as hard as she could, racing back to the jam-making contest.

"You knew he wasn't going to give me the book, didn't you?" Jake asked as the truck rattled toward Nehalem.

"That is correct," his aunt said.

"Then why did we drive two hours out of our way just to go to the museum?"

Hettle glanced over at Jake for a hair of a second. "Did Robert like you?"

Jake shrugged one shoulder. "I mean . . . We joked about a few things during the tour. He's an Oregon Duck fan."

"Then perhaps he will hesitate before showing the book to anyone else who might come inquiring."

"Anyone like the Magnussons," Jake muttered. "Or Edna. Or Stick."

"Precisely."

The jam jars below his feet tinkled together in a strange chorus as the truck rambled on. The voice warbling out from the tape deck hit a high note that made Jake feel lonely and strangely sad. He wondered what his parents were up to—this was the longest he'd ever gone without talking to them.

"Mia will likely be at the event today," Hettle said as they drove past the estuary an hour later.

Jake didn't answer. He knew he needed to apologize to Mia, but just thinking about it left him with a blunt, heavy pressure behind his eyes. He wasn't sure what to say and didn't want to face her with a crowd of people around.

He swallowed. "She might not even be mad anymore."

"That is possible," Hettle said, giving Jake a side-eye, "but it sounds quite unlike her."

As they turned down Foss Road, Jake was lost in thought, watching the fog rise off the Nehalem River. Then, without warning, Hettle hooked a sharp left turn and skidded into a gravel parking lot. The truck shuddered to a stop.

"Look at it, Jacob," Hettle said.

Jake looked up to see the mining camp he'd passed with his parents on the way to Hettle's house. The one that Hettle had sabotaged. It definitely wasn't shut down anymore—giant excavators and backhoe compactors chewed the side of the hill. The exposed hillside was slate gray with huge machines crunching across it.

Hettle gripped the steering wheel with both hands. Her breaths came tight and heavy, like a bull's.

"Are you okay?" Jake asked.

"You will always have to fight to preserve this forest," Hettle said. "Nice people will find excuses to support mines. Fine families will come up with reasons to sell their land for tremendous profit. Your heart will be broken as you watch those who claim to love the natural world make compromise after compromise until every forest has been clawed to shreds and every rare species dies out. This is what you are up against."

Watching Hettle's face fill with rage as she watched the miners made something click in Jake's brain. "It was always about more than just the turtle."

"That is correct, Jacob. The turtle is but one battle. The real war is for all of the wilderness—the trees and streams and salamanders."

Jake saw a flicker of movement to his left. Two men in a forklift were pointing at Hettle's truck. One of them, wearing a blue hardhat, hopped out of the cab and ran toward them.

"We know who you are! Get out of here! We have a restraining order."

Hettle jammed her gearshift into Forward and idled the truck for a long moment before dragging it down to Reverse. Then she cursed under her breath in what Jake assumed was Finnish. Finally, the truck rumbled away from the mine.

Less than a minute later, they were pulling off the road again, this time at the park. As they crunched into the parking lot, Jake spotted Yu-Jun getting out of an SUV with his mom. He pushed his hair out of his eyes, then waved at someone.

Jake followed Yu-Jun's sight line to see Mia. Her gaze landed on Hettle's truck for just the briefest of moments; then she turned her back. She didn't even wave.

"Okay, so she's probably at least a little mad still," Jake said.

As Hettle started to unload the jam jars, Jake saw other people he recognized. There was the man with the long, scraggly beard who looked like an old-timey gold miner and the hacky sack guy in patchwork pants. He saw a few of Mia's classmates who he recognized and Myron standing tall above the crowd.

Jake figured there were at least a hundred people altogether, but definitely fewer than the opening ceremony.

"People lose interest quickly," Hettle said, when he asked her about it. "With any luck they will all be gone quite soon."

As he carried a box loaded full of clinking jam jars across the field, Jake found himself looking up at a towering pole, surrounded by green and blue ribbons and decorated in a giant crown of flowers. The ribbons were held to the ground with stakes—making a colorful upside-down cone.

"That is the Maypole," Hettle said, before Jake even

asked. "It is a traditional dance from Europe—perhaps you would enjoy taking part."

Jake didn't say anything; he just kept lugging his box until they reached a canvas canopy covering a long line of tables. Every table had two rows of jars lined up on it. A group of older women shuffled around the tables, opening each one and putting a tiny wooden ice-cream-tasting spoon inside.

"You have to taste *all* these?" Jake asked. He guessed there were at least fifty entries, maybe a hundred.

"It is not what I consider torture," Hettle said.

Underneath the same tree where Jake and Mia had watched the opening ceremony, the members of the band Fifty Dollar Crab were busy tuning their instruments. There was already a microphone sitting in a stand, with a cord jacked into a tall amplifier.

Hettle piled her jam on one of the tables. "Do not look now, but Stick is standing beside the river, watching our every move."

Jake couldn't help but turn—though he tried to be sly about it. Sure enough, there was Stick with one hand on his knife sheath.

"Do not let him see you staring."

Jake pivoted away, and his eyes immediately caught on two matching crew cuts bobbing above the tops of cars in the parking lot.

"There are the Magnussons," he said under his breath. The brothers stepped into the field, squinting against the sun. Angus started filming Ragnar, who was gesturing toward the Maypole.

"See how they're always filming?" Jake said to Hettle. "If you had internet I bet I could find their YouTube channel."

Feedback squealed out of the amplifier, grabbing everyone's attention. Keona Choi held the microphone.

"Hey, everyone," she said, waving at the crowd, "as you all know, we do our best to hold the Maypole dance on the sunniest day of the festival every year, and it doesn't get much sunnier than this, does it?"

She gestured up to the sky, and the crowd cheered. The sun glinted off the surface of the river—making every ripple look like it had been flecked with gold.

"Since we have a lot of guests this year, I'm going to do a little refresher on the Maypole dance. There are thirty-two ribbons staked into the ground there—who's brave enough to grab a ribbon?"

Myron was the first to move. He strolled out into the clearing and stooped to pick up a stake, tossing it aside and keeping hold of the ribbon. The crowd cheered. The man with the wild beard skipped out next.

"All right, Myron and Zane!" Keona said, smile beaming. "Who else?"

A few people entered the clearing around the pole and picked up ribbons at once, including the Magnusson twins, still filming each other.

"How about some younger people? Yu-Jun, why don't you get out there!"

Yu-Jun seemed annoyed about getting put on the spot, but a long look from his mom was enough to make him trot out and find a ribbon. Mia jogged out next.

"There you go, Mia!" Keona said. "Let's get some more brave girls!"

Jake stood in the shadow of the jam tent watching Mia, waiting to make eye contact. She wouldn't look anywhere near his direction. When he heard scattered applause, he turned his attention to find Stick loping out toward the Maypole.

"Why would he . . . ?" Jake began under his breath.

But the question was answered immediately as the park ranger found a spot right next to Edna Blodgett, who'd also taken up a ribbon. Stick seemed to know she was his only hope besides Hettle for uncovering some clue about the turtle.

"JAKE!" came a booming voice. "JAKE RIZZI, COME HAVE A GO!"

It was Myron, and he was echoed by the Ragnar Magnusson. "YES! COME DANCE, JACOB! WE WILL ALL HAVE A MERRY TIME!"

36
All Around the Maypole

Jake looked at the dancers. Almost every ribbon had someone holding it, and they were all looking at him. Everyone except Mia.

Yu-Jun's ribbon was close to the jam tent, and he called over. "It's kinda fun! I promise!"

Without much of a choice, Jake jogged to pick up the last ribbon still staked in the ground. He tossed the stake into the grass and held the ribbon in both hands, the way he'd seen the others do. The Magnussons cheered for him, and Myron smiled from across the field.

"The steps are easy, but we'll start slow," Keona announced over the microphone. "People with the blue ribbons and the green ribbons face each other—you'll do the dance in opposite directions."

Keona explained the steps and demonstrated them. Then she had everyone practice without music.

"Now let's bring out Nehalem's own, the Fifty Dollar Crab! Can we all give them a hand?"

Everyone watching cheered as the band strode out from the shade of the spreading oak tree. First came a small woman with purple hair, carrying an accordion. She was followed by two men with big bushy beards. The larger man held a delicate fiddle, and the other carried a strange-looking guitar, shaped like a teardrop.

The woman with the purple hair stepped up to the microphone and said, "Welcome, everyone! We've got some good news—our band is complete today for the first time in a year! Our friend Hope Carter drove all the way down from Portland to be here with us! Can everyone give her a round of applause?"

A woman stepped out from behind the oak tree. She was wearing a big bass drum and spinning a drumstick in each hand.

"Mia!" Yu-Jun yelled. "Your mom!"

The woman with the drum spotted Mia among the dancers, smiled at her, and twirled one of her drumsticks, sort of like a wave.

"Okay, now don't forget your steps," Keona called. "And away we go!"

The music started slow—just the fiddle. Jake surprised himself by how easily he kept up. The pattern was simple and it repeated over and over. Soon, he even found himself having fun.

Step out, feet together. To the middle, feet together. Step in, feet together.

He came face-to-face with Stick. The park ranger's jaw

was set and he was wearing his reflective sunglasses. He didn't say anything and stepped briskly past Jake.

Now it was Mia facing him.

"Hey," Jake said, "could I talk to you after—"

She stepped away, arching her ribbon over Jake's head without a single glance. Like they'd never met.

Step in, feet together. To the middle, feet together.

He stood across from Yu-Jun now. The surfer offered a wide smile, like they were old pals, and Jake smiled back.

I'm in no position to turn down friendliness.

"Hallo there," Ragnar said, stepping in front of Jake. "Why have you run from us yesterday, in the forest?"

Except from these two.

"Yes, we are your excellent pals from Sweden," Angus added, coming right on his brother's heels. "What made you hide from such friendly fellows as us?"

Jake stumbled a little and then found his rhythm again, gliding past Edna Blodgett without slowing down.

"STOP!" Keona Choi called.

The music halted mid-note.

"Look at that beautiful Maypole! You're all doing a great job!"

The top few feet of the pole were now covered with a diamond pattern of blue and green, made by the ribbons weaving together.

"Now, let's have everyone change directions," Keona called into the microphone. "And, Hope, I don't think you came all the way from Portland to sit on the sidelines. Want to help our dancers pick up the pace a little?"

Mia's mom started a bright, crisp drumbeat, and the purple-haired woman mashed the two ends of her accordion together. The two men with string instruments joined last. The pace hadn't just doubled; it had tripled.

Jake managed to keep his steps in time with the music as the plait at the top of the pole unwound and then started weaving again in the other direction. There was Edna Blodgett, offering a polite nod. Then the Magnussons—still trying to talk to him.

"Told you it was kinda fun," Yu-Jun said as they crossed their ribbons.

Jake didn't have time to answer, but he smiled and kept smiling until he met up with Mia again.

"Mia, I—"

She was gone. Two steps later, Jake found himself facing Stick again. The park ranger held his ribbon in one hand; the other hand fiddled with the bowie knife on his hip.

He's trying to scare you. Keep moving.

Jake glanced around the circle—he wasn't the only one struggling to keep the beat. But the musicians didn't slow their pace one bit. If anything, Mia's mom increased the tempo, drumming like she was leading a battalion.

RAT-RATATAT-TAT-RATARATATA-*TAT-TAT!*

The reedy, bellowing notes of the accordion twined between the pops and taps of the drum. The violinist attacked the strings with his bow while the man on the strange guitar plucked high, soaring notes. The audience began to clap in rhythm.

As the pace continued to quicken, the man with the wild beard leapt up, clicked his heels, and gave a *whoop.* Jake didn't have time for kicking his heels—he was getting dizzy and practically had to run to keep up now. A few of the dancers had already let their ribbons fall and stepped to the outside of the ring as the audience cheered for those who remained.

The pattern of green-and-blue diamonds ran farther down the length of the Maypole. As their ribbons pulled tight, the dancers crowded closer. Jake had to lift his ribbon as high as he could to get over someone and duck low to the ground to get under them.

When Edna and Jake came face-to-face again, he noticed that she looked like she was dragging. Had she been up all night, hunting for a nocturnal turtle?

She doesn't know where to look. Don't get distracted.

But he couldn't help glancing back over his shoulder as Edna stepped past. She was facing Myron now, and the mycologist had to practically fold himself in half to make it under her ribbon.

"Careful, Jacob," Ragnar warned.

Jake swiveled forward and almost crashed into one Magnusson, then the other. He found himself so far behind that by the time he got to Yu-Jun, he was a full step back.

Can you get carsick from dancing?

RAT-RATATAT-TAT-RATATA-TAT-TAT! *RA-TAT! RA-TAT!*

Jake's mouth filled with sweet saliva. He stumbled

forward, shoes catching each other, almost tripping right into Mia. They'd been friends just yesterday, but now? The look on her face made it crystal clear that she wasn't going to move a muscle to steady him.

Jake dropped his ribbon and managed to careen haphazardly away from her.

"STOP!" Keona Choi yelled. Everyone froze.

Everyone except for Jake, whose momentum carried him straight into the chest of Stick Stamper. It felt like running into a tree.

"OOF!" Jake grunted.

He was dizzy and began to crumple to the ground when Stick grabbed him under both his armpits and yanked him to his feet. As he did, the park ranger leaned to whisper in the boy's ear. His breath was hot and smelled like campfire.

"I keep telling you to be careful. You're gonna get yourself hurt."

Jake managed to lift his head. Mia was finally looking at him. Her eyebrow was arched, but he had no idea what the expression meant and his stomach was tangled worse than the Maypole ribbons.

As Keona Choi congratulated all the dancers, Jake wrenched himself out of Stick's arms, lurched away from the circle, and staggered through the gathered crowd. He wasn't thinking of Hettle or Mia or Stick. He needed to be alone and didn't stop running until he passed the boat ramp, crashing through a small stand of oak saplings that grew along the banks of the river, and coming to a stop as soon as he knew he was out of sight.

You're just motion sick. Breathe. Everything is going to be okay.

Everything except that Stick had threatened him, Mia hated him, and everyone watched him mess up the dance.

At least you didn't get so dizzy that you threw up.

Exactly two seconds later, he was crouched and heaving.

"Wrong again," Jake grunted.

Nehalem—1:18 p.m., THURSDAY

Stick followed Jake as the boy bolted toward the river. No more "Mr. Nice Park Ranger." It was time to scare the kid into talking about the turtle.

One hand fell to his hip. The button on the knife sheath snapped open and shut, in time with his steps. His jaw gripped tight.

After ten feet, Stick gave a glance over his shoulder. That was when he saw her. Glaring at him with all the heat of the Scrub Pine sun on the Fourth of July. Mia, the mushroom hunter's kid.

She was standing with her parents and a cluster of friends but kept her focus right on Stick. Never even blinked. Stick bit his thumb and thought for a second.

"Dang kid looks ready to yell her head off." He kicked the dirt. "And that sure ain't the attention I need."

After watching Mia watch him for another full minute, Stick decided the only way forward was to switch courses. He jogged across the field to the jam tent. He decided to take one more shot with Hettle Olsson, spotting her in a sea of elderly men and women.

She saw him, scowled, then announced the award for "Best Orange Marmalade." There were so many people crowded around that Stick couldn't get within ten feet of her. Flummoxed again, he stepped out of the tent, spat in the dirt, and wiped his mouth with the back of his arm.

"That old grizzly isn't gonna tell me a thing anyway," he grunted.

That was when he noticed Edna Blodgett—the short, curly-haired Vermonter with the turtle foundation—storming away from the jam tent in a huff. Clearly, she'd been trying to talk to Hettle Olsson, too. As Edna got into a squat little rental car and headed toward town, Stick ambled over to his truck and slid in the cab.

"That crunchy old Vermonter knows about turtles," he said. "She might just be some help."

One look in the rearview mirror showed Mia still watching him—jaw as tight as ever. But he wasn't about to let a kid change his plans a second time in one day. He threw his truck into Drive and followed Edna toward Nehalem's tiny downtown.

"Ruby-rippled fudge—now that seems like it could lift my spirits," Stick heard Edna say as he entered Buttercup Ice Creams and Chowders ten minutes later. She was on her tiptoes, peering into the freezer case. "I'll try a tester of that, if you don't mind. Though I am tempted by the crab bisque, too."

“We’re only supposed to give three testers,” said the teenage girl behind the counter. “This is your fifth.”

Edna didn’t respond. The teen waited a moment, before sighing and scooping up a bite of ice cream on a neon plastic spoon.

“See that?” Edna said. “Everyone is so piping *friendly* here in Oree-gone.”

The girl winced. Edna licked the spoon clean, then inspected the freezer case again.

“Now this vanilla with blackberry jam—is that the famous jam Hettle Olsson makes?”

“I think it’s just regular jam,” the teen said.

“Well . . . I’ll try a tester of it anyhoo!”

Stick gave a polite cough. “Tell you what, Vermonter, you choose your flavor and let me pay. Get three scoops if you can’t decide. I fear I wasn’t as polite as I could’ve been the first time we met.”

Edna turned, saw Stick smiling at her, and looked taken aback. “Well, aren’t you suddenly the dashing gentleman, Mister Park Ranger.” She was holding a change purse and gave it a shake. “This trip hasn’t been easy on my pocketbook.”

Minutes later, Stick and Edna sat on a wooden bench in front of the shop.

“Well, ma’am, I’ll admit it,” Stick said, slapping his thigh. “I can’t help but be intrigued about this turtle story. So I reckoned since this old crab Hettle Olsson won’t share the tale, you could tell me what you know and, in return, I would donate to your . . . you have some sort of turtle foundation, ain't that right?"

Edna's brow furrowed.

"To help you keep up the good work," Stick assured her.

He reached into his wallet, took out a check, and started scrawling in a dollar amount.

"How does one thousand dollars sound?"

The way Edna's eyes bulged could only be described as turtle-like. Stick couldn't help but smile at the resemblance.

"That's very—quite . . . ," she stammered, ". . . quite generous of you, Mister . . . Stamper, was it?"

"Stamper is the last name," said Stick, waving the check toward her without handing it over. "It's right there in my signature."

Without needing any more encouragement, Edna regaled her new friend with everything she knew for certain about the Ruby-Backed Turtle. Not a word of which had been left out of her article online. There was nothing new, nothing that would help him much, and Stick knew it.

When the conservationist changed the subject to rare Ecuadorian tortoises, Stick looked down at the check.

"Well, dang," he said morosely. "I want to be generous, really, I do. But now that I think of it, one thousand dollars feels like it might leave me stretched mighty thin this month. I'd better just cut this donation down to five hundred. Of course, you can't change a check . . . but I have another one in my truck. Or, come to think of it, do I?" He tapped his chin. "Well, I reckon I could go to my bank maybe on Monday. Say, you don't figure they have a branch of the First National Bank of El Paso here in Nehalem, Oree-gone, do you, Ms. Blodgett?"

Edna gulped. "I very much doubt they have any branches of that bank in Oree-gone."

"Double dang!" Stick said, clapping his hands together. He rose to his feet. "Well, it's a shame! We tried, didn't we? Anyhow, I'll be seeing you."

Edna watched desperately as Stick meticulously folded the check in half, then quarters, just inches from her face, and stuffed it into the pocket of his tan shorts. She kept watching as he began to walk away—flipping the button on his knife sheath open and shut with every step.

"Wait!" Edna called, her voice bordering on desperation. "I have a few hunches about the turtle I could share . . ."

Stick wheeled around. "Hunches? Well, consider me intrigued."

"*If*," Edna said, "you were able to let your donation stand."

Stick strode right back to the bench, snapping and unsnapping his sheath button in time with his quickened pace. He sat back down, and Edna told him all about the Vietnamese black-breasted leaf turtle and the Sulawesi forest turtle. She explained how a population of endangered turtles that small could stay hidden for decades. Longer even. She noted that the real turtles that resembled what she'd read of Gustav Olsson's description often lived in leaf litter, though they'd certainly be found close to a stream or creek.

None of it helped Stick as much as he'd hoped, but he unfolded the check and handed it over anyway. Edna beamed at it and called her new friend "a true lover of Testudines."

"Quite the compliment," Stick drawled.

Later, Stick wondered if it was the sight of the dollar amount or the joy she got from meeting someone who listened to everything she had to say about turtles, but as he ambled away, Edna Blodgett blurted, "One more little tidbit, if you're not in a rush, Mister Stamper."

Stick turned to face her.

"That boy, Jake," she said, "the nephew of Hettle Olsson, have you seen him?"

Stick nodded.

"He asked me the other day about turtles that are *nocturnal*. That is to say, they're most active at night. And the way he behaved afterward . . . getting all panicky and jumping off that high rock to make a scene—bruising his chin. Well, it seemed to me that maybe he regretted making that query."

37
Ditched Again

By the time Jake calmed down and walked back up to the jam-tasting tent, his aunt wasn't there. In fact, he hardly saw anyone he knew—not Hettle, Mia, or Myron. Stick Stamper and Edna Blodgett were nowhere to be seen. Even the Magnusson brothers were gone, and they *always* seemed to be beaming at him with their sharky smiles.

Finally, he spotted Yu-Jun and some other boys skipping stones into the river. He went to talk to them.

"Hey, Yu-Jun!" Jake called from ten feet away.

The older boy spun around, his hair swinging dramatically. "Oh, hey! I thought you were coming surfing with us yesterday!"

"My chin," Jake said, pointing to his bruise. "Sorry."

Yu-Jun smiled. "Mia stood up on her first try—I got a video of it on my drone. Waves always look a little bigger from above, so she's gonna be stoked."

"It must be cool to see everything from above like that,"

Jake muttered—his brain was racing, but Yu-Jun was easy to talk to.

"We could try again tomorrow if you want. My drone is already charging!"

Jake felt himself getting overwhelmed—his brain was bouncing between imagining the drone flying above a bunch of surfers, the mention of Mia, and looking for Hettle.

"Hey . . . um, did you see my aunt?"

Yu-Jun looked caught off guard by the change of subject but smiled anyway. "She left with Mia in her truck a few minutes ago."

Why would Hettle . . . ? And why would she bring . . . ?

"You okay?" Yu-Jun asked.

Jake forced a weak grin. "For sure," he said, turning away. He felt dizzy again, but this time it wasn't motion sickness.

"Let me know if you want to surf tomorrow!" Yu-Jun called.

Jake stumbled up onto the road in a daze and started walking toward the cabin.

Mia hates me. Hettle ditched me. What am I even still doing here?

He'd only just made it back to the cabin and was letting Singer run in the front yard a little when his aunt's blue truck came screaming down the road and skidded into the gravel driveway. Hettle rushed into the house with Jake on her heels.

"What's going on?" Jake asked. "Why did you and Mia ditch me?"

Without answering, Hettle limped up the stairs to her room. She returned with a slender wooden box gripped tightly in her fist.

"We must assume Stick knows the turtle is nocturnal," she said. "Mia saw him follow Edna away from the festival and came to get me. We were not able to find you at the time, so I assumed you had come back here. We arrived in town just in time to see him leaving her side after eating ice cream together. He had quite a satisfied grin on his face."

Jake watched her closely. Even the day before, she hadn't seemed so panicked.

"You think she told him that the turtle is nocturnal?" he asked.

Hettle had already grabbed her keys off the table and was headed back for the door.

"Stay here," she said. "This land is now in a trust in your name. So it would not be wise for you to do something illegal."

Jake frowned in confusion.

"I am going back to town," Hettle continued. "My leg is too weak to venture into the forest at night. If we are going to stop Stick from looking for the turtle, we must sabotage him now, before he drives this direction."

"Sabotage him how?" Jake asked. "What do you mean? What happened to you telling me everything?"

Hettle slid open the box in her hand. Inside was a folding

razor with a long bone handle. With the slightest movement of her thumb, his aunt flipped it open. The blade gleamed from across the room.

"It was handed down from my father," Hettle said. "I happen to know that the only mechanic in Nehalem Bay closes at five p.m., so I am going to find where Stick's car is parked and slash his tires to ribbons."

Jake's first thought was to argue with his aunt, but he could see in her eyes that there was no point. Besides, they *did* need to stop Stick, and if Hettle couldn't go into the forest, her plan made sense.

"Mia has been researching him," Hettle continued. "She discovered that he poaches and sells rare pets all over the world. She found an interview of a movie producer telling a story about purchasing a tiger from this very same rogue. I gather that he is not a man to be trifled with, nor is he likely to leave Nehalem when the festival is over."

Jake's brain raced to put all the pieces together.

"Meaning," Hettle continued, still huffing, "that we need more than just a plan for tonight—we need to get rid of him once and for all. You should put your mind to that while I am gone."

She turned to leave, swinging the front door wide.

"At least take Singer," Jake called. "He can be pretty scary when he wants to be."

Hettle paused for a moment, then gave a low whistle. Singer sprung to his feet and trotted out the door on her heels, leaving Jake alone in the house just as the rain started again.

38
Into the Woods

As soon as Hettle was gone, Jake found a few books that seemed like they might help him make a plan. He spread a half dozen of them out on the coffee table. In the center of them all sat *Homesteading on the Nehalem*, opened to the chapter on the turtle. If the secret to getting rid of Stick was going to be anywhere, Jake figured it would be there.

"Focus," he imagined his parents saying.

But this time, he didn't want to focus. Jake's best ideas always seemed to come when he let his thoughts run and there was no one around to tell him not to. He read snippets from different books. He flipped around to random chapters. He paced back and forth through the living room.

One minute Jake read a folktale about trolls in *Homesteading on the Nehalem*, and the next he read about famous lighthouses of the Oregon Coast. He even pored through the book he'd picked up on his first night in Nehalem,

Bring 'Em Back Alive by Frank Buck, flipping through chapters on tapir and crocodiles and a close encounter the author had with an elephant.

". . . the beast was ensconced in dense jungle and though I couldn't see him, I could hear him trumpeting and trampling the bamboo. There is perhaps no sound so terrifying as a perturbed pachyderm preparing to charge."

Jake read that sentence twice. He frowned. There were no elephants in Nehalem. But . . . Maybe he could make Stick think that there was an elk in the forest. Or even a moose.

Something big.

And angry.

Jake started racing around the house looking for something that might imitate the sound of the antler of an angry elk banging a tree trunk. He tried to remember the Animal Planet show he'd seen about imitating moose calls. By the time Hettle's truck pulled back into the driveway, he didn't have a plan, exactly . . . But he had a seed of something.

He could try to stay out of sight and scare Stick with animal calls and sounds.

"The fake park ranger's tires are no longer intact," Hettle announced with a hint of pride as she threw the door open. She was limping more than ever and grimacing with each step.

Jake rushed over to help her. "Did he see you? Where was his truck? Did you wait to catch his reaction?"

Hettle leaned on Jake until they reached the bottom stair. "He did not see me and will not be driving that truck tonight. However, I am in quite a bit of pain and truly must rest. Tomorrow we will trade stories."

Groaning with each step, Hettle climbed the stairs. Jake found himself alone again. He made himself a snack in the kitchen and decided he'd go to sleep too. He could attack the problem of how to imitate the sound of an elk horn the next morning, when he was fresh.

The fading embers of the fire warmed Jake as he curled up on the couch. The rhythm of Singer's snores felt peaceful. But sleep didn't come.

Not even close.

There was a movie playing in Jake's mind that he couldn't distract himself from. He imagined his great-aunt at Stick's truck. He saw her slicing each tire. He envisioned Stick finding the flat tires and punching the side of his truck.

And I'd bet right after that he . . .

That was the bit that tripped Jake up. He couldn't see Stick calling it a night and going to sleep. Giving up and waiting for the next day. Backing off.

"I did not come all the way here from Scrub Pine, Texas, to have someone get the better of me in the middle of the night," Stick had said a few nights earlier, when Jake had tried to sneak up to his tent.

Had Hettle really gotten this rare animal poacher to skip a night of looking for the turtle because of some flat tires? Did that sound like Stick, who'd seemed so menacing every time they met?

This was a man who carried a giant knife on his hip. The man who'd broken into the cabin.

Do you really think he can be stopped that easily?

"Not now that he's seen the map and knows the turtle is nocturnal," Jake said aloud. "Both of which are my fault."

With nervous energy surging through his veins, Jake rose to his feet. If he wanted to protect the turtle, he needed to go into the woods. Not tomorrow; *tonight*. There was no avoiding that. But it scared him so much that he could feel his whole body trembling.

It's your fault Stick knows where to look. So you're the one who has to fix it.

Jake slipped on pants, a long shirt, and two pairs of socks, to make up for the fact that his shoes were still soaked. He found Hettle's flashlight in the spot she'd showed him, under the sink, and slid out the front door. Alone.

39
The Longest Night

A cold shiver raced up Jake's spine. He was sitting on a patch of moss at the base of a giant pine tree. Its branches were his only protection from the steady rain.

In one hand, he gripped Hettle's flashlight. In the other, he held a shoot of bamboo about as wide as a baseball bat. The idea of using bamboo to imitate elk horns hitting trees had come to Jake as he passed the Magnusson camp. He'd crossed the bridge to forage for a piece from the bamboo stand that grew on that side of the river.

Banging it against the trunks of trees would make a hollow *thunk*.

Stick might not think it's a moose or an elk . . . But it will definitely get his attention.

From where Jake sat, he could see the hill where the mudslide had washed out the train tracks. If Stick came looking for the turtle, Jake would be able to spot him when he scrambled up that mound and down the other side. Then he'd follow at a distance before hitting trees with the bamboo and imitating the moose calls he'd seen on a TV show more than a year before.

"Easy as cake," Jake lied to himself, his heart racing.

Jake let the bamboo and the flashlight slip out of his hands and onto the ground. Suddenly the idea of being in charge of Hettle's land felt like it was going to swallow him. How would he stop Stick? Not just tonight but *forever.* And even if he did, what about whoever came next?

And after that?

And after—

Breathe.

Jake's heart felt like it was skipping beats now. All week, being alone in the forest had calmed him down. Now, in the dead of night, it made him feel more ramped up than ever. He snapped his head left and right at every sound and twitch of movement.

The hoots of owls made him shiver. He flinched when a tree branch fell in the distance. A small part of him wished Stick would show up already, just so he wasn't alone in the endless forest.

"Breathe," Jake said aloud.

He drew deep breaths in through his nose. He tapped his cheeks. He closed his eyes and visualized things that had made him feel calm that week, just like the resource teacher at school taught him to do.

"Hiking in the woods with Singer," he said. "Sitting in the tree with Mia. Making jam with Hettle."

But Singer wasn't with him, Mia wouldn't talk to him, and Hettle was sleeping at the cabin. His parents were off at their retreat—probably relaxing in one mineral pool or another.

Jake felt more alone than he'd ever been.

"I was the one who forgot to cover the map," he said. "I was the one who told Edna that the turtle is nocturnal." He hesitated, then added, "I was the one who didn't give a copy of Gustav's book to Mia."

His words made him wince. He felt the same way he had after the Whole Saturday Market Fiasco. When he was so embarrassed at his mistakes that he just wanted to shrink into nothing.

But there was something else. Something bigger.

He'd been talking to himself out loud but couldn't bear to speak the next words that came to mind. Still, they rang in his ears so clearly that it was as if he'd screamed them.

This is all because of my ADHD brain. My disorganized, forgetful, never-thinks-things-through brain. My ramped-up "Jake, what were you thinking?" brain.

Tears welled in his eyes.

My brain that's not normal. My brain that makes me need extra help. My brain that makes my parents have to remind me to focus a hundred times a day. And makes other kids think I'm weird.

And then the loudest words of all.

I hate this stupid brain.

Who cared about having a lot of ideas? Who cared about being able to notice small things other people didn't? Who cared about having a memory full of random facts?

"I just want to be able to focus," Jake said aloud. "Like everyone else."

The forest didn't answer. It was eerily silent. As if all the sound had been sucked from the air. It made Jake's skin crawl. He realized that no one on earth knew exactly where he was right now.

Not Hettle. Not Mia. Not his parents. No one.

Jake wiped his eyes with the sleeve of his shirt. "I'm not taking the land."

That was it. That was the answer. It felt right.

"I'll tell Hettle I can't take it."

Just saying it made Jake feel like a weight had been lifted from him.

He sunk his hands into the moss to push himself to his feet. He'd go back to Hettle's in the morning and tell her what he'd decided. Then he'd ask her to call his parents to come get him.

"I screwed it all up," he said, looking down at his hands in the moss. "Now I just want it to be over."

That was when Jake saw it. A weak flashlight beam bouncing left and right. It was held by someone climbing over the mound of debris where the train tracks had been swallowed by the mudslide.

A man. Slender in the shoulders with a slight paunch. Walking slightly hunched in the rain.

One hand on his hip. Fiddling with the button of a knife sheath.

Stick.

Nehalem—12:06 a.m., FRIDAY

Stick was closing in on the blank area shown on Hettle Olsson's map. He hadn't been sure that was the right spot to look for the turtle until he found his tires slashed—then he felt certain that he was on the right track. So certain that he'd walked eight miles from town.

The rain had only gotten worse as Stick entered the Nehalem Valley. This wasn't a drizzle, and it definitely wasn't a mist. It was what someone back in Scrub Pine, Texas, might call a "toad-strangling rain" or "a great gully washer."

As he scaled a small hill, where the train tracks had been swallowed by a mudslide, Stick couldn't help but chuckle. He had a rain slicker . . . back in the truck. He had mud boots . . . back in the truck. He had extra flashlight batteries . . . back in the truck.

The truck with the four sliced tires. Tires that must've been cut by that boy Jake and his little girlfriend, Mia. Or maybe by that old badger Hettle Olsson.

Click-click went the knife sheath. The rain hammered all around him.

When Stick felt like he'd found the right place, he plunged into the woods. When his flashlight battery started to flicker, he pushed on. When the thorns of a blackberry bush scraped deep into his skin, he kept at it. When he slipped into the creek and twisted his ankle, he gathered himself and scrambled back onto the bank.

"What else you got?" he bellowed into the dense forest. "It's gonna take more than that to slow me down!"

Almost as if in reply, strange moans began to echo from the undergrowth. Then the sound of something—maybe an antler?—hitting a tree. Stick wasn't sure what exactly the noises were or what animal they belonged to.

But he didn't like them one bit. He knew better than to get charged by any animal with antlers.

40
Pick Someone Else

It was nearly sunrise when Jake finally left the woods.

He'd followed Stick through the forest all night—through streams and over ridges. He kept after him until the storm cleared and the sky turned purple in the east. Banging bamboo and doing anything else he could think of.

When Stick had waded into a creek searching for the turtle, Jake had dodged upstream and kicked up as much mud as he could to make the water murky. When Stick set his flashlight down, Jake snuck up and flipped it into a stream with a long tree branch. When Stick finally sat down to rest, Jake made loud long moans through cupped hands.

He wasn't sure if Stick thought he was a moose or a baby bear or a dying Sasquatch. All he knew was that somehow he'd made it to morning without Stick finding the Ruby-Backed Turtle. And he'd done it alone.

But he was tired. Not just sleepy but exhausted, right

down to his bones. And he couldn't imagine what he'd do the next night. Or the next.

Body aching and clothes dripping wet, Jake arrived at the cabin ready to collapse into bed. He longed to curl under the covers. But first, he had to talk to his aunt.

He walked upstairs and rapped a knuckle against her door.

"Hallo, Jacob?" came Hettle's sleepy, confused voice.

"Aunt Hettle," Jake said, "I was in the forest all night, chasing Stick."

The bed groaned. Jake thought his aunt might come to the door, but the movement in the room fell silent.

"He didn't find the turtle," Jake said.

"What did you do?" Hettle's voice seemed a little clearer now; Jake figured she was sitting up.

"I pretended to be a moose. And I made the water muddy. And I pushed his flashlight into the creek when he went to pee."

"This sounds incredibly brave."

"Yeah, but . . ." Jake hesitated. "Aunt Hettle, you have to give your land to someone else. Someone who won't ask a stranger about nocturnal turtles or jump off big rocks and almost break his chin or forget to pull the curtains shut on your map. With how my brain works—my attention stuff—it just can't be me. I'm going to screw it up. I know it."

There was a long pause. Jake wondered if his aunt had fallen back to sleep.

"You make quite a convincing argument," Hettle finally said. "Perhaps I will find someone else."

"You really have to," Jake said.

"As you say, I should find someone who is not impulsive," Hettle said. She paused. "Of course, they must also be brave enough to face an animal poacher head-on in the middle of the night and willing to sneak up on the tent of two quite intimidating Swedes."

Jake frowned. Inside the room, Hettle's bed groaned again. The next time she spoke, her voice was much clearer. He could tell she was standing up.

"I will seek out someone who is never distracted. This is what you want, correct?"

"Yeah," Jake muttered. "I just keep messing things up."

"Yet, I must also make sure that this person is able to quickly come up with ideas. Like pretending to be a moose and making the water murky. I am sure that exact variety of cleverness will be quite simple to find."

Jake knew what she was doing. But he also felt sure that he wasn't the best person to protect the turtle or be the caretaker for Hettle's land.

"I would like for them to have an excellent memory for small details," his aunt added. "And notice sounds and movements that others do not."

"Everything Stick knows is my fault," Jake said, with a lump in his throat. "He wouldn't know *anything* if it weren't for me."

"Jacob," Hettle said. Her voice sounded softer than he'd

ever heard it; it came from just on the other side of the door. "When we find a new person to look after this land, one thing is most crucial. It is paramount."

Jake nodded, forgetting that his aunt couldn't see him. He was so tired that he let his whole body sag against the doorframe.

"Whoever it is that takes your place must also believe that newts and salamanders are enchanting, as you once said to me. Gustav knew that the only way to protect the natural world is to love it. I am afraid I cannot accept anyone who does not find wonder in these forests."

"Lots of people like newts and salamanders."

The door swung open. If Hettle looked large at her front door, here she seemed like an absolute giant. A giant in a faded cotton nightgown. Singer stood beside her with a heavy bone in his mouth.

"I will find this person straightaway, Jacob," Hettle said. "As you said, they must not be impulsive or get distracted or ever dare to forget things. Meanwhile, they also must have good ideas and a superb memory. Brave. Creative. In love with the natural world. Perhaps we should write this down?"

Jake opened his mouth to speak, but Hettle charged on.

"I shall put up a flyer at the Food Mart."

Jake wanted to argue with her, but he was so wet and cold and tired that he simply stayed slumped against the doorframe. "Aunt Hettle, I just can't . . ."

"Or maybe I shall advertise in the local newspaper."

She was teasing him and he knew it.

“I CAN’T!” Jake’s voice cracked. He swallowed hard. “I can’t protect the turtle alone.”

Hettle looked at him solemnly. She set a hand on his shoulder.

“That much is true,” she said, “you cannot protect the turtle alone.” She smiled. “But if you will recall, no one ever said you had to.”

41
"Sorry"

Jake slept fitfully for three hours. Even when he tried to drift off, his mind seemed to race. Ideas sparked like little flashes of lightning. When he got out of bed at 10:40 a.m., he still didn't have a plan for how to stop Stick once and for all.

But he knew exactly what he needed to do next.

He raced toward the door without slowing down to even brush his teeth. Hettle convinced him to eat a poppyseed muffin, which he devoured in three bites. Then he sprinted down the train tracks as fast as his feet would carry him, leaving Singer back at the cabin.

"What *happened* to you?" Myron gasped when he opened the door to Jake's insistent knocking.

Jake had seen his reflection in the screen door glass but hadn't thought of how it must look to an adult. His face was muddy from the night before and there was a blackberry thorn scratch across his forehead that had left a dotted line of dried blood. The bruise on his chin from a few days earlier had gone greenish purple.

"Oh . . ." Jake looked down at his soggy sneakers. "Just . . . you know . . . I was looking for the turtle."

Myron reached out and slapped his back. "You know that's a myth, right? Might not be worth getting bruised up for."

"Fair point," Jake said with a forced half grin. "Is Mia here? I have to talk to her right way."

Myron shook his head. "She's at the Big Nehalem River Inner Tube Float."

"Oh yeah," Jake said, "like from the flyer."

"Exactly," Myron said. "It's always been her favorite part of the festival." He checked his watch. "They probably haven't left yet, if you want to go—it's fun!"

Jake considered this. "Would it be a hassle to drive me down there? I really have to talk to her."

Myron smiled. "I can do you one better, buddy—I'll even loan you a tube."

By the time Myron's car pulled up to the boat launch, most of the people with inner tubes, paddleboards, and rafts were already in the water. Mia stood with Yu-Jun and a crowd of their friends by the shore. Jake dove out of the car, got his tube from Myron's trunk, and started hustling toward them.

"Thanks!" he called over his shoulder to Myron with a wave.

When Mia saw Jake, she hopped onto her tube and

started paddling downstream. He kicked off his shoes and wriggled out of his sweatshirt.

"Mia, wait!"

Jake peeled off his socks and rolled up his pants; Mia paddled farther away. He jumped on his tube and raced downstream. Yu-Jun gave him a friendly wave and mouthed, "Good luck."

"Mia!" he called. "I have to talk to you."

A few of the girls Jake hadn't met yet looked back at him and giggled. He only paddled faster.

"Just give me one minute," he urged. "*Please*!"

Suddenly, Mia spun around in her tube and stopped paddling. "You're embarrassing me in front of my friends!"

"I'm really sorry," Jake said. "I should have brought a copy of Gustav's book right away. And told you about the map."

Mia turned to motion to her friends that she'd only be a minute. They paddled downstream while she treaded water just long enough for Jake to catch up.

"It's whatever," she said, eyes cold. "It's not like we're close or anything."

Jake winced. "I want to be."

Mia pounced on this. "Then why didn't you bring me a book like Hettle said or come over when you found out about the map?"

Jake hesitated. He'd spent the past few days trying to figure that out. He shrugged one shoulder.

Mia sneered, spun in her tube, and started paddling away. Jake watched her for a few strokes, then raced after her.

Of all the times to not be able to come up with something to say!

"I wasn't trying to leave you out!" he said.

Mia turned in her tube again. "Then why though? Why *did* you leave me out if you didn't want to?"

This time the words came. "I wanted to be alone without you asking questions about me jumping off the ledge the day before. And . . ."

Mia waited.

"I thought if I could find the turtle, people would forget."

"Forget what?" Mia demanded.

Jake sighed. "My ADHD. Like how I need extra time on tests and forget to do little things and make weird decisions—like jumping off those rocks. All of it. I just want everyone to think I'm normal."

The words rang true to Jake, and he felt brave enough to lock eyes with Mia. Her face softened a little.

"Dude, do you really think there's such a thing as normal?" she asked.

Jake opened his mouth, then paused.

"Lots of people have ADHD, anyway," she said. "I looked it up."

Jake shook his head.

She's not getting it.

"You don't know what it's like to feel like you're always annoying people because they have to remind you about stuff or maybe you accidentally get distracted when they're talking. And then wondering if that's why people don't invite you to their houses or . . . ditch you when they're with their other friends." He hesitated. "I guess I just started feeling like finding the turtle could fix all that."

The lump in Jake's throat caught when he said the words. It made him feel embarrassed. He shielded his face as if the sun were in his eyes.

"You think everything's perfect for me?" Mia said. "My mom lives in Portland, and my sister was supposed to be here all summer, and then she decided to go on some road trip with her boyfriend. My dad is totally obsessed with mushrooms, and sometimes I feel super awkward around all these kids."

"They all love you!" Jake said.

"That's not what it's about. I've been in Portland and I miss things. I don't know the inside jokes."

Jake nodded.

"You know why I started that journal?" Mia asked. She was paddling toward Jake for the first time. "So that I'd have something to do this summer if my old friends didn't talk to me. Something to make me look busy—that's all it was."

"What about the tape recorder?"

"I just found it in my dad's stuff, and it seemed like it

would go with the notebook," Mia said. "I have a cell phone I could record on—I don't even need it."

Jake looked past her. Yu-Jun and Mia's other friends were about five hundred feet downstream, getting out of the water at a landing. Just past them were two tall men on paddleboards—Jake figured it must be the Magnussons.

"I really am sorry," he said to Mia. "It wasn't cool."

"It wasn't," she said. "Not at all."

"I don't know how to make it right," Jake said. "But I tried to stop Stick alone in the forest last night, and . . . honestly, I don't think I can do it again."

Mia spun around fully, so that she was facing downstream and floating next to Jake. She poked at his tube. "So, you're saying you can't help Hettle protect the turtle alone?"

"Definitely not. Last night was the worst night of my life."

Mia didn't look angry anymore. She didn't look happy, either, but . . . definitely not angry.

That's good enough for now.

"I have all sorts of ideas for how to stop Stick from looking for the turtle," Jake said after a minute of silently floating together.

"Yeah?"

"But I need you to help me turn it all into a plan."

"You do, huh?"

"The sort of plan that will make him rush home to Texas and not come back."

Mia smiled. "Okay, let's hear what you've got."

Jake had been too delirious to notice the weather since leaving Hettle's, but suddenly he felt the warmth of the sun falling across his bare shoulders. It shone bright overhead and threw a million twinkling reflections across the surface of the river—like scattered gold coins. At the landing downstream Mia's friends and the Magnusson twins were clambering out of the river with their tubes and boards.

"Well, for starters," Jake said, motioning in their direction, "I think you'll be pretty surprised about who I think we should get to help us."

42
Scritch

After the float, Jake and Mia raced back to Myron's house. There was a lot more planning to do. Jake shared every idea he'd come up with for scaring Stick out of Nehalem for good and Mia helped him fit the best ones together like pieces of a puzzle.

By late afternoon, they had something that seemed like it could work.

"*Maybe*," Mia said.

"If we're really lucky," Jake added with a yawn. He was sprawled on the thick, avocado-green living room carpet.

After making some boxed mac and cheese, Mia found her dad in his greenhouse and told him she was headed "down to Hettle's place" with Jake. She didn't specify if she meant the cabin or the seemingly endless wilderness that bordered it. She did, however, promise to floss her teeth.

"I hoped I would see you two together again sooner

than later," Hettle said when the two friends burst through the cabin door.

Singer raced past them, out into the front yard.

Hettle's leg was up on a pillow, with a bag of ice on her knee.

"Are you okay?" Mia asked.

"I am afraid I will not be able to venture into the woods tonight," Hettle said.

"It's okay," Jake said. "We came up with a plan to stop Stick once and for all. Together."

Hettle shook her head. "All week, I have endangered you both. It was foolish, and I am sorry. I cannot let you go back into the woods."

"We won't be alone," Mia said.

"Still, I am in charge of this property, and my responsi—"

Jake cut her off. "You said *I'm* in charge now, right? And like Mia said, we won't be alone—just wait 'til you hear who we have helping us."

Jake and Mia raced around the cabin collecting everything they needed for their plan while occasionally explaining bits and pieces to Hettle. A half hour later, there was a knock on the door. Jake opened it.

Yu-Jun stepped inside, wearing a rain slicker and a backpack. Mia introduced him to Hettle.

"Did you bring it?" Jake asked.

"It's all charged up," Yu-Jun said, taking his drone out of his backpack. "I put in a fresh memory card, too."

"Perfect," Jake said. It was already dusk and getting darker by the minute.

Mia looked at Hettle. "It's time for us to go."

"One moment," Hettle said. "I do have one idea that might help you."

She stood up from her recliner with a grunt and led Jake, Mia, and Yu-Jun outside, to her shed, limping badly the whole way. The door groaned as it opened. The space was dank with the smell of mildew. Unseen animals scurried into the corners.

Yu-Jun flicked on his phone's flashlight, lighting up a thicket of cobwebs. Hettle knocked them down with the handle of a rake and approached an object hidden under a tarp. She steadied herself against it for a moment, then jerked the tarp away.

Mia leaned close to the iron contraption that had been hidden by the tarp. "It's . . ."

"Cool," Yu-Jun said.

"Definitely," Jake agreed. "But what exactly . . . *is it*?"

"This is a rail cart," Hettle said. "It was made by myself and my brothers many, many years ago. Set it on the train tracks and pump the handle to gain speed. It will prove much faster than walking."

"I wish I had known about it before," Jake said. "I've been walking all over Nehalem."

"By the time I remembered it, you and Mia were at odds," Hettle said. "It is not made to accommodate one person alone."

Jake, Mia, and Yu-Jun guided the rail cart out of the shed, dragged it across the lawn, and managed to lift it high enough to position it on the railroad tracks. Jake and Mia practiced seesawing the iron handle back and forth. Yu-Jun made last-minute adjustments to his drone.

"Be safe," Hettle said before nodding goodbye. "That is the highest priority."

Jake waved at his aunt as the cart creaked down the tracks. She gave him a solemn nod. Just before they lost sight of the cabin, Singer came bounding through the ferns and leapt right onto the cart—skidding into Yu-Jun's side.

"I guess you're coming then?" Jake asked with a smirk.

Singer looked right back at him and gave a long howl. Almost as if he was mad that they'd even considered leaving him behind.

With darkness falling all around, Jake, Mia, and Yu-Jun arrived at the spot where the mudslide had swallowed the train tracks. Jake and Yu-Jun picked around in the gullies and thickets for a place to hide the rail cart.

"Don't bother," Mia called to them in a hushed voice.

She was standing atop the mound of mud, facing the woods. Up in the hills, off in the deep forest, a flashlight beam bounced left and right.

"He's already here."

Jake gulped. He hadn't expected this part to happen so fast. He'd thought it might be hours before they confronted Stick.

Mia turned to him. "You good to go?"

Jake nodded. "I . . . I think so, yeah." He called to Yu-Jun, who was sitting with Singer on the rail cart, making final adjustments. "Good luck!"

Yu-Jun looked up and flipped his hair out of his eyes. "The eye in the sky will be watching you, dude. But I'll be flying pretty high, so you have to really wave the pillowcase when the moment comes. Then I'll zoom down."

Mia and Jake walked the first half hour together, upstream. They tried to stay dry by keeping to the banks of the creek, moving as quickly as they could. Singer trotted behind them at a distance, almost as if he sensed trouble ahead.

"How about here?" Mia asked, when they found a wide-open clearing where the stream was narrow. "There's space here so that he can't corner us."

The bone-white moon shone just one sliver less than full in the cloudless sky. Jake went to the edge of the creek and shined his flashlight into the water.

"Should work," he said.

"You good?" Mia asked.

Jake nodded. "I think so. What about you?"

Mia didn't answer, just pulled a walkie-talkie out of her windbreaker pocket and waggled it. "We'll always stay on channel three. If I lose range, don't worry. I should be able to give you plenty of warning."

"Yep."

Mia nodded and set off, upstream. After ten steps, she

wheeled back around. "He's got to believe you really have it, that's the key."

Jake smirked. For some reason, he didn't mind when she reminded him about things. It didn't feel like when other people did it.

Mia disappeared past a ledge, walking upstream. Jake whistled to Singer and motioned him to follow her. Their plan was based on her finding Stick, letting him spot her without her seeming to notice, then leading him back to the clearing where Jake would be waiting.

After a few silent minutes, Jake pressed his walkie-talkie button. "I have to say—this is one heck of a ruse."

The walkie-talkie crackled in response. "World-class stratagem."

If it works.

Jake turned his flashlight off and put it in his jacket pocket. The light of the moon was bright enough to see by, and he wanted to save battery power. The darkness the night before had felt like it was swallowing him—he wanted the comfort of a flashlight this time around.

He sat down on the bank of the creek and started feeling around for a ledge. When he found one, he took Hettle's wooden turtle figurine out of his pillowcase and set it a few inches underwater. He tested lighting up the shell with his flashlight. You could see shards of red glowing beneath the water. If Jake didn't know better, he'd have been fooled into thinking it was the real turtle.

Satisfied, he reviewed the plan in his head.

Mia comes. Motions that Stick is behind her. While she gets him to incriminate himself, I shine my light on the turtle shell. Then I reach down and shake out the pillowcase so Yu-Jun sees and I put the decoy inside.

There was more to it. And so much that had to go right for it to work.

"Stick has to admit to lying about being a park ranger," Mia had repeated over and over back at her house. "I read up on the law—it can't be vague."

With the fake turtle in the water, Jake scampered up a fallen log wedged between two rocks to the next clearing. He wanted to see if Stick and Mia were already headed his direction, but their flashlight beams were a long ways off. The sound coming over the walkie-talkie had faded to a faint, distant fuzz.

Jake hopped over to a rock, looking down at the clearing below. From this spot, he could see that running from Stick to the left would lead them up a ridge that disappeared into the undergrowth; it was hard to say where it would link back to the creek. Running to the right was safer and seemed to follow the water—but there were dense blackberry brambles.

Jake felt sick from nerves. As he stared down at these two paths, the whole idea—their "plan"—seemed to leave way too much chance. So many unknowns. So many pieces that could go wrong.

And if he actually catches us, then . . . Everything is out the window.

Jake had seen Stick limping heavily as he left the forest

that morning, after slipping into the creek the night before. But there was no predicting if that injury would slow him down. Somehow it felt doubtful.

Jake pressed the trigger of his walkie-talkie. "Mia, can you hear me? Come in, Mia."

Scritch. Scritch.

Jake shook his walkie-talkie, tapping the battery pack.

Scritch. Scritch. Scritch.

It wasn't static. He realized the sound was coming from closer to the ground.

Scritch.

Jake stooped down. There was an animal somewhere inside a hollowed-out branch of the same fallen tree he'd climbed up. He crouched down to try to see—the branch was too narrow for the animal to be a racoon or skunk. It was rotten, and with a little pressure he was able to pull it free from the larger log.

Once it was loose, Jake kept the branch balanced against the log but angled its opening toward the moon, to try to see what was inside. He lifted up on tiptoes.

A newt.

There was no mistaking the bright orange belly.

But then . . .

Is it crawling sideways?

Jake stepped back, right into the creek, so that he could angle the log down—making it easier for the newt to climb out.

Why is it moving like that?

The orange belly of the newt was facing up. Its body looked limp.

Scritch. Scritch.

Jake spun the branch slowly around so that the open end now emptied out onto the log. The newt appeared. It was dead. Upside down. Held in the mouth . . .

"Beak," actually.

Of a . . .

The world telescoped to one small point—the opening of the rotten branch. Jake's arms erupted in goose bumps. The sounds of the forest around him evaporated. He gasped.

The Ruby-Backed Turtle stepped into the moonlight. Jake steadied himself to keep from falling backward. He wanted to scream, to wave to Yu-Jun, to go find Mia and tell her the plan had just changed.

What do we do now?

It was exactly how Gustav had described it and strikingly like the sculpture hidden in the water just twenty feet away. And yet, it was so much more spectacular. Like night and day. The way the red sections of the tiny turtle's shell seemed to capture and reflect the light of the moon made Jake forget to breathe.

He couldn't help himself but to pick the reptile up by its shell to marvel at it. Even after hearing it compared to a leaf in Gustav's book, Jake was surprised by how delicate it was. How fragile. He wondered if some bug that it ate gave its shell that color.

The turtle's tiny legs pedaled the air. Its beak gripped the newt tightly, unwilling to give up its meal.

Jake leaned so close that the turtle could have bitten his nose. He'd never felt so focused in his life. It was like every idea and thought he'd had since arriving in Nehalem suddenly slipped neatly into place. He and Mia could change their plan. They could protect the *actual* turtle.

They would be famous together, *and* he'd never be the ADHD kid again. For a moment, he felt victorious.

But the whole world would know about the turtle.

How many more Sticks would come looking for it? Poachers. Hunters. Jake had read a story about the last northern white rhinos having around-the-clock guards.

How long before someone else found it? Sure, there could be others. But Jake knew that entire species can die out quickly. How many poachers would show up in Nehalem overnight?

"JAKE! JAKE, ARE YOU HEARING ME!" Mia snapped over the walkie-talkie. "Stick is behind me. You need to MOVE! NOW!"

43
Cleck

Jake couldn't leave the turtle. Not yet. He gripped the serrated edges of its shell tight in one hand and ran down the log to the lower clearing, skidding across the moss to where his flashlight lay on the banks of the creek.

"You found it?" Mia called over the airwaves.

Jake jammed down the button on his walkie-talkie. "Yes! It's amazing! I can't wait 'til you—"

He stopped. He'd forgotten that this was all part of their original plan—for Stick to hear Mia talking on the walkie-talkie. She didn't know he had the *real* turtle. He tried to remember the next step, but at that moment, everything seemed to snap into fast-forward.

Jake felt behind. His mind raced to catch up.

The pillowcase. Remember the pillowcase. Signal Yu-Jun.

He dragged it out of his pants pocket and held it in his right hand with the turtle in his left. Mia appeared on the ledge above him and shined her flashlight on Jake. He saw relief wash over her face for a moment when it caught on the turtle, then tremendous confusion.

"What the—"

He looked down. The turtle's legs were pedaling the air again. Its shell was brighter and more alive than the faded red of Hettle's figurine. But there was no time to explain anything.

Stick was already on top of them.

"Howdy, kiddos," the poacher drawled, striding along the opposite bank of the creek until he was only ten feet from Mia. "Did I hear someone say they found the Ruby Turtle?"

Singer moved between Stick and Mia and growled.

"It's ours!" Mia said. She shined her light on the shell of the turtle in Jake's hand, and it shone brilliant red. "We're going to be famous!"

Still holding the turtle in one hand, Jake waved the pillowcase at his side. "We're taking it to a zoo!"

"Now listen," Stick ordered, one hand on his knife sheath. "The only one leaving here with that turtle is me. I promise you that. If you two know what's good for you, you'll forget you ever saw it."

Singer began to bark frantically.

"But we found it!" Mia yelled. "You're a park ranger—you're supposed to be a good guy!"

"You're too smart to believe I'm really a park ranger, kid. Would a park ranger carry a knife like this?"

It was clear that Stick didn't want to get close to Singer

by climbing down the log. Instead, he hopped right off the ledge, just a few feet to the left of Mia, into the shallow pool. From that position, he moved slowly toward Jake—hand out, as if not to scare anyone.

Jake held steady. He drew deep breaths. Singer kept barking and snarling.

"Why would you lie about being a park ranger if you were only going to take the turtle from whoever found it?" Mia asked.

Stick glowered at the turtle in Jake's hand; he was fifteen feet away now and drawing ever closer.

"I guess I hoped it would make all you Oree-gone folks trust me," he said. "But now it's time for brute force. Get ready to hand me that turtle, pard, or I'm going to take it from you."

Click-cleck, click-cleck, went the knife sheath.

Singer's barks turned ever more urgent.

"Click" means the sheath is open. "Cleck" means it's closed. "Click" open; "cleck" closed.

Jake looked at the turtle in his hand. It had dropped the newt. Its mouth was open, and he could see its tiny tongue. He could put it in the pillowcase right now, before Stick got any closer.

"It belongs in a zoo!" he repeated.

Stick was only five feet away now. Mia shined her flashlight on Stick, buying Jake a few seconds cast in darkness.

You have to make a choice. You know what to do.

"OWWWWWW!" Jake screamed. "IT BIT ME!"

He dropped to his knees and plunged the hand holding the turtle into the water. When he found the ledge, he let it go, guiding it into the depths of the pool and stirring up as much silt as he could. Then he felt around the ledge for the carved figurine.

As soon as Jake brought Hettle's statuette to the surface, he held it up just long enough for Stick to see, then jammed it into the pillowcase.

Singer bounded down the log and skidded to Jake's side. The poacher was only three feet away.

"I've got the turtle," Jake yelled to Mia. "Let's go!"

Out of the corner of his eye, Jake saw Stick lunge, but Singer leapt up and snapped at the poacher's arm. With the second it bought them, they started running downstream. The blackberry thorns made a tunnel, and Jake and Singer wriggled under them. One caught on Jake's windbreaker; he could hear the fabric tear. The next one dug into his pants—he looked back, trying to shake free.

Stick wasn't there. Then Jake heard him—he was in the water, plunging down the cascades. The next clearing was wide. The stream spread out over flat rocks that reflected the moonlight. Jake and Singer were on one bank. Mia stood opposite them, on the ledge.

Overhead there was a loud buzzing, like a thousand mosquitos. Jake pointed skyward and Stick looked up to see the flashing red lights on the underside of Yu-Jun's drone. When he realized what it was, his face turned to a mask of rage.

“Bad news, kiddos,” he said. “As far as that camera can see up there, I haven’t done anything wrong . . . Yet.”

Mia reached into her windbreaker pocket and drew out a tape recorder. “That’s why we made sure to get what you said on tape, too. Impersonating a park ranger is against the law. So is selling endangered tigers in New York. We know all about you.”

Her words made something snap in Stick. He charged toward her without an ounce of hesitation. Mia backpedaled, but the moment she did, she lost footing—slipping down the ledge, crashing onto her wrist, and sending the tape recorder skidding across the slick, flat rocks.

Click.

Jake heard the button of the knife sheath open. The knife was out, raised high as Stick charged for the tape recorder.

“Mia!” Jake yelled. “Get up!”

Just feet from Mia, Stick stabbed the tape recorder—once, twice, three times, right through the middle—then looked up, eyes blazing. Mia was back on her feet but unsteady, holding her right wrist with her left hand and wincing.

Stick sunk the knife into the sheath, but there was still no “cleck.” It could be drawn again at a moment’s notice. He stalked toward her, hand on his hip.

“You two made a terrible mistake messing with me!”

Jake raced across the rocks, dropped the pillowcase, and slammed into Stick from behind.

"*GUH!*" the poacher groaned. His feet skidded out from under him and he went down on the rocks.

Jake leapt on top of Stick and grabbed the knife with his free hand. Stick caught his wrist and held it in an iron grip. He was stronger than Jake, and they both knew it.

"LET HIM GO!" Mia yelled.

She was standing over them, stomping down on Stick's arm. Then Singer sunk his teeth into the poacher's leg. Jake managed to wrench himself free and flung the knife skipping across the rocks, where it disappeared into a crevice.

He leapt to his feet, snatched up the pillowcase, and his eyes met Mia's.

"RUN!" he yelled.

44
Swedish Adventure Bros

Jake, Mia, and Singer ran in the stream until the bank on the left side of the river looked low enough to scale.

"There!" Jake yelled. "I'll shine a light!"

He yanked his flashlight out of his jacket pocket and shined it ahead so that Mia could see. Together, they crashed downhill for ten minutes straight, plowing over ferns and skidding across the loamy soil, never daring to slow down or look behind them. Finally, they burst through a wall of bushes and skidded into the clearing beside the train track.

Yu-Jun's drone hovered above, buzzing like a million bees.

Jake and Mia crossed the track to get farther from the woods. Singer stopped, turned, and barked fiercely toward the dense forest over and over, sharp and loud and angry.

"He's coming!" Jake yelled.

Two large bodies stepped forward from the shadows,

towering almost like twin trees themselves. When Stick emerged from the forest, limping, scratched, and panting, he was greeted by their shark-toothed grins.

"Hallo there," Angus said, "we are the Magnusson brothers, but most people know us as the Swedish Adventure Bros."

"Why were you chasing our supercool American friends?" Ragnar asked.

Stick was panting. "Well, pards . . . I was simply . . . I wanted to talk to them, is all. See, I—"

The buzzing of the drone distracted him, and he craned his neck to look up at it.

"We have a feeling you are not wanting people to see that video of you endangering these young people," Ragnar said.

"Is that correct?" Angus asked. "Because if it is, we will walk you to your car. And if you agree not to return, the video will not be shown."

"And I won't play anyone this backup recording of you admitting that you're a criminal!" Mia called, waving her cell phone toward Stick. "As long as we never see you back here."

The poacher hesitated. Jake tipped the pillowcase and the statue fell into his waiting palm.

"It's just wood," he said, tapping the figurine's head. "We tricked you."

"And you fell for it," Mia said.

Stick glared at them both. He watched as Yu-Jun's drone

buzzed overhead. He glanced down at Singer, ready to bite again. He sized up the towering Magnusson brothers.

Then he set his hand on his hip to grab for his knife.

It wasn't there.

"Well . . . ," Stick said, sucking his teeth. "Well, dang." He spat on the ground. "Dang it all!"

After another long pause, he started trudging down the train track. For the first hundred feet, Yu-Jun's drone floated over his head, recording his every move. Stick grabbed rocks and hurled them up at it, but soon he gave up.

When the defeated poacher passed the spot where the mudslide had buried the train tracks, Yu-Jun stepped out of the shadows, guided the drone back, and hovered it over the Magnussons.

"You guys ready for your close-up?" he said. "One, two . . . three!"

"And that's all for now, from Oree-gone with the Swedish Adventure Bros!" Angus and Ragnar boomed in unison with the drone just above them.

They gave four thumbs-up to the camera, and it zipped hundreds of feet high into the night sky. This piece of footage was the one thing the twins had asked for in exchange for their help defeating Stick.

"It will make the perfect ending for our next Swedish Adventure Bros video as we say goodbye to this forest!" Ragnar said.

"We have decided to look for the Sasquatch in our next series of videos!" Angus added.

That afternoon Jake and Mia had told the brothers just enough about their plan to get their help, while also convincing them the turtle had never existed in the first place.

"I'll email you guys a copy tomorrow morning," Yu-Jun promised.

The brothers nodded and started down the track, following Stick at a distance to make sure he left Nehalem right away.

When Jake, Mia, and Yu-Jun were finally alone, Mia crouched down, wincing in pain.

"We have to get you to a doctor," Jake said.

She flexed her hand. "I don't think it's broken." She fell back to the earth and stared up into the stars. "I just want to soak in the stars for a sec."

"It's a nice night," Yu-Jun said.

"It definitely is," Jake agreed.

Not long after, Jake and Yu-Jun were pumping the rail cart toward Nehalem and Mia was sitting with her feet dangling over the side, leaning against Singer. She wondered aloud if Hettle would agree to make them midnight pancakes.

"Smothered in her blackberry jam," she added.

"That sounds amazing," Yu-Jun said.

Jake smiled to himself as he pumped the handle of the rail cart. A quarter mile ahead, through the towering woods, he could already see the light glowing from inside his aunt's cabin.

Cannon Beach, Oregon—3:47 a.m., SATURDAY

"Hey, pal, you okay?"

Stick hadn't noticed anyone approach his booth. He also hadn't noticed his eggs getting cold or the fat on his bacon taking on an unappetizing sheen. He looked up to see a man close to his own age in a smudged, greasy apron with a name tag that read "Ken."

"Guess you didn't like the look of your food," the man said, nodding toward the untouched plate.

Click. Click. Click. Click, went the knife sheath. Stick kept forgetting that there was no knife inside.

"Everything was fine, pard," Stick said. "Bring the check and another coffee."

The man grunted and disappeared into the kitchen.

"Make it piping hot!" Stick called.

Click. Click. Click. Click. Click. Click. Click. Click.

Stick thought about driving back to Nehalem to look for the turtle. The problem was those two burly Swedes would have their eyes out for him. And whatever was on the drone and phone recordings felt like they could put him in prison.

Then of course there was the fact that he'd been writing checks all week on a bank in Texas that didn't actually exist. That Edna Blodgett woman seemed like just the sort of person who would try to deposit the money the very next morning and call the local authorities five minutes after that.

"Oh, just admit it," he mumbled to himself. "Those kids got you beat. They got aces and you got rags."

The man in the apron returned from the kitchen with a coffee and set it on the counter next to the cash register. Slowly, Stick limped over to the counter—his boots making a squelching sound with each step. He snatched up the bill.

"Looks like I owe you seventeen dollars, pard," he said. "Tell you what; why don't I add an extra hundred bucks."

The cook scowled for a moment. Then his facial muscles released. "You win the lotto or something, pal?"

"Nope," Stick said, "I guess I'm just glad to be headed back to Scrub Pine, Texas, is all. Not much for this Oree-gone weather."

He reached into his jacket pocket. It had been in the truck and was the only half-dry thing he had on.

"Now . . . let me see . . . are you okay to take a check from the First National Bank of El Paso?"

45
The Last

Jake's parents arrived Saturday morning to pick him up, and he brought them to the closing ceremony of the festival. Mia's mom had already headed back to Portland, but her sister showed up at the park as a surprise.

"Jake, meet Evie," Mia said with a proud smile.

"Mia has told me a lot about you," Jake said. "How is the camper van trip?"

"This is my favorite spot we've been so far," Evie said, winking at her sister.

Later, Hettle gave a speech, saying she was glad that her great-grandfather's *made-up* story of a turtle brought so much joy to so many. She even read a few sentences from *Homesteading on the Nehalem*, though not from the Ruby-Backed Turtle chapter. It was from the final chapter of the book, the one Gustav Olsson had decided to end with instead of the angrier version that was framed back at the cabin.

"Perhaps it was all the rain that helped the emerald

beauty of Nehalem seep into my bones," Hettle read, "or maybe it was the peace I found in these dank, mossy woods. What I am certain of is that I carry this place with me wherever I go. And that, with any luck, the generations that follow will have these same endless green spaces coursing through their veins."

As she read it, she leveled her eyes right at Jake. He was pretty sure he saw them welling with tears.

Later, there was more music and blackberry jam served on delicate white cookies, called meringues, which Hettle had made the night before when she was nervously waiting for Jake, Mia, and Yu-Jun to return. Myron had a paper bag full of lobster mushrooms and cooked them on a hot plate plugged into the Fifty Dollar Crab's electric generator.

Goodbyes came next. And promises to call. And inside jokes, shared in tiny snippets so no one would suspect what they were about.

"You did it," Mia said to Jake when they had a moment alone. "You saved the turtle."

"*We* did," Jake said. "Thanks for giving me another chance."

On the drive home, Jake leaned against Singer's warm body and stared out the window into the endless forest. It was so full of mystery and magic. So dense and green and wild.

"So you liked Hettle, didn't you?" his mom asked, turning in the passenger seat. "I thought she wasn't much of a hugger, but, wow . . . she sure wrapped you up tight when she said goodbye."

"Yeah," Jake said. "I want to visit her a lot. Mia's dad is in Portland for work all the time and he said he could drive me down."

"Sounds good, buddy," Jake's dad said. "But hang with us for a few days first."

His mom smiled at him. "We missed you."

On the second weekend of October, Jake was back in Nehalem for a long weekend. There was a birthday dinner for Mia at Hettle's cabin—a feast with Myron and Yu-Jun and Keona Choi. When it was over, Jake and Mia helped Hettle clean up. Yu-Jun had to leave early; he had plans to surf the next morning. "Gotta get those dawn patrol tube rides," he'd told them.

As soon as the other guests were gone, the two friends and Singer raced down the train track on the rail cart. They brought flashlights and some snacks but not much else. Except for Mia's notebook and a copy of *Homesteading on the Nehalem*.

As they waded into the forest, a yellow half-moon shone overhead. Soon, they came to the open glade where they'd confronted Stick. They rushed to the stream and peered with flashlights into the crystalline water.

No animal emerged. They paced up and down alongside it for an hour and looked in every rotten log they could find. Still nothing.

"What will we do if we see it again?" Mia asked.

Jake didn't imagine himself on TV shows and magazine covers anymore. Instead, he thought about turning the vast property into some sort of protected area. He'd already emailed a bunch of questions to Robert Bobb, wondering about making the land a Siletz Nature Reserve. Or maybe it could be managed by a conservation group—though not Edna Blodgett's; he didn't trust her to keep things secret.

"I'm not sure what to do," Jake said. "I have some ideas, but we need to come up with a plan." He paused. "Luckily, I'm friends with a very good planner."

"I do enjoy a good stratagem," Mia said with a wink.

After a few hours of poking around, they decided to head home. Singer was hungry and Hettle would be waiting up.

"What if we never see the turtle again?" Mia asked, looking over her shoulder at the clearing.

"We might not," Jake said. He made a "coo-eee" for Singer, and the dog trotted after them. "Gustav never saw another one alive. And Hettle hasn't ever seen one."

He and Mia left the clearing together, walking side by side.

"I guess it's enough just to know that a few turtles are still out there somewhere," Mia said, stepping around a spreading fern.

"Yeah," Jake agreed, "and that we did everything we could to keep it that way."

Acknowledgments

GRATITUDE:

I want to start, right off the top, with a shout-out to my wonderful editor, Mary Kate Castellani. Our collaborative relationship is one of the great joys of my creative life and your instincts about this book have been spot on since day one. I felt your love of Jake and Mia in every note and line edit—thank you.

To the whole Bloomsbury team: Thank you so very much for believing in this project. It's a true joy to work with all of you and have the privilege of representing you through my novels. I feel supported and heard by each of you and that means so very much. Also, huge shout to the copyediting team, who saved me multiple times and had a major impact on this novel's development.

To Rachel Hylton for giving the book that vital first read, demanding more where it was faltering, and letting me know when I got it right. To the entire Beverly Shores family for really feeling this one and being loud about it. And always, always, Varian Johnson for being a mentor in this industry to so many of us—urging caution when we're feeling brash, action when we're feeling disengaged, and (most important) believing in us right down to your bones.

Thanks to my wonderful agent, Sara Crowe, for pushing me in all the right ways. And a special salute to the team at the Laguna Beach Library, where this novel was written.

Huge cooo-eeeee to Forrest Galante, who was vital in creating the Ruby-Backed Turtle, explaining the good and bad aspects of rare/extinct species conservation, and adding general "that sounds like a book I would love" energy.

To Robert Kentta—who offered crucial insight about the geography and Indigenous Peoples of a region that I've loved for as long as I can remember. Double thanks for letting me base a character on him, and triple for walking the woods and rivers of the region with me. Robert, you made this book better from day one and the first email you wrote me marks the moment I realized the universe was smiling on this book. Thank you, a million times over.

To Nneka Gigi, thanks for your wisdom and warmth—shared in equal measure. I'm so thrilled that this book touched something in you and so grateful for your support. The character of Mia is realer and more resonant because of you.

Thanks to my sisters, cousins, aunts, uncles, nieces, and nephews—all of whom have explored the wilds of Oregon with me. My connection with the natural world is inextricably intertwined with the deep love I feel for all of you. I hope it manages to paint the coast in a way that feels real for each of you.

Endless love to Julien River and Zeela Sky, who have given me more reason than ever to protect the earth. I see how happy and peaceful you are out of doors and can't wait for the endless adventures to come. When life is overwhelming, try pressing your face against a tuft of moss. Take ten deep breaths. Peace will follow.

To my darling Nikta: You hold it together—balancing and juggling and managing and making it fun—so that I can chase my dreams. I can't wait to return the favor. And I love you!

This book starts and ends with my parents, who made me fall in love with nature. Dad, I wish you could read this one, but I believe in my heart of hearts that your spirit is in it. Whenever I falter, I look for you in the thin spaces. Mom, this book is for you most of all. You were the one who urged me to confront my ADHD. The one who set me on the path to turn it into something that enhances my "me"-ness rather than detracting from it, and who dealt with teenage me resenting you for all your efforts. I'm sorry and I love you. No matter what happens with this book, it's a smashing success because it's brought us so much closer. (Also, thanks for reading it over and over and over and loving it every time—it means the world.)

The shadow of my dear, late friend Anneliese Schimmelpfennig looms large over this book. She is the woman in the cabin lined with odd artifacts who is "not much of a hugger" but would weep at the sight of a tree being cut down. So much of Hettle's affect was taken from her and while I'm devastated that she won't get to see the novel out in the wild, I'm heartened by the fact that I got to hand it to her before she returned to the stardust.

Thank you to my readers—be there sixty or sixty thousand of you. You make me want to be a better storyteller. It is truly my deepest honor that you are eager to spend part of your one magical life reading my writing.

And finally, thank you to me. This book made me face things that were difficult. It taught me about myself and helped me reckon with how my unique brain operates. There are still times where ADHD trips me up and there likely always will be, but for the first time ever, I can proudly say: I wouldn't trade this brain for a second.

That alone is an accomplishment and I'm proud of myself for it. It only took forty-three years! For anyone else out there in the neurodiverse community—I hope you get there sooner and hope this book helps you along the way.